T0156966

A Vampire Fairy Tale

Melissa Hansen

iUniverse, Inc.
Bloomington

Taste
A Vampire Fairy Tale

iUniverse books may be ordered through booksellers or by contacting:

iUniverse
1663 Liberty Drive
Bloomington, IN 47403
www.iuniverse.com
1-800-Authors (1-800-288-4677)

ISBN: 978-1-4759-0268-6 (sc)
ISBN: 978-1-4759-0270-9 (hc)
ISBN: 978-1-4759-0269-3 (e)

Printed in the United States of America

iUniverse rev. date: 4/4/2012

For S, S, and M.
Your love inspires me …

Preface

I watched uneasily as he ran his icy fingers along the length of the body before reaching the shoulder. He grabbed its slender neck and grinned.

Baring his teeth, he sank his sharp incisors into the fleshy top and tore it open. A snapping sound split the silence while thick crimson rivulets oozed down the neck. I quivered as I stared, eyeballing the curious way he let it breathe for a moment.

The air was alive with blood scenting the room more bitingly than a crucible of metal in a foundry. I inhaled, watching him drink the liquid, devouring the sinful sustenance with elegance. The come-hither grin on his beautiful face made me melt inside. He licked the spill of blood from the corners of his mouth. He made it look easy, natural even.

The glorious grotesqueness of the moment roused me with hunger. Frightened and filled with fervor, my inner monster seethed to emerge, longing to satiate its indomitable thirst. This time, I couldn't fight it.

I watched him smear the scarlet stain of blood against his pink, pouted lips. My body swelled with a ravenous rage. I needed to submit to the craving. I hungered for a taste of it too.

1-Birthday

Once upon a time, I was a little girl, and the world was beautiful. The wind was warm and tickled my toes. The sun was balmy on my bare skin. I would lie all afternoon in my thick bed of grass, basking in the radiant rays. Oleander and saltwater fragranced the air, while giant marshmallow clouds sailed across blue sky. Tingles of sunbeams delighted my lily-white skin, and my cheeks blushed redder than a plump, ripe tomato.

It was time to explore. I sprang to my feet and giggled. The lawn tickled my feet; I liked it. Suddenly I spotted a pathway of pebbles. The tiny stones called out to me, their gravelly sound growing louder as I stepped upon them. The path was situated at the threshold to the forest. I wasn't supposed to go into the forest, but adventure beckoned.

I rushed across the jagged trail and stepped inside the forbidden forest. My pink dress swayed gracefully in the breeze as I leaped from little stone to big stone. The lapping of nearby water harmonized with the rhythmic hissing of the cicadas. It was an opus composed solely for my enchanted dance on tiptoes. The sun and I played peek-a-boo through the heavily hung Spanish moss that drooped from the scrawny pines. *This is a great adventure*, I thought to myself as I moved along.

Out of the corner of my eye, I noticed a beautiful blue flower. My ballet became a gallop as I breathlessly dashed toward it. I leaned over and ruthlessly snapped its tiny neck. "Gotcha," I giggled as the flower lay lifeless in the palm of my small hand.

Then suddenly the strangest sensation overwhelmed me. Someone was watching. I could feel it. I looked around and caught a fleeting glimpse of the most mesmerizing lady. She had long blond hair, fair skin, and honey-colored eyes. She was a golden princess. Our gaze met for a brief moment, and then she smiled at me before turning away. I watched the black butterfly on the back of her neck gleam in the sun between her gilded tresses as she fled though the forest. She was fast like an animal, and as I blinked, she disappeared.

I sighed to myself with a shrug and pressed on. My gaze shifted to the white flowers nearby. On tiptoes, I leaped toward the small, crooked stone ahead and landed with a thud. Like a rubber band at full extension, I stretched my skinny arm as far as it would go and struggled to snap the white one's neck. It wouldn't budge. I pulled harder, grunting and groaning, but it still wouldn't give. Then suddenly the stem snapped, thrusting me backward with tremendous force. I lost my balance and stumbled over the wiry tangle of mangrove roots underfoot.

I was an instant from plummeting into a cradle of water brimming with tiny sea creatures when suddenly time stood still, slowing to an almost motionless suspension. I had been swept up by strong, shielding arms and rescued from the ocean's stifling embrace. A most curious aroma filled my senses; a fragrant burst of metallic candy permeated the air. I inhaled the strange sweetness and watched the listless flitter of tiny insects floating in midair around me against the amber blaze of the evening sun. I looked to my left at a tiny hummingbird; even his hover appeared petrified. The world was more magical than I had ever thought possible.

Suddenly I was propelled through the air at an incredible speed. The wind whistled in my ears, and my body trembled with exhilaration while the woods sped past. Faster than the spread of fire, I soared through the pines as though upon the wings of a mythical bird. The swift motion overwhelmed me, and I could feel myself losing consciousness in the strong arms of my savior.

Eventually I awoke on a bed of grass. The world was running at normal speed again, and when I sat up, I noticed him. He was wearing all black, hiding behind the gnarly roots of a banyan tree. *My rescuer*, I thought to myself. A jagged snarl of dark hair hung in front of his pale face. Only his glorious green eyes were visible, peeking out at me from behind his unkempt tangle of tresses.

"Come out, come out, wherever you are," I whispered.

"Hello," he replied, slinking forward from behind the wiry tree roots.

I didn't know him, but I liked him already. He was beautiful, not quite a man, but not just a boy either—he was something in between.

"Do you know the golden princess?" I asked. "The one with the butterfly?"

He shook his head and grinned. "I don't think so." His voice was posh with an English accent. He sounded like royalty.

I sighed. He was like a knight from a fairy tale—tall and strong with the fairest skin I'd ever seen.

He cocked his mess of inky hair to the side and whispered, "Do *you* know the golden princess?" His lips were pressed together in a smile.

"No, silly!" I laughed, brushing the dirt and grass from my pink dress. "I don't know her either."

We smiled together.

"I'm Hope," I divulged, spinning around in circles on tiptoes. "Today is my birthday."

"Happy birthday," he said, his soft voice sailing upon the gentle current of the warm wind.

"I'm seven." I leaped through the air like a ballerina, his green eyes following my spin with a guarded gaze. "How old are you?"

He didn't respond.

"Well?" I insisted. The longer I stared at him, the more his featureless face fascinated me with its vagueness. He was beautiful, yes, but nothing more than an enigmatic blur of imprecise pink lips, a nice, notable nose, and jaw-length rumpled hair.

"I'm *very* old," he finally replied with a smile.

"Funny," I said, "you don't look very old."

"Why aren't you at the party?" he said, changing the subject.

I shrugged. "I didn't want to be there." My eyes swelled with sadness. "It's not a birthday party, you know." I leaned in closer, fighting back tears. "It's the other kind of party—a sad party."

He nodded knowingly, his green eyes radiating.

I twirled around again. "Thank you for saving me."

"You're welcome."

A gust of warm wind carried the familiar scent of metallic sweetmeats in my direction. A surge of tin and cinnamon saturated my senses with its peculiar potency. It was *his* scent. I stopped twirling and inhaled him deeply. I giggled.

"What is it … the golden princess?" he teased in his elegant voice.

"No, silly!" I laughed, looking up at his broad shoulders blocking the sun's rays like a tall tower. "It's you." I inhaled again and smiled before spinning around in a circle. I laughed and stopped. I was a little dizzy and off kilter.

He laughed too.

I watched him brush his pale arms with his hands, as though he was brushing dirt from his skin, and then I noticed something. Two small objects were tucked in the crook of his arm. "What are you holding?" I asked.

"Books," he replied, taking them in his pale hand. "My sketchbook," he said, sliding a small, red, leather book into his back pocket. "And this …," he said, holding out an antique book with a brown, leather cover. "This is one of my favorites."

"What is it?" I asked, taking the old book from him.

"Romeo and Juliet," he replied tenderly.

I shrugged, thumbing through the pages. The book smelled like a stale cellar, and the parchment practically crumbled with the touch of my tiny fingers. "It smells funny." I grimaced.

"It's old." He laughed.

I stopped smelling the book and looked up at him. "Well what's it about?"

"Um …" He grinned awkwardly, his white teeth sparkling. "Forbidden love," he replied.

I swallowed uneasily, my cheeks flushing with chagrin.

"And death." His voice grew grimmer and his face more rigid.

My expression dropped. I nervously handed the book back to him.

He laughed under his breath. "It's a pleasure to meet you," he said, extending his pale hand toward me.

I perked up immediately with the sweet sound of his voice and timidly slid my tiny hand into the palm of his. I gasped. He was cold like ice, and his touch startled me with a terrifying fright. I looked up at him again. He was still beautiful, but a hardened kind of beautiful. The emerald green of his eyes had been replaced by a mesmerizing metallic shine. “Oh my,” I whispered, my eyes glued to his in a magnetic stare.

“You’ve been injured,” he snapped, his tone severe.

“I—I am?” I said nervously, noticing the thin streaks of blood that seeped along my wrist in steady trails like vines.

He nodded slowly, his eyes suddenly fixed on my arm.

I swallowed hard, feeling my heart pound inside of my tiny body. Then faster than my eyes could process, the beautiful stranger suddenly tore off a piece of my dress to wrap my wound. I stood paralyzed before him, vulnerable, watching the way he inhaled the scent of my blood that now stained his snow-white fingertips.

“Ah,” he moaned quietly, licking the fresh droplets from his skin.

I shuddered. Tears welled in my eyes, fright and fascination immobilizing me. I tried to look away, but I was rapt, spellbound by his most terrifying behavior. He savored the drops of my blood on his lips and continued despoiling me with his ravenous stare as though he was waiting for more.

“Just a dream.” I sighed, snapping out of my reverie. I tried to catch my breath. I was inebriated, my body deadened, stupefied with inertia. Where was I? I blinked a few times, and when my eyes finally focused, I realized I was still at the bar, in the lavatory, shoved up against the stall door and staring into the brown eyes of a guy I vaguely recognized.

“Thought you’d passed out,” he teased with a grin.

“I think I did,” I answered groggily.

“Happy twenty-ninth birthday, Miss Havergale,” he whispered, his warm breath tickling my cheek as he spoke.

I sighed. “First, never talk about a woman’s age—my birthday is actually tomorrow. And secondly,” I teased, now recognizing his young face, “don’t call me Miss Havergale.”

“But I like it,” he purred, stroking the sides of my body with his hands.

His touch was clammy and clumsy. “We shouldn’t do this,” I asserted, my words sloppy as they spilled from my lips.

“Why? Because I’m your student?”

I laughed, eyeballing his pretty-boy good looks.

“I’m twenty-one,” he defended eagerly.

"Oh I can see that," I laughed.

"What's the big deal?" he said, his straggly, blond hair brushing against my cheek.

I looked at the spattering of graffiti on the walls. My eyes focused in on a ramshackle drawing of a heart with the words *true love* scribed into the center. The image had been stroked out and scribbled over. *True love,* I thought to myself. My body trembled with a strange elation as though the words themselves somehow summoned a physical response from deep within me, and suddenly I was desperate to slip away to my dream world again.

"C'mon," he urged. "I'm not trying to marry you. I just wanted to have some fun."

I laughed again. Cheap booze and stale sweat seeped through his pores. His warm body reeked of inexperience, and I liked it.

"What are you waiting for?" he taunted impatiently.

I shrugged, tracing the graffiti heart with my finger. "The man of my dreams …"

"He's not me."

"No. He's not," I snapped.

"But maybe I could—"

"Shh," I whispered, cutting him off. "Don't ruin this." I pressed myself against his taut body, surges of regret coursing through me the moment our lips met. His kiss was sloppy and impatient and immediately confirmed the magnitude of my mistake. Just as I began pushing him off of me, my phone started ringing from inside my pocket. "I have to take this."

"Now?" he whined.

"Yeah. Now. See you at school," I said, pushing him toward the door.

I sighed the moment he left and brought the phone to my ear. It was my father calling. "Hi, Richard," I said. The day my mother died was the last time I used the word dad to his face—that was over twenty years ago. "Don't you have something special to say to your daughter?" I said, assuming he was calling to wish me a happy birthday and take the liberty of slamming my age.

His voice was more curt than normal.

"What's going on?" I asked. Something wasn't right; I could feel it.

"My *grandmother* died?" I said. "I don't have a grandmother." I could feel the alcohol in me working its foggy magic, boiling my blood like wildfire as my emotions swelled. "Slow down," I demanded, struggling to resume clear-headedness. "A property in her will? But why would she leave it to me?" I took a deep breath. "I'm not going to your office tonight. It's late and ..." Tears welled in my eyes. It was clear that the bastard forgot my birthday. I groaned with frustration. "How long have you known I had a grandmother out there?" The phone went silent, and when he finally spoke, his answer enraged me. "I can't talk to you right now," I said. "Why? Because you're an insensitive—oh forget it," and then I hung up on him.

I tossed the phone to the floor as though it was trash and slammed my back against the stall door. Hate rose in my throat. "Selfish prick," I seethed. "He knew about her. Damn him for not telling me sooner." Saliva burning with rage slithered down the back of my throat. Tears of pain poured from my eyes.

Today I was that much closer to death. I could almost smell its rotting odor creeping nearer and feel its vacant eyes upon my aging flesh. I despised the fact that birthdays were a reminder of what time you had left to live.

I was twenty-nine. My mother was twenty-nine when she died. It was a frightening thought, one that I was struggling to keep at bay. My father, Richard, never spoke of her anymore. He detached emotionally from everything after her death—*even me*. For him, love was a punch line, and honesty was more of a commodity, but to ignore the fact that I had a grandmother out there all of these years was despicable, even for him.

I felt sick. My emotions were twisted tightly. I slept late, but not late enough. I wanted to go back to bed and forget that today even existed. I took a deep breath before studying my reflection in the mirror.

"Almost invisible," I said to myself. The youthful roundness of my face was starting to sag. My skin was a ghastly shade of pale, and thin wrinkles feathered the corners of my eyes. I ran my fingers through my long blond hair and gawked at the cavalcade of lotions organized on the counter; they stood row upon row like an army of promises, and today was as worthy a battle as any. It was my birthday. I needed every ounce of help I could get. The armada of anti-aging defense beckoned me with its cadence call. I grabbed the stout bottle that promised rejuvenation and globbed it on my face. Then suddenly I heard my phone ringing. I sprinted into the living room and grabbed it from my purse.

"Oh, Bradley, it's you." My tone was terse. Bradley was the classic ex-boyfriend that didn't seem to know how to take a hint. No matter how many times I insisted we break up, he maintained that we were soul mates and meant to be together. "You're canceling? Don't feel bad. It's only a birthday," I said, relieved. "I'll have others."

I sauntered across my sparsely decorated loft space toward the oversized windows. I wasn't much for tchotchkes. The rugged charm of the original wooden beams and red brick walls seemed décor enough for my part-time teacher's salary at the college.

"So what's the excuse this time?" I teased. "Working late?" I peered out at the shadow of grayness that cloaked the city. "I understand. You're a doctor … saving lives and all." It was hard trying to soften the sarcasm in my voice. I watched the legion of tiny people below with umbrellas, marching in unison like little ants. "*Richard* is the one keeping you at the hospital?" My eyes narrowed. "On *my* birthday. My father is incredibly inconsiderate." I took a deep breath. "Don't defend him." But I knew Bradley had no other choice; he was an overpaid protégée working under my father at the hospital. He was the son my father wished he'd had.

"Look, Bradley, I'm fine," I interjected. "Work late. Do what you have to do." I hung up and took another deep breath. In all honesty, I was glad he cancelled. I dreaded the thought of spending more time with him.

I turned away from the window and flopped down on my orange, vintage, vinyl excuse-for-a-couch. I pressed my face against the sticky cushions and inhaled. It was fragranced with Bradley's man-flowery cologne. I hated his scent. It reeked of ambition and narcissism. I wondered how I managed to date him for as long as I did. He wasn't my type. Not even close. He was big and boorish and beastly even. There was nothing tender about him—not the smell of his skin or the tone of his voice—nothing.

I rolled onto my back. "Working late at the hospital …" I had grown up hearing the excuse every time there was a concert at school, a dance recital, or even a birthday.

I closed my eyes and tried to ignore the nauseating smell of Bradley's scent on my furniture while visions of my eighth birthday flooded my thoughts. I remembered Richard promising me a box of freshly baked cinnamon buns from this little bakery on the corner before getting the call. His presence was required at the hospital. It was late, and there was no one to watch me, so he took me with him. I remembered the way he seduced some young, cute brunette nurse into keeping an eye on me. After a while, the nurse got busy with her own duties, and I got bored.

I roamed the long, sterile corridors, stowing away in bedding carts and hiding within supply cupboards, pretending I was on a secret mission to eradicate evil and protect the patients. It was my birthday, after all, and I deserved to have a little fun. At some point in my adventure, I happened upon the most peculiar room. It was cold, dimly lit, and stock piled with fridges and freezers. I'd been gone for a long time, and after a while, Richard's brigade of maudlin medical personnel finally went ballistic, scouring the hospital for me. But it was Richard who found me, crouched in the corner of the dimly lit room, surrounded by bags of blood. I was slathered in the stuff, using it to create drawings on the floor as though it were finger paint.

I'd never seen Richard so angry. He glared at me and muttered, "I knew this would happen," before pulling me from the floor by the collar of my shirt and dragging me away from the blood and through the hospital. We went straight home that night. We never talked about what happened, and we never had the freshly baked cinnamon buns from the little bakery on the corner like he promised. From that day on, he relinquished his efforts as a parent. It was the death of my childhood.

I swallowed the lump in my throat and struggled to bury the recollection of that dark day somewhere deep down inside me. *Freshly baked cinnamon buns.* A subtle smile eased the hardness in my face. I imagined I was breathing in the robust sweetness of cinnamon, letting it tickle my nose and fill me with delight. Soon my thoughts were flooded with images of my beautiful stranger, the one that smelled of tin-cinnamon from my dreams—the Tin Man as I so fondly called him.

I could feel myself escaping reality and slipping away again to my happy place, my dreams. I could almost feel the humidity in the air the moment I let go. The warmth of the sun on my face and the gentleness of the breeze against my skin made my body flutter with delight. I loved it here. It was my personal paradise, a playground for my most decadent desires. I listened as the cicadas' hiss smothered the drone of the gloomy city beyond my window. I was going in deep this time. I would surrender to the dream, letting myself marinate in every sensation for as long as possible.

And then *he* appeared, the sweetness of his scent floating toward me like a snowflake in the wind. I inhaled deeply. My body trembled with exhilaration. He was sitting down, leaning against the sinewy roots of the banyan tree, his small, red book opened across his lap and a pencil in his thin, pale hand. I watched the incredible speed with which his fingers controlled the pencil. The pointy lead tip fluttered along the surface of the paper faster than a humming bird's wings. It was inhuman.

"Can I see it yet?" I asked impatiently, my voice airy and childlike—because in my dreams, I was always a child.

The Tin Man looked up at me, his emerald green eyes sparkling. He grinned before running his hand through his unkempt hair.

"What are you drawing?" I insisted.

He laughed softly. "My muse, of course."

I could feel my mouth pulling up into a smile. I loved it when he called me his muse. I giggled and tried to peek over the edge of his sketchbook. "Are you finished *now*?" I asked, watching his pencil flitter against the paper.

"Patience," he whispered calmly, his hand frantically flickering like a rattlesnake's tail as he sketched.

I sighed loudly and threw my arms into the air, overwhelmed with anticipation. I spun around like a ballerina again and again. The warm wind soared through my hair, whistling its song as I twirled—when suddenly I stopped. I felt his icy breath on the back of my neck. I turned around to face him.

"It's a good thing I'm fast," he said in his crisp English accent, "because you are incredibly impatient!"

He grinned and handed me his red sketchbook. I reached out and snatched it from him with my tiny fingers. As I stared at the paper, my eyes widened. It was enchanting, like a page from a storybook. Each detail of the forest was captured with the utmost ethereal authenticity. To look at his art was to peek into the marvel that was his glorious imagination. Then suddenly a tiny charcoal butterfly landed on the tip of his pencil, and a blast of icy air distracted me.

My body shivered as a layer of goose bumps blanketed my skin. I could feel myself fighting against the horrible cold current while it pulled me away from the dream world and back to the real one. I fought and fought, but with little success, and when my eyes finally opened, I noticed the front door to my loft swinging open, a rush of icy air streaming in with it. My eyes struggled to focus on the pretty woman with the chin-length black hair standing in the doorframe. It was my friend Ryan. She looked like Cleopatra with a little less eyeliner and was wearing the most dynamite white dress I'd ever seen.

"Happy birthday, Sleeping Beauty," she said in her deep sultry voice as she swaggered across the wood floors in her red stilettos. "My god," she snickered, "you haven't even recovered from last night!"

I propped myself up on the couch, wiping my eyes as the image of my Tin Man faded from my thoughts.

"Honey, you have to get going."

I grimaced, feeling the stiffness in my limbs and the sickness in my stomach. "How do you do this every night?"

Ryan laughed. "I tend bar every night. I don't go out and celebrate my friend's birthday every night." She ran the tip of her thin pale finger along my cheek. "What the hell did you do to your face?"

I laughed, wiping some of the anti-aging goop into my hand. "I was trying to keep it from looking thirty."

Ryan laughed. "You're not thirty. You're only a baby, for crying out loud." She slumped down on the couch beside me and grinned devilishly. "So," she said, clapping her hands together. "Was it the one when the Tin Man saves you or the one with his sketchbook? Or maybe it was the reading one. I just love how perversely romantic the reading one is."

"How do you know I was dreaming about *him*? Maybe it was the drowning dream again."

"Yeah right. You're way too happy for the drowning dream." She grinned. "Look, if I had reoccurring dreams about a guy like your beautiful stranger, I'd nod off all the time too."

"You think I'm crazy."

"What—holding out for a figment of your imagination?"

The Tin Man really was everything, and no one could compare to him. Every fiber of my being wanted to believe in him, to believe that he was out there somewhere waiting for me. I sighed and bowed my head, a swell of seriousness suddenly consuming my thoughts. "Richard cancelled," I said.

"Good. He'd ruin your birthday with that bimbo fiancée of his. It's bad enough he's subjecting you to yet another one of his pretentious weddings with his latest Barbie doll."

I nodded. "Bradley cancelled too."

"Even better!" she cheered. "I can't stand that caveman."

"He said he was working late."

"Good." Her face suddenly hardened. "By the way, what happened last night? You didn't even bother to say good-bye. In fact, you didn't even acknowledge me when you stormed out of the bar."

"I know. I'm sorry." I smiled. "Good-bye. See ya. Ciao. Until we meet again."

"Too little too late, my friend," she replied. "Make it up to me then." Her eyes sparkled with flecks of luster like star sapphires as she spoke. "Indulge me with the naughty details," she insisted. "I saw you sneaking into the ladies' room with that pretty boy."

"What pretty boy?" I teased.

"Oh don't pretend like you don't know what I'm talking about."

I laughed. "He's just this guy from school. He's in my class. *Nothing* happened."

"He's not your classmate, sweetie—he's your student! And your version of nothing happened and my version of nothing happened are two very different things. So … which is it?"

"My version. Nothing happened. Seriously."

"Too bad. He *was* cute. Was he even legal?"

I tossed a vinyl pillow at her and laughed, recalling the unrefined smell of his warm skin against me. "I just needed to get Bradley out of my head." I exhaled with frustration. "He's all over me. All the time."

"Neanderthal."

"He's using me to impress Richard." I laughed. "As if anything I do has *any* effect on my father."

Ryan stiffened and placed her hand on my knee. She was cold; she was always cold, but today even more so. She quickly retracted her hand from my skin. "Sorry. I've been freezing all day. Hope I'm not getting sick," she blathered defensively.

"You can't get sick," I pleaded, tossing her the red hoodie that was hanging from the end of the couch. "One of us has to stay strong."

Ryan eyed the hoodie and flashed me a funny smile before draping it around her gaunt frame. "At least one of us *is* strong," she assured me. "There's absolutely nothing wrong with you." She smirked. "Well other than the fact that you're obsessed with the mystery man from your dreams!"

I laughed.

"What really happened to you last night?" Her voice softened. "I was worried. The way you left was … I don't know. It wasn't like you."

I shifted uneasily. "I got a call from my father when I was with the pretty boy. Something happened."

"What?"

"I inherited a property. Apparently, my late grandmother left her estate to me."

"What grandmother?"

"Exactly!"

"Richard knew you had a grandmother out there and didn't tell you?"

I nodded. "This is by far the lowest he's ever stooped."

"So who's this grandmother? What did he tell you about her?"

"Nothing other than the fact that she was my mother's mother, and apparently he knew her—a long time ago."

"Unbelievable," Ryan muttered, grasping her face with her hands.

"He was blabbering about a bunch of stuff on the phone last night, but I wasn't in any condition to process what he was saying."

"Did you call him back today?"

"No," I said, pulling my knees to my chest and hugging them.

Ryan shook her head. "That's it." She tore the red hoodie from her thin shoulders and let it fall to the floor. "C'mon." She grabbed me by the hand and pulled me from the couch. "You need to go out and have some fun. It's your birthday. Pity parties are for the weak. You, my friend, are strong, gorgeous, smart, and young! And you just inherited a windfall. We're celebrating."

"I just want to stay here …"

"And what? Go back to your Tin Man?" She grabbed my face with her cold hands. "That isn't reality, honey. You have to get out there and live your life before—"

"Before what?" I said. "Before it's too late?"

"I didn't say that," she snapped.

"You know my mother was twenty-nine when she died." My tone was somber.

"I know," Ryan replied. "But *you* are not your mother."

I nodded with a half-smile.

Ryan grabbed me by the shoulders and coerced me into the bedroom. "C'mon, you," she insisted. "No one ever succeeded in reality by living in their dreams."

"But my dreams are so much better than my reality!"

Ryan flicked me in the forehead with her long fingernail.

"Ouch!" I complained overdramatically, reaching for a pair of my comfiest blue jeans.

"No way!" she barked in reply, tearing the jeans from my hand and passing me something much tighter and more uncomfortable instead.

"This is torture, pure torture," I moaned.

"Suck it up, sweetheart. It's time for you to find your *real* Tin Man." And then she winked.

3-Choice

The music was so loud it drowned out my thoughts. I took another swig of my drink and smiled. Ryan knew how to take care of me. She was my apothecary, and this place was a most perfect elixir.

I finished the last drop of wine in my glass and straightened the red bow on my black, barely-there mini-dress. I sighed, noticing a young couple engrossed in each other at the bar. I could hardly tell where he ended and she began. He was tall and slim. She was adorable with the loveliest red hair I'd ever seen. He was slathering the little rose tattoo she had on her neck in a tongue bath. They were oblivious to everything around them.

"What are you staring at?" Ryan interrupted, arriving back at our table with another bottle of wine.

"The lovers over there."

She turned to look and cackled. "You think *that's* love?"

I shrugged.

"That's drunk and barely twenty-one."

I laughed. "Wish I could be—"

"What, drunk and twenty-one?"

"I was going to say I wish I could be so free. Imagine being so in love with someone that nothing else mattered."

Ryan rolled her eyes.

I smirked. "It's *my* birthday. I can dream."

"All you do is dream," she replied, pouring the wine into our glasses.

"At least the dreams make up for the nightmares," I noted.

"I don't know anyone who does either as much as you do." She laughed.

My thoughts drifted back to my beautiful stranger, the gentleness of his manner and the sweet crispness of his voice.

"What is it that he has over you?" she said, as though she was somehow privy to my thoughts. "He's not even real."

I beamed. "Oh he's real, all right. And he's out there somewhere waiting for me."

"I envy your optimism," she said.

"It's not optimism. It's something more ... a feeling. And I know you think I'm nuts, so I'm not going to talk about him anymore tonight."

"I don't think you're nuts," she whispered. "I think you're romantic—a *hopeful* romantic." She grinned. "And if you tell anyone I said that, I'll be forced to kill you. C'mon, I have a reputation to keep." She reached into her purse and pulled out a tiny white box with a red ribbon on it. She placed it on the table and stared at me.

"What's this?"

"A steak dinner," she joked.

I gently tugged on the red ribbon, letting it unfurl until it fell to the table. I pried the box open. "Ryan!" I gasped, ogling the splendor of the necklace inside. It was beautiful, resting peacefully on a soft bed of satin.

"It *is* beautiful, isn't it," she said.

It wasn't any ordinary necklace. The pendant was circular, about the size of a dime, adorned with tiny rubies and diamonds and decorated with extremely ornate filigree. It was opulent, exquisite, and obviously antique.

"You like it?" Ryan shifted awkwardly in her seat. "I had to pull a few strings to get it." "What strings?" I asked, continuing to scrutinize the extraordinary piece.

"This guy owed me a favor."

"A favor—huh?" I held the pendant up to the light and watched as the rubies and diamonds shimmered like miniature fireworks. "This isn't a necklace—it's an artifact. It belongs in a museum."

"Oh probably," Ryan replied casually. "But what fun is there in being held captive in a museum." She smiled deviously. "Wear it. Show it a good time. It's so old, it probably can't remember what it's like to live."

I smiled. "I can't accept it." I handed the necklace back.

"You *will* accept it," she insisted, pushing my hand away. Ryan grabbed her glass of wine. "I didn't steal it, and if you don't wear it, I will be terribly offended. Besides," she whispered, urging me closer, "I happen to know that this particular necklace has special powers."

"Don't be ridicul—"

"I'm serious!" she said, trying to tame her giggling. "It has a long history. If you wear it upon your chest, true love will find its way into your heart."

"C'mon, Ryan. That sounds like the message in a greeting card."

"I know, I know," she laughed. "But I'm not kidding."

"Then why are you laughing?"

"Because you're making me feel like I'm lying—but I'm not." She tried to stop herself from smiling.

I heaved a sigh and laughed with her.

"Look," she insisted. "Just wear the thing—okay?"

"Okay."

"Now let's toast!" Ryan extended her brimming glass. "To your birthday and," she hesitated, "to destiny. Whatever mysteries lay ahead, may they overflow with pleasure and swelter with passion!"

We clinked glasses together and took a drink.

"C'mon," she said. "Try it on." She grabbed the necklace from my hand.

My gaze flitted back to the bar as she placed the cold platinum chain around my neck. "No! No! No!" I exclaimed suddenly. It was Bradley. Dressed in a white button-up shirt and perfectly pressed, tan chinos, he was standing at the bar groping a pretty brunette. They were laughing, flirting, and whispering to each other.

Ryan finished securing the clasp and ran her cold hands along my shoulder blades. "Are you seeing what I'm seeing?" she asked heatedly.

"Couldn't miss it if I were blind."

"Do something!"

"Like what?" I said, fear surging through my body like poison.

"Well if you're not going to do something," she said, "then I will."

I placed my hands on her bony shoulders in a bold effort to stop her.

"Now that's more like it," she said, urging me on.

I took a deep breath and started walking toward Bradley inhaling the noxious odor of his man-flowery cologne as I neared.

"Hope!" he said nervously as I approached.

"Working late?" I scoffed.

"I *am* working," he pleaded. He grabbed the brunette by the arm and turned her toward me as though she was a rag doll. "This is Jenna … the new intern. Richard told me to get her acclimated."

The brunette belittled me with her smug smile before fluffing her bushy, brown hair.

"I don't care, Bradley. We broke up—remember? It's your life. I just hate the lying."

"I wasn't really lying," he argued.

I rolled my eyes.

"What? That was an apology."

"Ugh."

He grabbed my arm.

"Let go of me," I ordered.

"Not until I ask you something." He swallowed nervously. "I didn't want to do it this way, but here it goes." He let go of my arm and fumbled through his pockets before getting down on one knee in the middle of the crowded bar. He extended his hand to me, grasping a large diamond ring between his index finger and his thumb.

I gasped—paralyzed with panic.

"This is so hard for me, but I'll do it because I know that you're good for me." He exhaled deeply. "Hope Havergale, I know you love me, so I guess it's time that you marry me."

My face contorted as I stared at the ring. It was huge, ghastly, and more menacing than the thought of a handcuff being secured around my wrist. The room went silent.

"Well that was the most vainglorious proposal I've ever heard," Ryan jibed, cutting the silence. Her laugh was harsh. "Oh, Bradley," she razzed, "you really are incredibly good at this—although I think you could have said *me* a few more times."

"You," he raged, pointing at Ryan. "Stay out of this." His gaze shifted back to me. "And you," he said like a threat, pulling himself from the dirty floor, "put this ring on." He grabbed my finger and forced the giant diamond into place.

"She didn't say yes, you moronic ape," Ryan snapped.

He scowled at her with his bulging blue eyes.

"Meathead," she muttered under her breath.

At that moment, Jenna, the cute brunette, grabbed her purse and started walking away.

"Hey, Jenna!" Bradley called out. "Don't leave, honey. What's the problem? Let's finish our drinks!" He dropped my hand and tore off after her.

I bit my lip and stared at Ryan. "Did that just happen?"

"What—the part when the caveman proposed or the part when he blew you off for a mistress already?"

I shook my head with disbelief. "Can we please get out of here before he comes back?"

A huge smile stretched across Ryan's gaunt face. "Drats," she teased. "It was just getting good."

"I'm glad my life amuses you," I said, pulling her though the crowd of inebriated bodies toward the exit.

I wanted nothing more than to head home and hide. I wanted to wrap myself in a cocoon of blankets and stay there until I was ready to emerge a beautiful, confident butterfly. But Ryan insisted that the only way to becoming a butterfly was to set myself free. She wouldn't let me go home. And so we found another bar a little less complicated and tried to salvage what remained of my birthday.

"So where is this property you've inherited?"

"Please don't talk about anything serious," I begged.

"You have to talk about it. You have to make a decision." She grabbed my hand. "You believe in fate and destiny and all that mumbo jumbo, right?"

I nodded.

"Well then you have to do this. It's a sign." She smiled.

I stared down at the ring on my finger. The large, round diamond was faultless, refracting with thousands of tiny prisms. It was firmly cradled within the grasp of six platinum claws upon a solid band. I contemplated whether Mother Nature was being sassy when she saw to it that time and pressure had the capacity to produce something so lovely. I sighed as I stared. This ring would make any normal twenty-nine-year-old woman giddy with delight, but I wasn't any normal twenty-nine-year-old woman. I was different, and like the diamond, I worried that time and pressure would eventually force me to become something other than myself.

"You okay?" Ryan asked.

"Yeah." I took a deep breath. "It's a little place called Perish Key," I muttered reluctantly. "In Florida."

"The Florida Keys," Ryan purred. "That sounds like fun."

"I can't go."

"Why the hell not?"

"My job," I claimed. "This might be the year they finally give me tenure."

"So? Is that what you really want? *Tenure*? What about some fiber cereal and mothballs to go with it?" Ryan laughed. "Look, you're twenty-nine, remember? You should want excitement, passion, and adventure—not tenure."

"Don't mock me," I begged. "I don't think I can bear it today."

Her dark eyes narrowed. "I'm not trying to hurt you. I just want you to be happy. Get out there and live your life before settling down and becoming a schoolmarm."

"Schoolmarm?" I rolled my eyes. "Gee thanks."

"Look, all I'm saying is that it's an opportunity. You've never had a sense of family—well not a real sense of family anyway because Richard and his poor excuses for wives certainly don't count." Ryan grabbed my hand. "This could be that thing you've been missing. That sense of family."

I sighed. "But she's dead."

"Yeah obviously, but her stuff is probably still there. And maybe she had neighbors and friends and, well you get the idea."

"I don't know. It's not like me to do something this—"

"Exciting?" she said, cutting me off.

"Irrational."

"Oh, Hope, it's a chance to escape reality." She smiled and added, "*Without* dreaming."

"Maybe you're right."

"Wait. Stop. Is that a smile I see on your pretty face?" she jeered.

"Don't tease me," I said, struggling to fight the ridiculous grin that was creeping its way across my face.

"So you'll go?" she asked with anticipation.

Suddenly the weight of the world had been lifted. I beamed with excitement. My decision was made. I would test my new wings and seize my destiny. I would buy a plane ticket and discover something about my past, the grandmother I didn't know existed and the remnants of a life I never had the pleasure of knowing. I would discover something about family—*my* family.

4-Blood Pact

I was a weightless cloud floating through a sea of blue sky. And suddenly, like in any dream, nonsense became sense. The hissing cicadas and the whispering wind tickled my eardrums like an enchanted overture. I inhaled deeply. The familiar fusion of ocean water and oleander filled my nose. I licked my little-girl lips to taste the soft tang of salt in the air while a tropical gust blew the heady scent of tin cinnamon toward me.

My tiny body came alive, electric with excitement. I opened my eyes faster than a falling star. And there he was, just as perfect as the moment I left him, his vague face radiating with a magnificent splendor.

"Try it again," he whispered tenderly.

I looked down at the book in front of me and focused in on the words above my finger. "For saints have hands, um, that … pilgrims' hands do touch." I sighed. "And palm to palm is holy palmers' kiss."

"Good," he murmured, gently putting down his pencil and pausing to look up from his red sketchbook.

"What does it mean?"

He grinned. "You really want to know?"

I nodded.

"Juliet is telling Romeo that the virtuous way to profess their love is by holding hands."

"Holding hands?"

"Yes," he laughed.

"Let's do it."

"Hold hands?" His voice cracked awkwardly like a nervous adolescent.

"Yes, silly boy," I replied eagerly. I dropped the book by my side and started raking the sand with my fingertips until the rough ridges of a piece of coral grazed my soft skin. I held up the coral and smiled serenely at the Tin Man before dragging the serrated edge along the inside of my palm and slicing it like a razor.

"Hope, stop!" he raged, moving toward me.

Blood oozed from my tiny hand like a river. I tossed the piece of coral at his chest. "Now you," I insisted.

"No!" His tone was hard and his eyes wild.

"Do it," I said.

"No!"

"Don't make me do it for you," I seethed.

"It could be dangerous if—"

"I don't care. We've been over this. Just do it," I maintained, cutting him off. I grinned mischievously and began playing with the curls in my hair, twisting them coyly around my fingers, completely unmindful of the bloody gash on my hand and the spill of blood that was staining my blond strands.

He moaned a strange frustrated groan.

"I thought you were my friend," I said.

"Don't," he pleaded.

"I just want you to prove it." I bit my lip. "Swear your eternal friendship to me." I batted my lashes at him. "Please."

"Oh, Hope," he said, an agonizing expression on his face.

"Do this for me. Do this one thing, not because you want to or even understand why, but because I'm asking you to." I smiled coyly. "And I've never asked you to do anything."

"Oh why do you torture me like this?" he muttered under his breath.

I smiled, staring into the metallic shine of his eyes.

He sighed and shook his head, reluctantly taking the sharp coral ridge and pressing it into the pale skin on his palm. It bled instantly with a peculiar thick, viscous crimson.

I was elated with his willingness to please me and inhaled the scent of his blood. I stared into his eyes and quickly pressed my hand against his.

He gasped with my touch.

The cold of his skin against the warmth of mine felt electric like an effervescent sting, but soon our touch befell a much greater intensity. Our wounds fused together in a seamless union, our blood mixing and congealing as one. But before long, the force of him within my bloodstream burned like a firestorm, making my tiny veins smolder with pain. At first I wanted to scream, pull away, but the longer I held on, the stronger I felt. And soon I could perceive his feelings through the touch, like he was somehow speaking to me using the connection between our hands.

My heartbeat intensified, and I watched as he opened his beautiful iridescent eyes wider than normal and gazed like he was glimpsing into my very being.

"*I can feel your heart*," he said without speaking.

"*I can feel yours too*," I replied without a single sound leaving my lips.

The thump of his barely palpable pulse beat lethargically in the palm of my hand while the fire raged inside of my veins, boiling my blood as it coursed through my body. It was painful, yes, but also very wonderful with an addictive quality that made me crave more.

"Hope," he uttered tenderly, "you must let go."

I strained to stay fastened to him, but his tremendous physical strength was no match for my feeble determination. The moment our palms parted, the burning ceased. I watched as his cut miraculously repaired itself, and then I unclenched my fist. My wound was still gaping and oozing with blood. At that moment, something intrinsic and powerful from deep within me took over, guiding my actions. I extended my bloody hand to him like a leaf reaching for the nourishment of the sun. I closed my eyes, and when I opened them again, my wound had been cleaned. There was not a drop of blood except for the small scarlet smear that was left on his bottom lip. He licked it with his tongue and grimaced with shame.

A blush coloring suddenly replaced the bluish tones of his lips and cheeks. He seemed energized and renewed, and I knew that it was because of me. I shifted my gaze ahead to the glorious golden sun and watched as it bid a final farewell to the day.

"What have I done?" he muttered, his head in his hands.

"You've done nothing," I shot back exuberantly.

He shook his head from side to side.

I pressed my cheek against his strong shoulder and said, "Why can't it be like this forever?"

"Why would you want *this*?" he asked, withdrawing a little.

I looked into his eyes. "I want you."

"Hope, you shouldn't say things like that."

"Why not?"

"Because you're just a child, that's why. I know it's difficult for you to understand, but you *must* wait."

"I won't," I insisted.

"You will," he replied.

"Well I can't wait," I confessed, heartbroken.

He turned toward me and gazed into my eyes. His look was impassioned, sending charges of emotion through to the very core of me.

"I'm not going anywhere," he whispered. "I'll be waiting for you."

I could feel my eyes starting to swell with tears. I swallowed hard.

He touched my chin with his icy fingertip. "Do this for me," he pleaded. "Do this one thing, not because you want to or even understand why, but because I'm asking you to." He smiled. "And I've never asked you to do anything."

I bit my bottom lip and grinned a little.

He smiled back.

I leaned my head against his shoulder again and looked up at his boyish face. It was still indistinct and relatively featureless and yet somehow beautiful and lovelier than everything in the world.

"Patience," he whispered gently. He was aglow with the light of dusk. His jet-black hair seemed almost auburn now and his lips a happy shade of pink.

"I can't be patient. I'm only a child, remember." A solitary tear emerged from my eye and slid down my cheek.

Faster than speed itself, he caught my tear in his pale hand just as it was about to drop. He held it tightly, and when he opened his hand again, the tiny symbol of my sadness sat comfortably upon the freshly healed scar in the center of his palm like a diamond, glistening in the bronze blaze of the setting sun.

I looked into his eyes, and as I gazed into their strange iridescence, I could feel my own eyes glazing over. Like Dorothy in the poppy field just outside of the Emerald City, I surrendered to the overwhelming sedative power. The truth swirled in a circular motion with the deadening darkness of his pupils. The tall grass and palm trees seceded into millions of miniscule particles dissolving before my eyes. The sounds of songbirds and whispering wind suddenly turned to soothing silence, while the savory smell of saltwater and cinnamon became a distant recollection of a scentless perfume. Like a ghost, I drifted somewhere between imagination and truth. And when I awoke, I had arrived.

"Hey, lady," a crotchety voice said. "You're here."

I rubbed my eyes and straightened my posture. I peered out the window of the cab. It was dark and late, but I could see the silhouettes of palms and pines up ahead, and I could hear the whooshing of ocean water through the opened window.

"This is it?" I asked skeptically, gazing out at the dense wooded area cloaked in shadow.

"This is as far as I'm going," the cab driver replied ominously.

"But there's no house?" I said, more to myself than to him. I handed him the money, the aged scar in the center of my palm shimmering in the moonlight. I pressed my tired face to the glass and suddenly saw the outline of a large structure in the distance, almost like a castle rising through the darkened pines. My heart thumped its clumsy beat.

5-Fog

I wasn't particularly fond of water. I never much cared for swimming and always had an irrational fear of falling in and drowning. Nightmares plagued me since childhood. Every dream was always the same: sinking deeper and deeper into the water, drawn by the compelling call of death as it pressed upon my chest and appropriated my last breaths. And now I was in the Florida Keys, nestled between the Gulf of Mexico and the Atlantic Ocean. The chain of islands, connected by bridges like the bones of a skeleton, was surrounded by water.

When I got out of the cab, I stretched my arms and watched as the beautiful night materialized before me. Stars flickered in the black velvet sky above. The soothing sounds of waves crashing against the shore in the distance calmed my nerves while heat bugs hissed to an intermittent rhythm around me. It was humid for so late at night and so late in the season. I inhaled deeply, sensing all that fragranced the air.

The house was barely visible though the patches of dark forest up ahead. I immediately resented tipping that cab driver; he could have dropped me off a little closer to my destination. I dreaded the thought of treading through the thicket in the dark.

I grabbed my purse, slung it across my chest, and tugged on my large, designer suitcase. The case was a gift from Richard. It was a lot like his latest fiancée actually: pretty to look at but utterly useless. Its tiny golden wheels struggled to spin along the stone pathway. Every few inches, the case fell, and I was forced to prop it back up again.

Eventually, I stopped to take a break. I sat on the suitcase instead of propping it back up. When I looked around, I was surprised by the darkness. There were no streetlamps; there was barely even a street for that matter. Moonlight was my only guide. A jolt of nervousness shot through me. I was alone, and there was no one anywhere for miles; here, the mosquitoes significantly outnumbered the people.

"I've a feeling we're not in Kansas anymore," I whispered as I ruthlessly exterminated insects against my skin, their tiny corpses sticking to my clammy flesh.

I stretched my arms out, closed my eyelids, and tilted my head to the sky. And with a deep exhale, I opened my eyes to the splendor of the heavens. The darkened cerulean night was nothing like the muted haze of pollution that shrouded the city at night. And the sounds were like something from one of those corny relaxation compilations, except that this was real and there was nothing cheesy about the live performance of a choir of frogs and chorus of cicadas.

I breathed in the salty humidity and sweet florid aroma. The tranquility and simplicity was impressive, otherworldly even.

In many ways, Perish felt like the place that time forgot. I knew it was one of the smaller keys in the archipelago, far less popular than Marathon and Key Largo and not nearly as exciting as Key West.

A cool breeze caressed my skin, and suddenly my tank top and jeans didn't seem warm enough. I needed a jacket. I unzipped my overstuffed suitcase just a crack and felt around for a sweater. When my fingers finally graced the velour of my favorite red hoodie, I tugged on the arm, prying it out between the clenches of the zipper's teeth. Once free, I swung the red sweater around my shoulders and slipped inside it.

The chilly warmth to the wind felt like summer's last breath. It was autumn, and yet the foliage was still alive with a burgeoning vigor. I liked being distanced from the gloomy browns of fall. Back home, the leaves had already changed, and the air was bitter and angry, raging for winter's welcome. It was almost as though I was on a vacation, like an extraordinary spell of stolen time mysteriously bestowed by an estranged grandmother.

I propped my hood over my head and sighed. "Grandmother," I whispered, feeling like Little Red Riding Hood, "what strange taste in real estate you have."

Suddenly I noticed a peculiar low-lying fog approaching. The mist crept nearer, stroking my arms with its cool, moist tendrils. The fog was undeniably inauspicious. I apprehensively scanned the surroundings.

"Hello?" I called out, dreading a response. "Somebody there?" I swallowed hard. It was silent. Dead silent. And soon the fog surrounded me. "Show yourself," I demanded, my voice wavering.

Looking into the thick miasma was like staring down evil's throat and becoming suffocated by its intoxicating breath. I felt as though I needed to succumb to it. Lightheadedness was beginning to consume me, and unconsciousness was only a gasp away. I closed my eyes for a moment, feeling a return to my dream world just within reach. I was a child again and back with my beautiful stranger. My eyes opened to him. He was sitting by the banyan tree, staring at me.

"Are you finished yet?" his delicate voice beckoned.

I looked at him with confusion before realizing that I was holding his red sketchbook in my lap. I was doodling a black butterfly on the first page.

"I don't have all day," he badgered playfully.

"All right, all right." I thumbed through his collection of beautiful sketches; there were some of me and some of our forest. Then I turned to an empty page. I gently stroked the tip of the pencil across the paper in a single line, waving it slightly for hair and fingers, while curving it considerably for shoulders and ears.

"Ready now?" he jeered.

"No!" I shouted in my juvenile tone. "I never seem to get your face right."

He smiled. "Let me see it so far."

I rolled my eyes and grunted, embarrassed by my pathetic portrait.

"C'mon," he pleaded, extending his hand to me.

I eyeballed the familiar scar in the center of his palm before reluctantly placing the red book in his hand.

"It's brilliant," he said, scrutinizing my infantile drawing.

I turned the book around and took another look. My drawing was a one-line silhouette. It was terrible, even for a kid. "Have you gone mad?" I asked.

He laughed sweetly.

I rolled my eyes and grinned. "I *am* rather proud of the other one though."

"What other one?" he asked.

"The butterfly … on the first page of your book."

He turned to it. "Black butterfly." He sighed.

"What's wrong with it?" I asked self-consciously.

"Nothing." His voice was stern. "It's just …"

"What?"

"Well," he whispered, "some say that the black butterfly is a harbinger of death."

"A *what-in-ger*?"

"A harbinger," he said, "a warning that death is near."

I swallowed uneasily. "Death doesn't frighten me, you know."

"Is that so?" He smirked.

A rush of warm wind soared past, ruffling the pages of his sketchbook. Scraps of loose paper suddenly sprung free, floating through the air like confetti.

We dashed through the woods in an effort to collect the fallen pages.

"Is it true?" I asked breathlessly.

"Is what true?"

"That ghosts live here." I reached out and grabbed hold of a paper just as it was about to take flight. It was a sketch of an old ship.

He took the page from my hand. "There are stories."

"Are they true?"

He hesitated for a moment.

"Well are they?" I persisted.

"That depends," he replied.

"On what?"

"On your definition of a ghost."

At that moment, the loud cry of a bird startled me. I opened my eyes and gasped. I was back on the dark pathway sitting on my suitcase. The fog was retreating. I watched as it slowly slinked its way past me and onward. Then I heard the bird again. Its call was jarring like a crow, but much more hoarse and abrasive. I looked around but saw only darkness. I hurried to my feet and dragged the ridiculously useless suitcase behind me. *Ghosts*. I sighed. This was definitely not the time to be thinking about ghosts, but I couldn't seem to help it. I recalled the cornucopia of folklore I had inundated myself with prior to the trip; ghosts were a big part of that legacy.

"*To perish on Perish*," I mumbled over and over again like a nervous mantra as I stumbled along the stone pathway, fear driving my every step. It was something I remembered reading before I left—something published in a less respectable digest and not one of those run-of-the-mill tour books from the travel association.

Perish Key was aptly named for its unrivaled aptitude for disemboweling over a dozen ships in the last two hundred years. I recalled reading about the malicious way affluent settlers at the turn of the century perpetuated such silly sayings and refused to make their homes on Perish Key, asserting that it was plagued with a terrifying legacy of tragedy, misfortune, and above all, death. I remembered seeing claims made by the brave few that actually lived on the key over the years, avowing that they had in fact seen the souls of deceased sailors roaming about. Others swore off swimming and even sailing near Perish Key for fear that the fallen vessels were haunted like morbid ghost ships laid to rest in a crowded graveyard on the seabed floor. A chill ran up my spine.

And then like a glimmer of hope, the house suddenly came into view. The dramatic glow of the big auburn moon above obliterated the murkiness of the fog. I rushed ahead, dragging the futile suitcase behind me like a sack of potatoes.

The tawny moonlight illuminated the historic abode like a shimmering jewel. My eyes lingered on each glorious detail as though it were the Sistine Chapel. It was striking and much larger than I had imagined and sat proudly like a queen on its rather substantial plot of land. It was elegant: a Victorian gingerbread house without the candy trimmings. It had two floors, quaint windows with louvered shutters, and an old-fashioned wrap around veranda. The spires and turrets were reminiscent of a mythical castle while the sloped roof was evocative of Snow White's cottage. I could envision ferns hanging from the porch, swaying in the tropical breeze while Grandma, reclined in her rocking chair of course, listened to the frog calls and crickets like a serenade.

The house was dark both inside and out. Only the moon, the brilliant twinkling of the stars above, and the tiniest flashes from fireflies illuminated my way as I neared the front steps. A sharp breeze soared between the palms like whispers as I rummaged through my purse for the key. The unsettling mixture of smells and sounds coming from the shadowy woods propelled me to get moving. I contemplated what creatures might be out there, both earthly and ethereal, and dreaded to imagine what they fed upon.

No one was around, and yet I had a funny feeling like someone was watching again. My skin tingled with nervous exhilaration as I approached the house—*my house.*

The exterior was tired. Not so much dilapidated, but rather more neglected, like a little elbow grease could easily restore it to its former glory. The old white paint was flaking. The cement steps at the front were cracked and crumbling. The wooden floor planks around the porch were splintered and warped. Even the front entryway looked like the sad skeleton of a once exquisite threshold.

I abandoned my purse and suitcase at the foot of the cement steps and headed to the front door. A weathered metal plaque, oval in shape, next to the door read: Ambrose House.

"A house with a name," I said. "That's different." I took the key out of my coin purse and carefully pushed it into the lock. It didn't turn. I heaved a sigh before twisting it harder from side to side, but stopped when I felt as though it was about to break off. I pulled the key out and groaned. I tried again, straining to turn it with all my might, but nothing happened.

I kicked off my shoes and flexed my tired toes on the warped, wooden porch planks before considering the likelihood of another entrance. With a renewed vigor, I walked barefoot down the steps around to the side of the house. The sounds of the night grew louder as I neared the corner, resonating like an ominous orchestra rehearsing for an impending performance. A large bullfrog cleared his throat while a pair of bats swooped over me. I gasped nervously.

Just then an eerie silence resounded. My body trembled as I listened to the sound of my shallow breath harmonizing with the hushed shuffle of my feet against the dirt path. And suddenly a boom of thunder echoed like shattering timber. An unbelievable rush of rain ensued. I put my red hood over my head and hurried along the strange, spongy grass. The force of the falling drops was so hard I was compelled to take immediate cover. I felt like an unarmed soldier under open fire.

A huge, gnarly rooted tree at the threshold to the forest seemed my closest cover. The trip back around the house to the porch was a long one, and the strange tree seemed safer than the dark woods. I darted toward the tree and nestled myself within its sinewy roots in an effort to stay dry.

I bit down on my bottom lip to hamper the trembling while beads of rain teased my eyelashes like falling diamonds, blurring my vision with a glittery gleam. I glimpsed at the moon as it hung in the sky like a celestial jack-o-lantern, bearing its defiant smile to the world. The heavy rainfall entranced me with its audible aria. The longer I eavesdropped the more it sounded like the applause of an audience, and suddenly the loneliness became tolerable.

6-Visitor

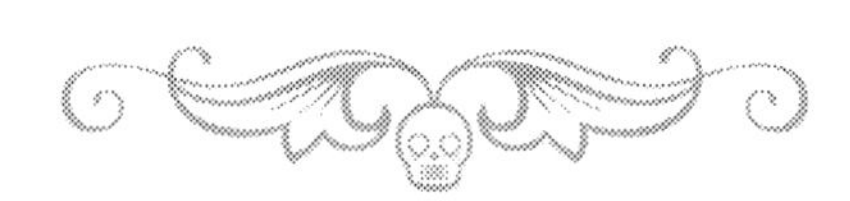

When the rain finally let up, I rushed toward the side door as fast as my feet would allow. My toes skimmed across the grass with a slippery step as I headed for the narrow entranceway. I was determined to get inside the house. I inhaled the sweet scent of jasmine that fragranced the evening air as I soared. The delectable aroma of honeysuckle was present too, its potency somehow enlivening the damp darkness of the night like a ray of light—a glimmer of hope.

As I sped across the grass, I eyed the ramshackle pool. It was empty and dilapidated. The fallen tiles and decaying cement walls were creepy. It reminded me of a giant crypt. I hated pools—even in the absence of water.

The house was quite a distance from the shelter of the tree and gave me ample opportunity to examine the expanse of my inheritance. The property itself was immense and resplendent with natural beauty. A forest full of trees fringed the estate; acreage abundant with tropical flora peppered the grounds while a bevy of wildlife thrived throughout. It was unquestionably beautiful in an eerie kind of way.

I tucked my hands inside of the front pockets of my red hoodie and eyed the rotting, retro patio furniture and old, ornate cement planters that sat in ruins like tombstones across the lawn. When I finally reached the side door, I froze. An unexpected visitor halted me at the steps. It was the most unusual bird I'd ever seen, much larger and sleeker than a crow. A raven, I realized. I had never seen a real raven before. I swallowed nervously as I stared into its strange eyes. They were tiny and whitish like two gleaming pearls. And the more I stared, the more I realized how glazed over they appeared. I watched the way his iridescent black feathers shone with a purplish color in the moonlight. He was fascinating, and like a royal guard, he was perched majestically upon the top step, forbidding my entry into the house.

"So?" I asked, feeling like Alice arriving in her Wonderland. "Why *is* a raven like a writing desk?"

And then he cawed at me. I gasped with fright. Apparently he wasn't a Lewis Carroll fan. I swallowed nervously, my eyes fixed on the peculiar bird. The strange sound of his voice intrigued me. It was low and guttural and reminiscent of the birdcall I'd heard on the path. Then he cawed again, bobbing his head back and forth, his large pointy feathers shifting against one another like overlapping louvers as he continued to thwart my entry. I tried shooing him away. It didn't work. Suddenly he moved closer, studying me with his peculiar eyes before belting out yet another raspy caw.

"What?" I demanded, fear coursing through me.

Slowly he toddled toward me, and then he lunged, tearing a snake from my shoulder with his mouth. I yelped, watching in awe as he flew away into the night with the snake dangling from his beak.

Boom went the loud thumping of my heart, resonating like an uncoordinated drumbeat in my chest. I hurried up the steps toward the old, wooden side door, slipped the key into the lock, and exhaled with relief when the handle actually turned. I rushed inside the house, and immediately a strong surge of wind slammed the door shut behind me.

I gasped.

It was dark. Incredibly dark.

I tried to push the door open again but quickly realized that the force of the wind had lodged it on a splinter of wood. It was stuck. I pressed with all my might, but the door wouldn't budge. Only a thin crack of light beamed through a small opening at the top. The wind raged through the tiny gap like the whistle of an angry teakettle. I shuddered with fright, lingering in the darkness and deliberating whether to venture forth.

An instant later, I shed my hood and pressed on. I extended my hands and searched the walls with the tips of my trembling fingers for a light switch but felt only the soft flocking of ancient wallpaper. It was dark, and I was scared. The smidgen of moonlight from the crack in the doorframe was barely enough to see what was right in front of my face, let alone what was up ahead. I continued on my way, slowly shuffling my feet along the cold tile floor.

The fact that I was barefoot terrified me. My toes became the most sensitive part of my body, apperceiving everything with the perception of my eyes. Every granule of dirt and cluster of dust horrified me, feeling as though I was treading upon the bones of rotting rodents and spongy insect corpses. And as my footfalls quickened, so did my breathing.

Boom. Boom. My heart thumped quickly. I was in a hallway—narrow with a low ceiling. It was claustrophobic, and I knew I had to get out of there as soon as I could when all of a sudden the most surprising smell caught my attention. It was cloying and heavy like molasses and made my mouth water. My body came alive when I reached what felt like a doorframe. It smelled good in there. I ran my hand down the length of the door until I touched the large knob. I embraced the handle and turned hard, but nothing happened. The door was locked.

Just then a blast of wind suddenly pushed the side door open with the force of a slap. A tunnel of amber light illuminated the narrow corridor. I pulled myself away from the strange door and forced my body to move ahead. I had to continue on; I had to get out of the hallway and into the main part of the house before the door became stuck again and I was once more caught in the darkness. I sped through the corridor, away from the smell and deeper along the arteries of the house.

I ascended several steps and found myself at the backend of what seemed like the living room. I flicked on the light switch, but nothing happened. My eyes scanned the shadowy surroundings. I felt like Pip from *Great Expectations*, half expecting to see the likes of Satis House—Miss Havisham's crusty wedding gown and cobwebs—but this was altogether something else. It was elegant and eclectic, smoldering with history like a museum. Metal floor candelabras, strange pegs wrapped in rope, curved walls, and an immense wooden lady like a mermaid from an ancient ship immediately caught my attention.

My heartbeat slowed as I looked around. Fascination overcame fear. I took a deep breath, my senses coming alive with smells. I immediately identified an understated metallic aroma; it was faint, but it was definitely present. Mustiness also imbued the air like rain against pavement. Clearly the place had been vacant for some time. I closed my eyes for a moment, marinating in the redolence, wondering when I'd happen upon the fragrance *she* left behind—my grandmother's scent.

Persian rugs were scattered across the floorboards like lily pads in a pond. I leaped from one to the next, trying not to touch the hardwood with my messy feet, when suddenly I realized that the carpets were actually covering deep-set water stains. I pulled back the edge of one of the carpets and eyed some of the damage. "Flood?" I whispered with uncertainty, but the stains were quite profound, as though they were the outcome from years of consistent saturation. I flipped the carpet back into place and sauntered gingerly through the darkness toward the entryway.

The house was divided up the middle by an impressive wooden staircase. The two rooms flanking the stairs were of utmost peculiarity. The room to the left was lined with countless books like an extensive library while the room to the right, the living room, was more decadent than a turn-of-the-century boudoir. It was decorated with impeccable Victorian furniture, boasting a bevy of exquisite antiquities, floor candelabras, and gilded mirrors. Rich ruby velvets filled the interior with an undeniable seductiveness. It was almost too provocative for a living room and definitely too provocative for a grandmother's house.

My eyes flitted back to the focal point of the entryway: the wooden lady. As though liberated from an old pirate ship on its return from Peter Pan's Neverland, the carved mermaid was affixed to the wall next to the staircase. She was elegant, angelic even. With scales like plates of armor and hair the faded tone of gold, she was larger than life, crafted with an utmost realism. She stared at me with a look of melancholy in her vacant eyes. I was more enchanted than frightened, and the longer I stared, the more I felt as though this wasn't the first time our eyes had met—but that was ridiculous.

I turned around, unlocked the front door, and stepped outside. The air was ripe with the rich reek of rain. A storm still hung on the horizon. I walked across the rickety porch planks and down the crumbling cement steps to get my stuff. After looping my arm through my purse and dragging the suitcase inside, I sighed a breath of relief the moment I shut the door behind me.

"Home," I whispered.

I secured the old, cast iron deadbolt and moved toward the living room. It was dark, and yet somehow I could still see the mermaid's empty eyes following my every move with their ghostly gaze.

The Victorian couch opposite the huge window looked enticing. I fell into the fold of its crimson arms and sighed with exhaustion. The couch was soft and unexpectedly comfortable. I tried to relax. I rummaged through my purse for my phone. There were four messages—all from Ryan. I vowed to call her in the morning. My eyelids were heavy. It was a concerted effort to blink. I stuffed the phone into the front pocket of my jeans and exhaled loudly. I felt the slithering sensation of my necklace falling along my chest before landing in the little niche at my collarbone. I took the pendant into my hand and stroked the exquisite jewels, feeling the rough ridges of each tiny ruby and diamond. "True love," I said to myself longingly. "Wonder if this thing really works …"

At that moment, a flash of lightning streaked the sky, illuminating the wooded area just beyond the window. My body trembled. I kept my eyes to the glass, watching. The black sky lit up again. This time, the flash exposed the silhouette of a raven sitting on the porch rail. I gasped, jolting to a sitting position. I waited for the next flash, gnawing my nails to the edge of my skin. A boom of thunder rumbled through the house like the hum of a dragon. Then there was nothing—nothing but quiet, and soon the silence swallowed me whole. And while I fretted anxiously in the belly of the calm, without warning, a brilliant strike of lightning illuminated the room with a grand blaze.

There was a man in place of the raven on the porch. My body faded into unconsciousness, floating like a feather into the graceful arms of the velvety red couch.

7-Love

My pulse struggled to pound to the sound of a steady rhythm. *Thump. Thump. Bang. Thump. Thump. Bang.* I exhaled deeply and opened my weary eyes.

"What the hell is that noise?" I sauntered over to peer out of the huge window in front of me. I rubbed my eyes. The sun had barely risen behind the scrawny pines. I watched as the surplus blues and grays of night mingled with the gentle, early morning sun. I was captivated by the ease with which night became light and dawn become day; it was poetic.

I didn't need a clock to tell me that it was early. I needed a few more hours of uninterrupted rest, but the banging continued, insisting that there would be no more sleep for me this morning.

I ruffled my tangled hair and followed the sound of the steady banging up the large staircase, past the wooden lady, to the second floor. The old floorboards creaked beneath my feet as I leaped upon them.

When I reached the landing, I noticed the large master suite to one side and three smaller rooms to the other. The doors were all slightly ajar. I started peeking inside of the rooms as I passed by when suddenly the wretched sound of the banging increased in speed.

"What the ..." I muttered, storming down the corridor toward the source of the sound. It was coming from the last of the smaller rooms at the end of the hall. I pushed the heavy door open and was surprised by the splendor of sunlight as it bathed the room in a golden glow. The cheery yellow walls and furnishings reminded me of a field of dandelions; it was incredibly lovely and almost made me forget about the banging—but then the dreaded sound continued. I shaded my face to dim the brightness of the sun, and as I looked across the room to the window, I noticed the silhouette of a person standing outside on a ladder. "That's it!" I said, moving toward the shadowy figure, watching as each pound coincided with the strike of the hammer.

And then I froze.

It was a man—a beautiful, young man, and I couldn't take my eyes off of him. A blast of emotions surged through me. I didn't know whether I wanted to scream or laugh or cry. My breathing quickened, and the palm of my hand suddenly started throbbing. "Holy sh …," I started to say, watching wide-eyed as the early light of dawn blazed upon his faultless chest like sunbeams on sand. And with each strike of his arm, his strong shoulders vibrated like the strings of a cello, coercing my graceless heart to synchronize in rhythm. His black eye-length hair playfully flickered with hues of auburn as the gentle light diffused each splendid strand. And as I looked closer, I noticed the pale pallor of his exposed skin. It was soft and delicate, almost featherlike. He was like an angel—a dream. I stared, spellbound. He was exquisite and left me breathless. A most ridiculous grin forced its way across my face, and I let it happen because in all of my life, I had never seen anyone so splendid; no one had ever made me feel so emotionally charged before. He was unbelievable.

I might have stayed forever between the door and the armoire just watching if he hadn't moved closer to the glass, looking in as though he had suddenly become aware of me. Mortified, I thrust my back against the wall, hopeful that he hadn't seen me—hopeful that my honey colored hair blended in with the rest of the golden room.

"Tell me he didn't see me," I pleaded with myself before trying to sneak another look. I stuck my head out a little, and then it happened: our eyes met. And it was beautiful, like the world suddenly stopped spinning for a moment and time was standing still.

And then he smiled.

I gasped, humiliated, and pulled back to the shelter of the golden wall again. Fear hit me like a fever. My face flushed, my skin crawled with clamminess, and chills surged through my body. "My god," I said. "Who is he?" I'd never felt this way before. I'd never known love at first sight, and the thought of it, the incredibly preposterous thought of it, terrified me.

In a moment of frayed emotions, I fled the golden room and moved to the landing, but by the time I reached the end of hall, I wanted more of him. My lovesick heart craved another look. I needed to see if he was real—if that beautiful vision beyond my window was more than just a figment of my overactive imagination.

I hurried into the room beside the staircase, desperate for another glimpse. The pleasing scent of gardenias graced my nostrils the moment I entered. I inhaled and smiled. The sun sparkled brilliantly throughout the pure white room as though it was shining on a blanket of freshly fallen snow. It was heavenly. With the skillfulness of a snake, I slithered across the ivory colored canopy bed to the window and furtively pressed my face to the glass. "He *is* real," I said, watching him hang off of the ladder, his strong upper body flexing as he descended the rungs. "But where is he going?" I muttered nervously. "To the porch—the front door." I panicked, and yet I wanted to see him again. I fled the room and charged down the staircase more eager than a giddy schoolgirl, a rush of adrenaline pushing me onward.

When I reached the main floor, I leaped like a dancer across the pathway of Persian carpets toward the large window opposite the velvet couch. I looked through the glass and scanned the surroundings. I couldn't see him anywhere. The ladder was empty, and the porch was vacant too. "Where is he?" I muttered, confused, when suddenly the shrill sound of a pebble striking the windowpane startled me. I turned to the glass and saw him, pebbles in hand, standing on the lawn just below my window. I watched in awe as he leaped from the ground up to the porch with unbelievable dexterity, suspended from the railing by the crushing grip of his left hand. Then he pulled himself up to the veranda with the ease of an adolescent on the monkey bars.

"Oh my …," I mumbled, impressed. He was tall and somewhat lean with beautiful broad shoulders that framed the fine figure of his physique. His strong, pale arms peeked out from beneath the black shirt he suddenly seemed to be wearing. He was leaning comfortably against the porch railing, his shiny black hair hiding his face, making it difficult to see anything beyond his sweet smile. I giggled a little at the thought of how refreshing it was seeing someone so attractive without a tan. And then he shifted his position. I swallowed nervously, drawn by the compelling manner of his stance, my eyes rapt by the tender way his jeans sat just below his hips, displaying the refined contours of his lower abdomen. He was gorgeous to look at, that was obvious, but there was something more there, like a rush of feelings that he invoked in me—and *that* seemed crazy. I felt like an adolescent with a crush, panging for some cute guy, some stranger I didn't even know, and the impulsiveness of it all frightened me.

He wanted me to look. I could feel it. He made my bones ache and my pulse pound, and when he ran his long, pallid fingers though his dark hair, I had to gasp—I was unable to contain it any longer. I watched as his hair fell into place, dangling in front of his eyes, imploring me to come closer and sweep them back with my hand. "Oh," I said, breathlessly. He laughed in response, flashing me a smile, his perfect teeth even whiter than his pale skin.

And then he gestured for me to come around to the front door.

I froze, reality suddenly hitting me. "He wants to talk to me—in person!" Fear folded its frightening arms around me, crushing me with its unforgiving grasp. I struggled to breathe while butterflies wrestled in the pit of my stomach. "I don't think I can do this," I said to myself, moving away from the window and dropping pathetically to the floor. "Damn it!" I whined, biting down on my bottom lip. "Why do I have to be so scared all the time—why do I have to be so—" And then I stopped myself. I took a deep breath and swallowed hard. I tore off my red hoodie and pulled myself from the wooden floorboards, forcing my frightened body forward. I unfastened the deadbolt, opened the front door, and stepped across the threshold onto the porch.

The sweet scent of salt and citrus hung in the morning air like fog. It was pleasing and eased my nerves. I closed my eyes for a moment and inhaled, fear finally releasing me from its grasp. I smiled as I opened my eyes again, feeling renewed and full of confidence, and suddenly he was there, leaning against a pillar on the cement steps just below the veranda. My heart swelled with excitement. He was even lovelier in person—without the glass between us.

"Hello," he said. His voice had an unexpected softness to it.

I smiled, ready to respond, when suddenly my phone started ringing from within the front pocket of my jeans. I pulled it out, dragging my eyes away from him for a moment. *Ryan.* I knew she was worried about me, but she'd have to wait. I shifted my gaze back to the pillar, but when I looked up again, he was gone. I rushed down the cement steps to where he had been standing, but it was already too late. He was nowhere to be seen. "Hello?" I called out. But there was no reply. I heaved a sigh and turned back to the house. A cool breeze soared past, sending shivers up my spine. I peered over my shoulder once more, hopeful that he would be there, but he wasn't. I was alone.

I exhaled with defeat before moving back inside the house. I shut the door tightly, securing the deadbolt across with a swift slide. Fear wasn't far behind. I could feel its devious fingers tickling the back of my neck, readying to take complete control—again.

8-Good Christian

I spent the rest of the day unpacking and exploring. The house was big and chocked full of strange stuff. I knew it was going to take me a while to get through everything, but then I wasn't on any particular schedule. There was no job waiting for me when I returned. And I didn't mind that. Time was on my side for a change.

I wanted to go out and enjoy the sunshine, but something about my liaison with the mystery man on the ladder tarnished my enthusiasm. I was a little uneasy with acknowledging that perhaps he didn't really exist. I tried to keep my thoughts from revisiting all the silly ghost stories about Perish and merely took the day to explore indoors instead.

The sky outside of the living room window was electric with color at dusk. I watched in awe as the brilliant orange sun descended beneath the skeletal pine needles of the trees. It was the end of the day, and it was beautiful. When nightfall approached, I cuddled up in the huge bed in the master suite. The sheets were dark burgundy and smelled of pennies. It was an unusual aroma but a pleasing one. It didn't take long for sleep to meet me. My eyes were heavy and fatigued from sifting and sorting through my grandmother's belongings. I slept peacefully—absent of dreams, which was most unusual for me. There was something about this place, the feeling of it, the smell of it even, that comforted me.

And when dawn broke, I awoke to the familiar, shrill sound of banging.

"It's him!" I sprang from the satiny sheets in my white T-shirt and pajama pants. "He *is* real."

I rushed down the stairs to the main floor of the house. The day was alive with vitality. Sunlight poured in like molten gold, illuminating the living room in a gilded sheen. I pressed my face to the window, my body tingling insatiably with exhilaration.

"*His* ladder," I said, spotting the immense metal apparatus leaning against the side of the house. "I knew it. I knew he'd come back."

I hurried toward the front door and tore it open, determination pushing me onward. The smell of morning caught my attention the moment I stepped outside. I inhaled the magnificent mugginess in the early air and grinned. The city didn't smell like this—not ever. This was fresh and clean, dreamlike even. I relished its purity, allowing the aroma to infuse my senses with its pleasant powerfulness. Then with a spring in my step, I scampered along the porch and through the spongy grass, making my way around the side of the house before fear had a chance to catch up to me.

"Good morning," a familiar voice called out from atop the old, rickety ladder.

And as I elevated my gaze, butterflies swiftly returned to my stomach, quivering with excitement. I blinked, and then suddenly, he appeared, standing in front of me on the grass, leaning casually against the side of the house.

I gasped, startled with his sudden presence on the lawn. "How'd you …," I started to say while becoming sidetracked by his beautiful body. His shirt was unbuttoned and hung loosely against his skin, presenting me with a generous glimpse of his well-sculpted chest.

He smiled. It was infectious. I couldn't help it. He laughed in response.

"I didn't wake you, did I?" I could hear the empathy in his voice in addition to the trace of an English accent.

"Not really," I lied, biting my lip and playing with a few strands of my disheveled hair as I struggled to conceal the fact that I was still in my pajamas.

"You're lying. I'm terribly sorry," he said, moving a little closer. He had the charisma of an old-time movie actor and the swagger of a rock star.

"Don't worry about it," I said, studying his face as he neared. His features were stunningly soft and his eyes an exquisite green.

"I'm not very good with time," he avowed.

"It's okay," I said. "I'm not either."

He grinned boyishly in response. I wanted to melt inside.

"Sorry about leaving yesterday." His voice was like poem, enchanting me with its splendiferous style.

"Yeah. I was starting to think I'd made you up." I eyeballed the way his jet-black hair framed his high cheekbones, drawing my attention down to his cushiony, full lips. Ah, his lips. They were perfect, soft and blush in color and beckoning me to press my own lips against them.

He smirked self-consciously.

I sighed, smiling back, and continued gazing at his unrefined youthfulness. He was mesmerizing—both childlike and mature simultaneously. While his body was muscular like a man, his face was angelic like a boy. My skin tingled with excitement the longer I looked. Emotions swelled inside of me like a storm. There was something compelling about him that attracted me with a fierceness I'd never felt before. I locked my hands together behind my back in a concerted effort to keep from lunging at him. And despite the fact that it seemed ridiculous, I really did want to charge him; I wanted to pounce upon the feather-like serenity of his sweet skin and feel the hard curvature of his muscular form pressing against me.

"So," he said, clearing his throat.

I laughed a little in reply and struggled to resume composure.

"Here you are then." His words were gentle. He smiled.

"Here I am," I uttered in reply.

"Actually," he whispered, "I didn't realize you had arrived."

"*Arrived*," I repeated like an imbecile, entranced by his enchanting allure. I flushed with mortification the moment the ridiculous word left my lips. "I mean, I got here last night." I was flustered. "Or was it the night before?"

"It must have been late," he said with a grin, running his fingers through his hair.

"Yeah," I uttered brainlessly, ogling his chest.

"Well," he said, "you're probably wondering why I'm here."

"Not really. I mean—" I took a deep breath and tried to compose myself. "Why are you here?" I had hit a low. An all-time low. Mortification didn't even begin to describe the way I felt at that moment.

"Moira hired me to fix the place up."

"Moira?"

"Your grandmother."

"Right," I said. I looked up at him again, my eyes suddenly somber. "You do know she—"

"Passed away," he said. "Yeah, I know." He bowed his head. "I'm very sorry for your loss."

"Thanks." I smiled demurely.

"But that doesn't mean I'm going to stop fixing Ambrose." He shifted his position against the wall and slipped his hands into the front pockets of his jeans.

His pants suddenly lowered a little as he tugged on them.

My god, I sighed in my thoughts. His body was making me behave like a lovestruck teenybopper. He had curves and definition in places I'd only ever seen in naked Ken dolls. I tried to look away. *Keep your eyes off his hips,* I told myself.

"Ambrose," he suddenly said.

"Ambrose?" I asked.

"It's Greek. It means immortal one."

"Hmm," I said.

"That wind is really picking up," he said, changing the subject.

"Yeah," I replied absentmindedly, as I continued eyeballing the divinity of his form.

"She won't need much to bring her back to life."

"The house?" I asked, a little startled.

"Yeah, the house," he replied with a grin.

I laughed a little and cleared my throat, avowing to finally start acting like an adult. "So," I said with resolution. "What exactly needs fixing?"

"Only a few things. She's a good old house." He took his hands from his pockets and planted them on his hips. The veins in his arms protruded as he pressed. "She's got lots of potential you know." His words were smooth like slipping into a warm bath.

And then I started blushing again. I didn't know whether it was his words or the damn veins in his arms this time that prompted my response, but there it was—the tingling beneath my skin, the aching in my bones, and the graceless pulse palpitations consuming my better judgment once more.

"But," he said, staring at me, "it's missing something."

He was fixed on me with a biting intensity. And even as I closed my eyes, I could feel the power of his stare upon my skin, sensing as he shifted his gaze from my mouth across my face and down my neck. It was like time had suddenly frozen again, and I was its prisoner, held captive—defenseless and vulnerable for all of eternity.

"It's hard to put my finger on it exactly," he continued, taunting me with subtext. "It needs the right kind of attention. It needs unwavering. Undivided. Undefiled attention."

My eyes flew opened. *Undefiled attention. This can't be real. He can't be real. Nobody speaks like that.*

"It's worth the work," he said suddenly, his tone brisk.

I felt the sting of his stare abate almost immediately. I looked into his eyes. They were vivid and splendid but definitely not as intense as before. He had the longest eyelashes I'd ever seen.

"You're not considering selling?" he implored running his long, pale fingers across his body as though he was wiping debris from his skin.

"Well—"

"Can you honestly say that wherever you're from is more beautiful than this?" He gestured to the lush surroundings as he spoke, but it was obvious that he was referring to himself.

He was smooth—I'd give him that.

"Look, just don't do anything you might regret." His manner was more confident than that of any young man I'd ever known.

I smiled.

"You look a lot like her, you know," he said.

"Who?"

He laughed. "It's in the eyes. You have her eyes."

"Really?"

He nodded.

"Had you known her long?"

"Yeah." He paused. "A long time."

"What—since you were like five?" I teased.

He raised his dark eyebrows and laughed. "I'm older than you think, Hope."

Hope. How'd he know my name?

"She spoke of you often," he said gently, as though in reply.

"She did?" A strange sense of pride surged through me.

He nodded.

"But she didn't even know me."

"*You* didn't know her," he corrected graciously before turning around and starting back up the ladder.

"Well," I rambled desperately, "can you tell me about her?"

He flashed me a sassy smile. "On one condition."

"Anything."

He looked at me, holding his gaze.

"Okay, maybe not anything," I corrected with a laugh. "C'mon then. What's the condition?"

"Don't sell the house. At least not right away anyhow. Give yourself a chance to get to know it first." He grinned. "Sometimes old things are the best things."

"All right," I said, nodding. "That sounds fair."

"Good."

"Hey," I called out, watching him ascend the ladder. "You never told me your—"

"It's Christian."

"Christian," I whispered. His name felt good on my lips.

He laughed quietly and popped a red, heart-shaped candy into his mouth before climbing further up the ladder.

A strong gust of wind suddenly sailed past. The unexpected hint of cinnamon in the air from his candy filled my nostrils, and when I smelled deeper, past the cinnamon, I detected the light tang of metallic rust.

I froze, feeling as though my skin suddenly turned paler than a ghost. I knew instantly that the face of fear was closing in again, taunting me with its evil eyes. My inelegant heart struggled to race as I watched the wings of the wind gracing Christian's body with its coiled current. It was though I could actually see the miniscule particles that composed his smell drifting from his skin like pollen toward me. I breathed in deeply. The succulent scent of tin-cinnamon saturated my senses with a frightening familiarity. And then suddenly like déjà vu, coincidence, and serendipity, my dreams became my reality.

The Tin Man. He had a face, and it was beautiful. He had a name, and it was Christian.

I closed my eyes for a moment, letting the sun soothe my skin. I contemplated my sanity and, above all, why fate was teasing me.

I rushed away from his ladder and back into the house. I didn't know how to talk to him—I simply couldn't. He was the manifestation of my imagination, the living incarnate of the man in my dreams. I was mortified, exhilarated, and above all confounded. I closed the front door, slid the deadbolt into place, and pressed my back against it, hopeful that he wasn't following behind.

My thoughts sped while my stomach churned. It was stupid to believe that Christian was the Tin Man. He was just a guy. Simply because he bore a resemblance to my beautiful stranger, the one I'd been dreaming about since I was a little girl, didn't mean anything.

Or did it?

The strident banging resumed. It was him—my Tin Man's swing of the axe, his strong arm striking the hammer. I listened to the sharp thump and envisioned the soft sunlight upon his pale frame. My anxiety turned to wanton curiosity. *I had to see him again*. I needed to know if what I was feeling was destiny's delicate hand sweeping through the contours of my life. I needed to know if my Tin Man was real.

I rushed past the wooden lady, up the staircase, and into the white room. It was still aglow with the luminous sun, gleaming with heavenliness. I leaped across the bed and toward the window, getting tangled in the slippery disarray of white satin sheets as I moved. I saw him just beyond the glass. He was balancing on the ladder as though he was floating high above the world.

"Angel," I said to myself. "*My* angel." And then I slinked closer, my stomach flitting with anticipation as I moved. I watched the tender way his dark hair fell into his beautiful eyelashes and the ease with which his muscles came alive as he swung the hammer.

"Why couldn't he be the Tin Man?" I mumbled under my breath. I'd always believed in his existence, so why now, now that I finally found him, did I suddenly start questioning everything—even my own heart?

The more I looked, the more euphoric I became. He was incredibly young and decidedly attractive. And yet there was something remarkable about him that extended beyond merely that of juvenescence. He had a tender allure. Outlined in a soft nimbus, his exquisite form appeared as though the surface of his skin were the edges of a quill. And like an archangel or story-bound character, he was more dreamy and enchanting than humanity seemed capable of—and yet he stood before me on a ladder just outside of my window, real. Real flesh. Real blood. Real bone. Real.

I sighed. "If this is a dream, I don't ever want to wake up."

And then he shifted his position on the ladder, leaving me a clear view of the right side of his body. His unbuttoned shirt blew like a sail in the breeze, and I noticed the elaborate image of a phoenix tattooed along the span of his ribcage. It caught me off guard. Completely off guard.

"Prince Charming never had one of those," I said, my eyes glued to his ribs while my skin quivered with a mischievous excitement. The smooth lines graced his fair skin like paint upon canvas, as though he himself was a work of art—a living work of art. I exhaled with delight. There was something arousing about the way the tattoo hardened the innocence of his appearance.

And then he saw me.

I wasn't ready to be seen. I moved away from the window and collapsed on the white canopy bed, falling into the tousled mess of sheets. They were slippery and cool and smelled of salty gardenias. I tried to clear my thoughts, but it was difficult. He was impossible to ignore.

"Christian," I rambled to myself. "Who are you? And why do you make me feel this way?" I smiled and stared aloft. I watched the shadows dance across the white ceiling in large broad swoops as the sun peeked in and out of the clouds. Light, dark, light, and then dark again. Sometimes the shadows even overlapped; the light became the dark, or perhaps it was the other way around. But even the arcane character of nature's splendor wasn't enough to distract me from the beauty of my Tin Man.

As I reclined on the bed, I could feel my necklace sliding forward from deep within my shirt. It stopped falling just as it approached the little hollow below my throat. The circular pendant found a comfortable way of lodging itself into place. I stroked the tiny rubies and diamonds with the tips of my fingers. "True love," I said. "Maybe I've—"

Suddenly there was a loud knocking at the door. I jumped. *It's him*, I thought, surges of fear and excitement coursing through me. I tousled my hair with my fingers and licked my lips as I hurried down the large wooden staircase toward the front door.

When I pulled the door open, my face dropped with disappointment.

"Good morning!" greeted the robust woman standing on the porch. "Expecting someone else?" Her voice was severe.

I shrugged. It was Christian I expected. Christian I wanted. But where was he? I sighed sorrowfully in my thoughts as the sweet sound of his hammer faded into the wind like smoke.

"I'm Shirley Powers," the colorful, big-boned woman asserted proudly, her voice wobbly like the gobble of a turkey.

I smiled awkwardly.

"I'm a real estate agent." She cleared her throat. "Word has it you're interested in selling."

"Really?"

"Oh yes, sweetheart," she replied, her stout frame jiggling like jelly as she laughed.

"You know now is not really a good—"

"I was in the neighborhood," she said, cutting me off. "And I thought I'd pay you a visit."

"You were in the neighborhood? *This* neighborhood?"

"Okay, you caught me. I wasn't in the neighborhood." She shook her head. "No one ever comes here. But I can get them here. Not to worry. I'm the best at what I do."

"Oh I bet you are."

"I can sell anything. Ice to an Eskimo … a corpse to a ghost."

"Corpse to a—I'm sorry, what did you say?" It was a bizarre expression and a rather insensitive one, considering the fact that I was recently bequeathed the property from my *deceased* grandmother.

"I won agent of the year three times in a row." She smiled. "And everyone loves me. Once I even …"

I could feel my eyes glazing over as I struggled to listen to her incessant rambling. She wasn't short on confidence, that was for certain, but she was weird, and weird wasn't always a good thing. She had a disposition that made insanity seem humdrum, and her dowdy clothes and out-of-style hairdo made her look like a bitter, middle-aged divorcee, despite the fact that she was probably younger than me. She was a train wreck without the carnage. She was, for lack of a better word, unexpected.

"So?" she said, bringing me back to reality.

I swallowed hard and directed my attention toward her.

"Can we close this deal or what?"

I looked at her with uncertainty. I had no idea what she was talking about.

She burst into an eruption of obnoxious laughter.

"What's so funny?"

"Your reaction! You weren't listening, were you?" she scolded. "You know, I didn't get your name." She extended her hand toward me.

"Hope," I mumbled, reluctantly reaching my hand out. She was cold and had a very firm grasp, like a man-shake. And as I neared, I wanted to sneeze. Her perfume was fetid, like a mélange of rotten eggs, lilies, and gardenias. I had to restrain myself from gagging.

"Perish is a small place," she said while straightening the large collar on her hideous hibiscus print blazer. "No one actually wants to *live* on Perish. How did you end up here? You strike me as more of a mainlander." Her eyes ignited with intrigue, highlighting the dreadful teal eye shadow that was caked across her large lids. "Oh right," she said. "*Beneficiary.* I forgot. Sad the way things work. Isn't it? Someone lives here their whole life, passes away, and then suddenly," she slapped her swollen hands together in a startling smack, "a *stranger* inherits everything."

"Um ..."

"I'm a conch?"

"A what?"

"A saltwater conch actually." She smiled, her swollen red lips twisted in a winding smirk. "It means I was born in Key West."

"Really?" I replied, pretending to be interested.

"Well," she giggled, suddenly easing up, "if anyone can do this job, I can. I've got the *Powers* to sell your home!" She grinned proudly at the irony in her overly rehearsed little spiel.

"Shirley *Powers*," I said uneasily. "Funny."

"Mind if I come inside and take a look around?"

I hesitated.

"I'll give you a free-of-charge, no-obligation evaluation of your home."

I thought of Christian—the promise I had made to him, the fact that I would give the old house a chance before putting it on the market.

"Hey, sweetheart," Shirley said, "can I come in and look around or what?" Her tone was hard.

"I guess," I said. "Come on in."

Shirley flashed me a phony smile before stepping across the threshold. She paused awkwardly for a moment, her foot lingering in the air.

"Now I have to go," she said abruptly.

"What? But, what about my no-obligation evaluation?"

"Some other time perhaps." And then she turned around and hurried away.

I tried to keep up with her, but she was incredibly swift for a woman of her stature. And when I moved outside to the veranda, she was already gone.

Just then, the sound of Christian's hammer suddenly resumed its sublime spot in my consciousness. The longer I listened, the less I thought about Shirley and her weirdness. The sound was loud from the porch and filled me with a joyous jubilance as I jaunted toward the side of the house to take a peek. I liked the fact that he was still here. It gave me comfort. And then I stopped myself mid-stride. I wanted to see him again. I was ready to see him again, but not in cruddy clothes. Christian deserved to see the real me—me with makeup.

I headed back inside the house and let the door swing shut behind me. I didn't fasten the deadbolt this time. Instead, I gleefully sauntered over to the staircase, pausing briefly at the scaly tail of the wooden lady. I scanned her ample timber bosom, scarlet wooden pout, and oak colored hair. She was beautiful, ancient and festering, but beautiful with a timeless opulence about her. I stroked the fine form of her scaly body. "Ready for some competition?" I taunted, and then I disappeared up the stairs, intent on readying myself for the man of my dreams.

10-Scars

I smelled like vanilla, and I felt pretty for the first time since arriving. Something about sliding into my white, cotton slip dress was rejuvenating. I rubbed my lips together and tasted the sweetness of the gloss. I was ready to see him.

Like sweet music, I followed the banging of his hammer through the house. I burst outside, leaped across the porch, and lunged down the crumbling front steps. *Christian*, I thought to myself, *are you the one—the one from my dreams?* My step quickened.

It was another gorgeous day; like paint by numbers, everything was perfect. It was October, and I was under the warm Florida sun staring at my private Garden of Eden.

Even the peculiar wooded area that fringed the estate was rather inviting in the daylight. I could hear the sound of water running ashore somewhere in the near distance as I inhaled the pleasant scent of salt and orange blossoms that imbued the cheery current. This was an autumn like no other; no falling leaves cracking beneath my feet, or chilly wet winds to remind me of summer's exodus. I was a tourist in my own home, a traveler with no itinerary. I felt alive for the first time in a long time.

Eventually, the loud banging of Christian's hammering distracted my fantasizing. I rushed ahead, and as I approached, something fascinating started to happen. My sense of smell suddenly became hypersensitive. Like tunnel vision, I was capable of ignoring all other aromas around me and purely focusing in on one scent alone—Christian's. Now that I knew his smell, it was effortless for me to find him.

Tin and cinnamon flooded my senses. Drawing in the aroma, I could feel my heartbeat accelerating, triggering something visceral from deep within me. I closed my eyes and allowed myself to surrender to every uncontainable sensation.

"Boo!" he suddenly whispered from behind me.

I gasped, pivoting around to face him. I had heard his hammering only a fraction of a second before and wondered how he could have gotten down from the ladder so quickly.

He smiled and winked at me.

"How did you do that?" I asked.

"Do what?"

"You were just …" I motioned to the ladder. "And now you're here."

"It's very hard to say really," he responded lightheartedly.

"It's very hard to say really," I mimicked in a dreadful attempt at his English accent. I smiled. "That's the best you can come up with?"

He laughed. "Is that actually what I sound like?"

I stared at him. The skin on his face was smooth and covered with only the faintest trace of stubble, an understated reminder that he was indeed a man amid the wholesomeness that made him look so boyish. His youth and perfection suddenly intimidated me. My insecurities felt indomitable in his presence. The crow's feet that feathered the corners of my eyes felt like roadside ditches.

"You look stunning today," he said in his airy accent.

I blushed. It bothered me that he was so blatantly flirtatious. I was way too old for him, and he knew that.

"Your dress is," he paused to scrutinize my body, "beautiful."

"It's rude to speak to your elders that way," I teased.

He laughed. "You're *not* older than me."

"Oh please, I'm *not* an idiot." I giggled, turning away.

He moved to stand in front of me, blocking the sun with his tall frame. "Hey," he whispered tenderly, the sound of his lovely voice quieter than the flutter of a butterfly's wings in the wind. "Time has treated you with soft hands." His tone was gentle, touching.

I sighed. It was an unfamiliar sincerity I wasn't accustomed to hearing from a man and left me somewhat breathless. I swallowed. "Nice try, handsome."

He laughed, running his thin, pale fingers through his dark hair. "*Handsome*," he mocked.

"Oh please."

We laughed in unison, the playful energy between us searing with intensity.

"You still didn't answer my question," I insisted.

"What question?"

"How did you get down from the ladder so fast?"

"Let me think about that." He pretended to study the height of the ladder and its distance from us with his hands.

I rolled my eyes.

"Hum," he teased, moving away a little to lean against the side of the house. "I'm fast," he said boldly.

"*Fast*," I said with disappointment.

"Yeah." He smiled.

I stared at him, into his eyes. They were electric. His dark pupils were surrounded by a remarkable blend of silvery green and yellow like the iridescent hues in an oil slick. They drew me in. I couldn't blink. And suddenly his feral eyes captivated me with a spellbinding shine worthy of stalking prey in the dark of night. I could feel myself conceding to dizziness—his stare and his scent compelling me. I was losing my balance and starting to fall.

"Hope," he called out, extending his left hand to catch me.

I was ready to reach for him when suddenly I noticed something.

"Your scar," I said, mystified.

He quickly clenched his fist.

"Wait a second," I pleaded, pulling myself back to a standing position. "Why do you have that scar in the center of your palm?"

He stayed quiet.

"Christian!"

He inhaled, his muscular chest inflating as his lungs filled with air. And then he exhaled with a sigh. "We've all got scars, Hope. Some deeper than others." His voice was haunting. He turned away and started back up the ladder.

"Wait!" I called out. But he didn't stop. "Don't leave," I said, as he continued up the ladder. "Christian," I whispered.

He stopped, the shine from his eyes refracting like a prism as he stared down upon me.

"Say it again," he said, the breeze carrying his words with the gentleness of a petal in the wind.

Our eyes locked. I could feel the magnetism from his stare coursing through my entire body.

"*Christian*," I replied, my lips quivering as his name escaped them.

Then, within a fraction of a second, he was standing next to me. I trembled with his nearness. I wanted to be frightened—but I wasn't. I looked at him, my body tingling with a peculiar blend of dread and desire as I stared. I wanted nothing more than to feel his mouth against mine. I wanted to allow myself to surrender to him. I wanted to let myself be impulsive. *Kiss me, beautiful stranger*, I implored in my thoughts. *Kiss me now.* I was ready and willing to receive him. I could feel his cool breath on my skin and sense that his lips were near. If this was destiny's plan, then I was eager to accept it with open arms.

Suddenly I felt him withdraw.

My eyes flew open.

He moaned softly, biting his bottom lip, a strange expression of restraint overwhelming his sweet face. "I should get back to work." The sun on his skin was divine, encircling him in a subtle yet sublime halo of fire.

I exhaled deeply. I was mortified and left with a hunger for his touch. I could feel beads of sweat trickling down my face and along my neck.

"I should go now," he insisted. His unyielding stare followed the droplets of sweat as they moved along my neck, pulsating as they traversed my jugular.

I watched as his beautiful long eyelashes fluttered like the wings of a monarch in flight when suddenly a subtle surge of movement overwhelmed me as though the world started working again. I wiped the sweat from my skin, closed my eyes for a moment, and heaved a sigh. I started thinking that maybe none of this was real—not the house, not the wind, not even the Tin Man. I considered that maybe I was lost in one of my dreams again. But this was different. I wasn't a little girl; I was an adult, and I was free to explore my temptations—free to explore my beautiful stranger whoever he was.

11-Sink or Swim

As I stood on the porch, I noticed that the sun was directly overhead. It was hot. A balmy breeze blew through my white, cotton slip dress. I couldn't keep hiding, pretending like he wasn't out there. If this was one of my dreams, then I deserved to enjoy it.

I tiptoed across the porch and down the cement steps. Music blared as I rounded the corner of the house. It was like I had stepped inside an old-time Hollywood movie. The big band sounds of lively trumpets and trombones boomed as I neared. *He filled the pool*, I realized as I wandered past it. The water sparkled like diamonds in the hot sun. It looked rather refreshing and inviting even to me, and I loathed the water.

I spotted Christian poolside. He looked splendid in his white T-shirt, jeans, and work boots. He was diligently revamping old patio furniture with the brightest red paint I'd ever seen. He didn't seem to notice me. The music was earsplitting, and he was lost in its melody. His body moved with a subtle grace to the rhythm of the tune. I giggled. I didn't take him for an old-time swing fan. My eyes lingered on the antique tabletop radio with the lovely carved wood chassis that was playing the music. It worked great considering its age. It was sitting atop a rusty, cast iron patio set. The furniture was distinctive and ornate—rusted butterflies and iron filigree. Christian was hard at work stroking one of the wings with the tip of his paintbrush, slathering it in a coat of shiny crimson.

I stepped off the grass and onto the sun scorched cement pool deck. The soles of my feet sizzled like bacon in a frying pan as I hurried.

"Hi!" he yelled over the music.

"Hi," I responded with a hint of anguish in my voice.

"Your feet must be burning!" He turned down the music a little. "Stand on the grass!"

I rushed to the lawn, letting its thick coolness squelch the fire. Christian neared, flopping down on the ground beside me. His scent was still highly aromatic and undeniably appealing. I inhaled discreetly, letting his tin cinnamon fragrance fill me with exhilaration.

"Ah," he groaned exhaustedly, tossing a wet paintbrush into the lawn before stretching his arms over his head.

I watched the way his chest heaved beneath his white shirt each time he took a breath. Quickly, I turned my attention back to the freshly painted patio furniture, a much needed distraction. "They sure don't make 'em like that anymore," I said.

"No, they certainly don't," he said with a laugh. He ran his paint-stained hands through his dark hair.

I clenched the thick, cool blades of grass between my toes.

"Do you have something against shoes?" he teased.

"No," I said, laughing, "I just couldn't find them." I watched the way his feet moved in time to the rhythm of the music.

"What?" he asked with chagrin.

"Nothing."

"C'mon."

"It's the music," I uttered timidly. "You really like it, don't you?"

His pale face flushed a little. "I can turn it off if you don't—"

"No," I interrupted. "Don't turn it off. It's nice."

He smirked. "Bet your boyfriend doesn't listen to this."

"*Boyfriend*," I giggled. "I don't have a boyfriend."

"I find that hard to believe."

"Oh really?" I nervously placed my hair behind my ears. "Why's that?"

He laughed, his long fingers tapping to the beat of the music. "Because you, my friend, are gorgeous." His lips curled into the most exquisite smile.

"Yeah sure."

"See that."

"What?" I asked, playing with a few strands of my hair.

"That modesty of yours." He bit his lower lip. "The fact that you don't even realize how beautiful you are makes you even more attractive."

I rolled my eyes, feeling my face blush. "Okay, Casanova." I leaned in closer. "Why are you so confident around women? You're just a kid."

He threw his head into the air with laughter before falling back onto the thick bed of grass. Reclined on the ground, he sat comfortably and silently with a stiff smirk stretched across his pretty face.

"Most *boys* your age would be tongue tied and tense around a woman. But you're different." I paused for a moment, watching the way he seemed to revel in my words. "Why?"

"Okay, it's a fair question," he said. He put his arms behind his neck and crossed his ankles. "It's simple really. I had two older sisters and a wonderful mother."

"Really?"

He nodded. "Mother was one of a kind." His eyes narrowed. "My sisters, however ..." He laughed. "They were another story."

"Were?"

"They died." He shielded his eyes with his hand from the blaze of the afternoon sun. "But that's life." He sat up. "And somehow we all manage to get through it."

He was so poised and sure of himself. I knew people much older than Christian, like my father, who could never express that kind of honesty. I smiled.

"So," Christian said, "how do you feel about a little elbow grease?"

"Well that depends," I replied, slyly searching the grass with my fingers for the loaded paintbrush.

"Depends on what?"

"On this!" I said, splattering a mass of red paint across his chest with the goopy brush.

He gasped. His white shirt stained instantly. It was red and looked like blood as it seeped through the fine fabric of his shirt. Suddenly his expression turned serious, his lips in a thin purse, his eyes electric with an eerie silver sheen. I trembled at the sight of him. He was both beautiful and terrifying.

"You," he threatened coldly, his voice deep and harsh. "You're so dead."

I turned pale, blood draining from my face, when suddenly his eyes brightened and he started laughing. A moment later, I watched as he ran across the pool deck for an opened can of paint.

"No!" I pleaded, trying to escape him.

"Hope," he insisted, "it's only fair." He held the nearly full can in his hands ready to hurl it at me.

"Please!" I shouted. "Don't!"

"Why not?" He retracted the can. "Give me one good reason, and maybe I'll change my mind."

"Because …," I said, tiptoeing across the grass away from him.

"That doesn't sound like the start of a very good answer," he taunted.

I laughed. "Okay, okay. Don't do it because … you're a gentleman."

He grinned. "Then I'll do it *gently*!"

I shrieked with laugher, dashing across the grass with the wet paintbrush fixed in the palm of my hand when suddenly I felt a damp, gooey sensation saturating the back of my white dress.

"I'm sorry," he said, trying to repress his laughter. "So sorry."

The red paint slithered down my body like syrup. "My turn now," I growled half-jokingly.

"Okay. I deserve it." He kicked off his work boots and inched closer to the edge of the pool.

I lunged forward like a jouster as though I was impaling him with my pathetic little paintbrush. He recoiled—a little. I charged him again, only this time taking what was left on the brush and painting a red stripe down the center of his face. He looked ridiculous. I started laughing when suddenly I felt him behind me. It was like magic, and I practically fainted when I felt him scoop me up in his strong arms. Suddenly we soared through the air like birds in flight toward the glassy surface of the pool. Fear squeezed me. I hated water, and here I was about to plummet into it. I closed my eyes, and everything went quiet: the water neglected to splash, the birds forgot to sing, and the wind suddenly lost its whistle. Silence echoed like clatter, and the world felt entirely wrong. I peeked out through my tightly clenched lashes and realized that we were hanging high above the pool airborne, lingering in a moment of static suspension. The icy coolness of Christian's breath fell gently against my skin. I looked up at him, trembling and wide-eyed, when suddenly our bodies plunged toward the water with the force of a missile. He wrapped himself around me like a shell, ready to absorb the shock from the slap. The impact was colossal; the upsurge on either side felt like the water's not so subtle way of grasping us within the palm of its hands.

And then we sank below the surface together. Sinking. Deep. Deeper. At first I could feel my body pushing to succumb to the lure of drowning. As in my nightmares, I felt my last breaths as they escaped my lungs, leaving me drained and weak. I wanted to submit to death's persuasive plea, but something inside of me burned with an invigorating compulsion to fight. I let go of Christian's hand and opened my eyes. Bright red paint sliced through the water like blood from a cut. I couldn't see him anywhere. I was running out of air when finally I coerced my defiant limbs to paddle.

I burst through the surface with a stupendous splash and gasped. Waist deep, I planted my feet on the bottom and brought myself to a standing position. Through the stream of water and tears in my eyes, I saw him. He was beneath the surface, circling me like a shark, a vivid trail of crimson paint following behind him as he swam. After a moment, he emerged laughing. Streaks of diluted red paint stained his face with a morbid eeriness. He stared at me, his eyes suddenly sympathetic.

"Oh no," he whispered, rushing through the water with an inexplicable swiftness.

I trembled, nervously hiding behind my wet, straggly tresses.

"What's wrong?" he asked, sweeping the soppy hair from my face with his cold fingers.

"I—I hate the water."

"You do?"

I nodded. "I've had nightmares about drowning," my teeth chattering as I spoke, "ever since I was a kid."

I lowered my gaze, and then I felt him, his cold fingers cutting through the water to interlock with mine. He pulled me close. I tried to pull away, but his hold was firm. And then he slipped back beneath the water again, his electric green eyes sitting just above the surface of the water while his mouth and nose remained submerged. Hints of red paint were speckled across his forehead like freckles while his hair stood on end in wild disarray. He was incredibly sexy and yet somehow innocent and adorable at the same time. And then he winked at me.

"Why does it seem like the world stops when I'm with you?" I said.

He stood up without answering, slow drips of water falling from his face. He tugged on my hand, pulling me toward him. I followed his lead and let him take me through the water like a rag doll. A moment later, he stopped moving. He ran his cold hand up my arm, along my shoulder blade and across my collarbone until his fingers met with my necklace. He stroked the chain a little before tugging on it to reveal the pendant. The tiny rubies and diamonds sparkled with the sunlight in the palm of his hand.

"Very beautiful," he said as he stared. "It's old and precious." He smiled. "Someone special must have given this to you."

"Ryan," I said, rapt by the sweet smell of his wet body.

"Ryan?"

"A friend. A *female* friend," I clarified.

He grinned, letting go of the weighty pendant. It fell against my chest with a tender thud. I swallowed nervously as he stroked the tips of his cold fingers along my back and up my spine. With a surge of confidence, I put my hands on his wet shirt and started tracing the contours of his strong, cold chest. Chills of elation ran though me as I touched him.

"Your heart," he whispered, staring at the throbbing of my pulse through the thin skin on my neck.

"It's an arrhythmia," I said, feeling the iciness of his breath against me. "My heart has an irregular beat. I've had it since I can remember." I closed my eyes when suddenly I could sense him pulling away.

My eyes flew open.

"I can't do this," he whispered, vaulting out of the pool with the ease of a gymnast.

I was bewildered. I wanted to ask him why, but then I wasn't sure

I really wanted to know. I feared that my weary lovesick heart wasn't prepared for the truth. I stayed silent watching the strong sun as it beamed against the red tinged water that dripped down Christian's body. His clothes were soaked, but he moved with effortlessness. And then he extended his hand to me. I glided through the water and took hold of him. He pulled me up with ease. At that moment, I turned his hand over—I had to see the scar again.

"Don't," he insisted sharply.

"I have to." And as I looked, I froze. The scar was practically identical to mine; it was in the same spot and about the same length, although his had healed much nicer than mine had.

The sun suddenly pierced through the clouds, and a singular shaft of light illuminated us with a sublime intensity. Instantly, I felt at peace, like this was meant to happen. *Destiny*, I thought to myself. *It's her!* And then the sun was gone, chased away by a cluster of smitten clouds.

"Let's see," Christian whispered. "Was it my turn?" He moved toward the cans of paint.

"No way!" I shouted.

"I don't know about that," he said teasingly, and then he tore off after me.

I could feel him at my heels, his laughter like the soft coo of a dove. I rounded the corner of the house, flew up the steps to the porch, and threw open the front door, hurrying inside. And then I stopped. I couldn't hear his laughter any longer. I turned around. He wasn't behind me. "Christian?" I called out. He was standing below the porch, at the foot of the cement steps. "What are you doing out there?"

He shrugged.

"Why don't you—" And then I stopped myself. It wasn't like me to be so forward.

"Hope …," he started to say.

'Yes," I answered eagerly.

But he didn't continue. He just shook his head before running his hands through his hair.

I turned away from him and moved back inside. I left the front door open, figuring that if he did decide to follow me in, I was okay with it. I ascended the stairs to the second floor and made my way into the master suite. The house was quiet, and after a while, it was clear that

Christian wasn't coming. I groaned with frustration. Maybe he was more of an old-fashioned gentleman, I thought to myself. I switched on the television and grabbed a towel from the adjoining bathroom. I peeled off my dress and listened to a local news report about the rising number of missing tourists in the area. The news was a total buzz-kill, so I quickly switched the station to something more mundane. The phony laugh track from an old sitcom was just what I needed. I heaved a sigh, my thoughts returning to Christian. I knew we'd have our moment. I was certain of it. I just had to find a way to convince the hands of time and the hand of fate to finally come together.

I let myself collapse onto the huge bed and inhaled the strange scent of pennies that fragranced the sheets. I stared up at the ceiling, watching dust dance in the columns of sunlight. The sheets were cool against my skin and reminded me of him. I smiled at the thought of Christian's icy breath against my neck and closed my eyes, ready to dream of what might have happened had he not been such a gentleman.

12-Truth

It was another scorcher. I could feel the heat creeping its way into my room uninvited. The humidity in the dawn air made me feel sticky and moist. It seemed like forever until daylight finally broke.

Would he come again today? I tossed around restlessly in my shroud of slippery satin and considered the many reasons why Christian didn't follow me into the house. What stopped him? I knew he liked me—I knew he more than liked me. I could feel it. The burning attraction between us was off the charts! So there had to be another reason—something, I suspected, far greater than simply his virtue as a gentleman.

After a big yawn, I emerged from the sheets and moved toward the window. I watched the lingering dark fade into first light. I imagined Christian propping his ladder up against my bedroom window like Romeo when suddenly the sound of loud, crotchety cawing interrupted my thoughts. It was that raven again. I couldn't see him, but I knew he was out there. I moved away from the window and back to the bed.

I switched on the antique jadeite radio that sat upon the night table. The low drone of an anchorperson's voice sliced through the static. The broadcast was local and more about missing tourists. I fiddled with the dial until I came upon an oldies station. *This is his music*, I thought to myself, and suddenly I couldn't help but smile. The dandy sounds of swing resonated throughout the room. Just then, the loud rumbling of a motorcycle engine distracted me. A moment later, I heard the distant racket of a ladder being positioned against the side of the house. "It's him!" I gushed with delight. I rushed to ready myself to the walloping beat of some big band song, squeezing into my jeans and sliding into a black, curve-hugging tank top.

Today would be a wonderful day. I was certain of it. I rushed down the stairs with an exhilarated anticipation when suddenly I stopped in my tracks.

"My god!" I gasped, eyeballing the wide-open front door. It was swinging a little with the early morning breeze. "I forgot to close it," I said under my breath. I was so entirely preoccupied with whether or not Christian was going to follow me inside, I actually forgot to close the door.

Golden sunlight poured inside the house as I skulked down the stairs. Just then, a humid breeze soared though the hall, carrying with it a mixture of sweet scents. I took a deep breath and slid into a pair of my flip-flops. "Lavender," I said. "Jasmine and lavender." The pleasant blend of smells filled me with an unexpected tranquility, and suddenly I wasn't so bothered by the fact that I had left the door open. Everything seemed fine. Nothing was moved or disrupted. I noticed my designer sunglasses still in place on the table by the door. They were sitting beside a little jar of heart-shaped candies. I laughed. They reminded me of Christian—their robust cinnamon taste. And then I heard the banging—Christian's banging. I grabbed my sunglasses and stepped outside.

Honeysuckle fragranced the air the moment my foot met the porch. Warblers and parakeets serenaded me with their lively songs as I strolled around to the side of the house. It was another perfect day in paradise. The sun had barely risen, and yet the humidity hung in the air with a heavy mugginess. And then I inhaled the most wonderful smell of all—his. I breathed him in deeply, closing my eyes, nearly tasting him in my mouth.

"Hello, beautiful," he said from atop the ladder, his words floating down as softly as snowflakes.

"Hi," I replied, watching the confident way he hung from the rungs. He was wearing an ordinary black T-shirt and pair of dark, torn blue jeans, and yet he looked sublime. His pants hung slightly lower than his waist, giving me a pleasant glimpse of his hips again as he moved down the ladder toward me.

"You recovered from the swim?" he said.

"Yeah," I replied, a little disappointed. Apparently he wasn't going to tell me the reason he didn't come after me.

"You control your fears. It's not the other way around."

"Easier said than done."

"I know it's hard."

I looked into his eyes. They were mesmerizing. "You know," I said, "there was a moment yesterday. I could swear we were floating."

"Yeah," he laughed. "That's what tends to happen in water."

"No. Not in the water." My eyes narrowed. "In the air."

He looked away and smiled. He didn't answer.

"I feel like I should thank you."

"For what?"

"For your patience with me in the pool. I felt … I felt strangely safe with you for some reason."

"Strangely safe, eh? Well if I hadn't thrown you in the water like that, then—"

"Let's just forget about it. Okay?"

He nodded in agreement. I could tell he was thinking about more than just the pool incident. I knew he was referring to the way he ditched me at the door.

A ray of sunlight suddenly refracted off the diamond engagement ring I was wearing. The ring! How could I have forgotten I was still wearing the stupid ring? I threw my hands behind my back and pried the shackle over my knuckle. It came off with ease. I slyly slipped the ring inside the front pocket of my jeans. A disturbing mix of nausea and nervousness began overwhelming me. I felt a sinking feeling in the pit of my stomach as images of Bradley cut through my thoughts like a knife.

"You okay?" Christian asked. "Here," he said offering me one of his little heart-shaped candies. "Eat this."

I smiled. "I'm not going to shrink to the size of a mouse, am I?"

"Not unless your name is Alice and you think this is Wonderland."

I popped the candy into my mouth and moaned the moment the sweet cinnamon stung my taste buds. "This little thing packs a punch."

"That's why I like them so much."

"Moira must have liked them too."

"What?"

"I noticed she had a jar of them inside the house."

He laughed. "Moira hated candy."

"She did?"

"She believed candy was for children."

"That makes sense," I teased eyeballing his youthfulness.

He laughed.

"Tell me more about her," I said. "You did promise."

"I did promise, didn't I? And I will, but today I've got something else in mind."

"You do?" I said, watching as he sucked on the last of his candy using his tongue to push it between his teeth.

He laughed for no apparent reason.

"What?" I asked defensively.

"Nothing," he replied, running his hands along his bare arms as though he was wiping them clean.

"Did I say something funny?"

"Not exactly."

My eyes narrowed suspiciously. I simply didn't understand why he continued to do that—why every so often he suddenly broke out into laugher as though he was listening to my inner thoughts. I widened my eyes and fixed my gaze upon his chiseled arms. If he wanted something worthy of laughing at, then I'd give it to him. I'd leer and gawk, making it unmistakable that I was indeed undressing him with my eyes!

And then I froze.

I noticed something sticking out of his back pocket—an old, red leather book, the Tin Man's sketchbook.

Christian grabbed me by the hand and pulled me against the icy freeze of his solid chest. "Don't deny what you're feeling inside," he mumbled tenderly, his mouth hovering just above my ear. "You know you belong here, Hope." His voice was barely a whisper. He brushed the hair out of my face with his cold hand. "You belong here … with me."

My heart was begging to believe in the fairy tale that were his words. I took a deep breath, reason suddenly seeping its way back into my consciousness. "But you don't even know me," I said.

"Is that what you've convinced yourself?"

His fingers reached for my cheek, and he started tracing the line of my jaw. His touch was soft yet unyielding.

"Let's get out of here," he insisted boldly.

"What?" I whispered, lost in the feeling of his fingertips against my flesh.

"I want to show you the Keys."

"What about house?"

"I don't want to show the house anything," he teased, withdrawing his hand from my face.

"But we can't just leave."

"Why not?" His lips stretched into a wide grin. "Who's stopping you?"

I thought about it for a moment. Who was stopping me? No one actually. I had no reason not to go with him. I shot him a sassy smile.

"Is that a yes then?" he asked.

We darted across the lawn like children. I felt free and capricious for the first time in a long time—maybe even ever.

We rounded the corner of the house and there, parked curbside, was his motorcycle. "Nice bike," I muttered, excitedly scrutinizing its sleek black curves.

"Thanks," he said. "Have you ever ridden on one of these?"

"Only in my dreams."

He laughed, hopped on his bike, and cranked the throttle. "What are you waiting for?"

The last time a guy asked me what I was waiting for, the answer had been the man of my dreams. I laughed a little. "Nothing," I said and jumped on the bike with him.

As I started putting my arms around him, I noticed the red book again, sticking out of the back pocket of his jeans. I wanted to ask him about it. I wanted to rip the book from his pocket and tear it open just to prove to myself that it was real, that everything was real, but I didn't. There was something much more significant at play between us. It was the sensation of feeling myself falling in love.

I held him tightly. I'd get my answers eventually, but for now, this was all I needed. And then with the force of a rocket, we peeled away, leaving Ambrose House in our dust.

13-Flash of Brilliance

Christian drove fast. We took in a lot of territory. At Bahia Honda, we sank our feet in the white sand and meandered along the water's edge. Christian told me about my grandmother's love for dolphins. Shortly thereafter, a family of bottlenose dolphins started playing offshore.

Christian nudged me in the arm. "It's a sign," he whispered. "She knows you're here."

I smiled with delight, wondering if he was right and hoping that he was. Our conversation flowed like a river, smooth and swift. He was so comfortable to be with, almost as though I'd known him all my life. *Maybe he's right,* I thought to myself. *Maybe I really do belong here with him.*

"I'd better get you out of the sun," he said.

"Yeah, I'm so pale. It's a wonder I haven't burned up completely out here."

He smiled in reply as we headed back to his bike along the beach.

"What about you? You're even paler than me—don't you burn?"

"It's all about moderation," he teased, taking me by the hand and twirling me around in a circle as though we were dancing.

I laughed freely as I spun, until my eyes met with an odd bridge in the distance. "What's that?" I asked.

"It's an old rail bridge. It's been there forever."

I scrutinized the unusual way a section of the bridge seemed missing. "What's with the gap?"

"It's for the boats to pass through."

"If you say so," I replied, but somehow I felt as though there was more to that story.

Christian tugged on my hand, and we ran along the sand together. I laughed and tried to keep up with his swift pace. It was fun. *He* was fun. And as I dashed along the white sand beside the water's edge, I became rapt by the vastness of the ocean and our tiny place within it. *This can't be real,* I thought. *A place like this with a boy like this can't possibly be real.* A moment later, he grabbed me by the waist and pulled me into the cold of his embrace.

"Everything is possible," he whispered in my ear.

"Everything?" I replied playfully.

We looked out at the horizon together. The sensation was humbling, and yet my mind was fixed on one thing and one thing alone: *when are you going to kiss me, Christian?* I heard him laughing to himself again as he helped me onto his bike, but he didn't explain why, and I didn't bother asking.

We drove off into the late afternoon, and when I convinced him to take me to Hemingway's house, we shared a most intimate moment petting the famed polydactyl cats. Our hands intertwined as we stroked their soft fur together, but not once did he try to kiss me. I giggled as his icy breath caressed my ear while he whispered sweet nothings to me over a cold glass of lemonade, but there was still no kiss. He leaned in close several times, his lips mere breaths away from mine, and yet he continued holding back, assuring that our mouths never touched.

Later as we strolled along Duval Street, I started feeling a little resentful. I was incredibly comfortable around him and absurdly attracted to him. I liked him—really liked him—and I thought he liked me too. I couldn't understand why he hadn't tried to kiss me.

Suddenly he reached for my hand, and I flinched a little with his touch.

"What's wrong?" he asked.

I smirked, biting my lower lip.

"C'mon," he badgered playfully.

"What am I doing with you?" I teased, giving in to him. I let him grasp my warm hand.

"What's wrong with me?" he asked.

"Nothing. It's just I'm way too old—"

"Don't say it," he said, cutting me off as we passed by a busy bar.

I tugged on his hand, forcing him to stop walking, and fixed my eyes ahead. I eyeballed the rowdy crowd having fun inside the bar. "Why don't we go in for a drink then?" I taunted.

He laughed. "I told you. I'm much older than you give me credit for."

"Okay, old-timer. Let's go in for a drink."

He squeezed my hand and laughed, pulling me along the street away from the bar. "That's not where you want to get a drink—believe me." He ran his long arm around my shoulders and pulled me close to his side.

With each passing moment, the attraction between us grew stronger. Time felt as though it stood still when I was with him. There were moments that seemed endless and instants that endured far beyond any normal measure I'd ever known. Being with Christian was surreal, almost like being in a dream. And then suddenly we diverted from the main road. He led me down a dingy alleyway toward a large, black door covered in graffiti. He unlocked the door and pulled me into a dark hallway to a red, velvet curtain. The robust reek of rust and disinfectant filled my nostrils the moment I entered while a numb, buzzing sound resonated in my eardrums. The smell was strong and sterile, evocative of a hospital, but the place seemed far too bedraggled to be any kind of hospital.

"Where are we?" I whispered nervously.

"A speakeasy," he replied. "Of sorts."

Speakeasy, I thought to myself. The word conjured images of prohibition in the Roaring Twenties.

"You *do* know what a speakeasy is—don't you?"

"Of course I know," I assured him. "It's a place that serves people under age. People like you!"

He smiled, condescension brimming in his grin. "Not exactly."

Christian pushed his head through the curtain and called out to someone. The buzzing noise was replaced by whispers. I tried to peek over his shoulder with little success. Christian was tall and deliberately trying to prevent me from eavesdropping.

"So?" I insisted as he turned back around. "Aren't we going in for a drink?"

He laughed. "I don't think you're ready."

"I'm ready," I said. "I'm not the one under age that has to go to a *speakeasy* to get served."

"That's not what I mean. I don't think you're ready to pull back the curtain just yet, Dorothy Gale." His voice was playful, but I knew he wasn't playing.

"You infuriate me, you know. All these secrets. Good thing you're cute; otherwise I'd—"

He pulled me by the hand against him. I stopped talking and stared into his electric green eyes, a jolt of excitement coursing through me. Was this it? The kiss I'd been waiting for?

He smiled, tracing the line of my jaw with his long index finger. "You're so pretty when you're angry."

I rolled my eyes. "If you weren't so … I mean …" My words were incoherent. I was distracted by the tantalizing smell of his skin. "Don't patronize me," I whispered.

"I'm not."

But I couldn't stay mad. Christian was far too persuasive. His disposition was remarkably charming and his scent far too irresistible to ignore.

"C'mon," he said, taking me by the hand back outside. We left the speakeasy behind us.

The sky was alive with color as the sun was on the verge of setting. The day was nearing an end. I didn't want it to be over. I didn't want to go back to Ambrose House. Not yet. Not without a kiss.

"I've saved the best for last," Christian purred in my ear.

We jumped back on his bike and tore off into the dusk together. A short while later, we reached the waterfront.

"This is Mallory Square," he said as we strolled the docks hand in hand.

The amber blaze of the setting sun illuminated everything around us as though we were looking though rose colored glasses.

"What are these people waiting for?" I asked, staring at the crowd in front of me.

"Sunset," he said with a smile.

I nodded even though I had no idea that people took the time to celebrate the setting of the sun. Droves of tourists in their Hawaiian shirts and flip-flops huddled together, eagerly anticipating the sun's farewell performance. Local eccentrics peppered the surroundings with their unique talents like opening acts before the sun was ready to take center stage.

"Do you like it?" he whispered.

"I think I'm starting to love it," I replied.

Christian beamed. He was radiant against the brilliant orange blaze of the sky. His skin wasn't as fair as usual in the amber light. And then suddenly he grimaced.

An old withered woman in gypsy clothing was waddling toward us. She was plump like a tomato and very short with the tough, wrinkly skin of an elephant on her aged face. She looked about ninety years old.

"Read your fortune?" she said in her broken-English accent.

"Okay," I said reluctantly. I reached for several bills from my back pocket and handed them to her. She stuffed the money into her blouse faster than a skilled magician. She was a peculiar woman, aggressive yet grandmotherly, and she smelled of garlic, limes, and bitter oranges.

"Oh please," Christian muttered curtly as he watched the olive-skinned lady take hold of my right hand. He shook his head with disapproval and started snickering.

"Let's see," the fortuneteller said as she traced her sharp fingernail across my palm. "Lifeline," she murmured, dragging her nail along the crease until it met with the scar in the center of my palm. She looked up at me, her swarthy skin now paler than a ghost. *"Mala suerte!"* she said, shaking her head, her old eyes consumed with dread. *"Mala suerte,"* she repeated, pointing to my palm.

"What?" I asked nervously. "What are you saying?" She pointed to my palm again. I looked closer, noticing the way my old scar severed my lifeline into two separate parts. I had two entirely disconnected lifelines.

She turned to Christian and glared. She grabbed his left hand without permission, took a deep, raspy breath, and began examining his palm. *"Muerto!"* she shrieked on first glance, letting go of his hand.

His hand fell through the air with the grace of a goose feather. Christian rolled his eyes.

"Muerto!" the fortuneteller repeated, her old eyes full of fury.

Christian growled at her playfully, flashing his white teeth as he snarled.

Her weathered fingers trembled at her sides, and yet she seemed resolved not to let him frighten her. *"No tiene alma!"* she spit out like a curse, moving back to me. Her voice was low, gravelly, and resolute. *"Raiz de la Vida,"* she whispered under her breath. She tugged on my shirt, waving me down to her level, her dark eyes staring into mine. *"Esperanza,"* she purred, ominously moving in close, her spicy breath against my cheek. *"Protejete,"* she whispered in my ear, her words like a warning. She grabbed hold of my hand with a force I didn't think she seemed capable of. *"Protejete,"* she repeated gravely. And when she pulled her hands away, I realized that she had returned my money. The bills fluttered in the evening breeze against my knuckles for a moment before taking flight. I chased the money through the air, and when I returned, the old fortuneteller was gone.

Christian was laughing when I reached him. I shoved the money in my back pocket and shrugged.

"I didn't think fortunetellers gave refunds," he teased.

"That was weird." I shook my head. "Do you know what she was saying?"

"A bunch of nothing."

"*Protejete?* She kept saying *Portejete*. What does it mean?"

Christian hesitated. "Protect yourself."

"Protect myself?" I said. "From what?"

"I don't know! Surely she's a fraud. A phony." He tugged on my hand, turning me around to face the sunset. "Forget about her—she's not why we came here."

I looked out at the water. The sun was drawing close to the horizon. An interesting buzz of excitement filled the air.

"See the sun?" Christian signaled toward the water. "And the horizon?"

"Yeah," I said, turning back to face him again.

"Hope, turn around or you'll miss it," he insisted.

"But everything I want to see is in this direction."

He smirked boyishly, biting his bottom lip, and placed his hands on my hips, turning me back around. "Some say that when the sun hits the horizon, a brilliant green flash appears." His voice was quixotic as though he was reciting poetry.

"A green flash?" I whispered while slipping myself into the space between his arms, feeling the coldness of his chest against my back.

"Legend has it that there was this captain who fell in love with a beautiful woman at sea."

"Go on," I whispered.

"He had already fallen deeply in love with her by the time he realized that she wasn't in fact a human, but a siren. Their love was powerful. They hoped it would conquer all that bound them both on land and beneath the water. But it didn't. The humans threatened to kill her, and her people threatened to eradicate humankind if they continued to live together in sin."

"But—"

"But nothing," he continued. "They were from different worlds, and it was against nature for them to be together."

"Star-crossed lovers," I lamented.

Christian nodded. "He retreated to the land, and she to the water. But legend has it that before they parted, she promised to visit him every night. And it was here that he would come and stare into the horizon at sunset, waiting for her. And every night she would appear to profess her love to him just as the sun touched the water."

"She's the green flash," I said, my heart swelling with exhilaration.

"Her *kiss* is the green flash," he corrected.

"Oh I love this story."

"It's terribly tragic really."

"Yes, but their love couldn't be stopped for that one brief moment of every day. That fleeting millisecond when the sun touches the water. It belonged to them and them alone!"

He nodded.

"So how exactly is the green flash her kiss?"

"Well some people believe that a kiss between lovers is the most significant of all physical acts."

"A kiss," I said. How desperately I yearned to feel his lips against mine. I swallowed hard and stiffened up a little, pretending as though a kiss didn't matter so much. "That's so old-fashioned," I said.

"Perhaps. But it sure as hell is romantic." His smooth voice curved into a whisper. "The mere exchange of breath in a kiss is like offering up a part of your soul to the person you love. Some say that if you listen closely, you can hear the siren's song."

"Now *that's* romantic," I gushed, focusing my attention on the sun's hasty decline.

Christian grinned.

"But what happened when he stopped coming?" I said suddenly. "I mean he was only human—eventually he would have died."

"It's only a story, Hope," he said.

"I know. But stories are usually grounded in some truth. Aren't they?" I wanted his story to be true.

Christian stared into my eyes, his sweet face afire in the setting sunlight. "What if death wasn't the end?" he asked.

"Don't be—"

"If you could live in a moment of happiness forever with your true love—would you?"

I was speechless. It was a beautiful idea. It was the kind of thing that sent shivers down my spine and left my knees feeling weak. My soul swelled with elation as I stared out at the horizon. And then I had the most brilliant idea. I slid my hand into the front pocket of my jeans and drew out the large, diamond engagement ring that Bradley had given to me. I held the ring in the palm of my hand for a moment and watched it sparkle with kaleidoscopic fire in the sunset. And then I tightened my fingers around it and closed my fist. With a deep breath I tossed the ring into the ocean. I turned to Christian and shrugged. "A sacrifice," I sighed, "for the siren and her sailor."

He smiled. "You astound me." He pulled me into the cold embrace of his strong arms.

We watched the ring disappear forever beneath the water. I took a deep breath and inhaled Christian's sweet metallic scent. *Why does this feel so right*? I thought to myself. *Why do I feel like I've known you forever?* And with a breath of confidence, I asked him. "What's the red leather book in your back pocket?"

"What book?"

"C'mon," I pressed. "Don't play coy."

"I'm not playing coy."

"Then show me the book." I tried to take it from his pocket, but he was quick, grabbing the book and holding it high above my head.

"Why do you want this?" he asked.

"Because. I want to see what's inside."

He lowered the book. "What if it's not what you think it is?"

My eyes turned serious. "What if it is?" I took the book from him with a hard tug. I touched the worn cover before stroking the edges of the yellowed parchment. My body quivered with a strange nervousness.

"Why aren't you opening it?"

"I—I'm afraid."

"Of what?"

"Of everything."

My fingers trembled as I forced myself to open the book. And there it was, on the first page in faded pencil, the drawing of a black butterfly—*my* black butterfly.

"Hope ..."

I thumbed through the pages, astounded. It was filled with his beautiful sketches, all of my beautiful dreams.

"I thought I was making it easier for you," he said, his voice nervous. "But I was wrong. I didn't realize that you ... us ... our bond was so strong that even over time you would be able to see through the veil."

"Veil?" A surge of tears rushed down my face soaking the sketchbook with their salty flow.

"But I can change all that now," he said, wiping the wetness from my cheek. "I'll fix it. I will." He took a deep breath. "Please forgive me."

And then he leaned in close and parted his perfect lips as though he was about to place them against mine. I closed my eyes. It was the most ethereal sensation ever, like a kiss from an angel, soft and sublime even though he wasn't touching me. The billowy air from his body transferred through my mouth like breathing outside on a cold, winter day. I could sense the vaporous wraithlike haze that connected us, regenerating me with life energy, full of detailed thoughts and feelings that once held their place in my assemblage of memories. And then, when the last fragmented breath of a memory was restored, he withdrew himself from me and I was whole again.

As I fought to open my eyes, I realized that I was caught within a lingering moment. Time really was standing still. It was like the very fiber of a second had been stretched to its most infinite extension, drawing out the subtlest of actions.

The brilliant green flash stained the sky in a searing surge. It was far too blinding to perceive fully. The siren's deafening shriek accompanied the flash, ricocheting through my eardrums at a pitch so high it was nearly inaudible. I was astounded by the volatility of the situation and wondered why no one else was affected by the beautiful violence around us.

An intoxicating burst of tin-cinnamon sailed past my nose. As I tried to inhale, my weak body tingled with a sudden numbness. I was starting to fade into unconsciousness. Just then, Christian picked me up in his arms and carried me away with him.

14-Affirmation

I was cold, and my head throbbed with pain. I could feel we were outside and moving very quickly. Christian's icy body was making me shiver. I fused myself to him, my face buried against his chest, my hand grasping his solid arm. I couldn't see where he was taking me, but I could hear and smell everything around us.

The hushed hum of birds hiding in their nests and the strong smell of rain looming about filled my senses. A few moments later, water descended from the sky, gently at first before quickly turning into a hammering downpour. I could feel as each droplet of rain touched my skin, bursting into minute splashes upon impact. Soon I was soaked. Its sound was like thousands of tiny fingers hitting keys upon keyboards, and yet if I listened carefully and focused my hearing, I could pinpoint the melodic quiver of each singular leaf and petal that had been graced by droplets of rainwater.

Christian's scent was more potent than ever, and the deeper I buried my face against him, the more I wanted a taste of him. *Taste*, I thought to myself with a surge of delight. I'd never thought of having a taste of anyone before; it was disturbing and yet somehow exciting. I ran my tongue inside my mouth, stroking it along edges of my sharp incisors. I was fighting the urge to bite into him when suddenly I felt his hold tighten. I sensed we were nearing something—*someone*. I could smell them too, mouthwatering and metallic like Christian, except less tin and more copper. I inhaled deeply letting the mélange of scents overwhelm me, practically satiating me like a meal.

We stopped moving. Christian leaned against the side of a large, gnarly rooted tree. There was silence for a while until finally footfalls replace the quietness. Resting upon his strong arms, I hid as much as I could against his body, pretending I was still unconscious. Then suddenly I heard a voice.

"Did you lift it?" a gentle male tone inquired.

"Yes," Christian replied.

I peeked out from beneath my hair. I saw a man, young like Christian, standing with his hands on his hips. He was blond, tired looking, and very pale.

"How much does she … will she remember?"

"Enough." Christian's voice was hard.

"She smells like her."

"Naturally," Christian asserted.

"Can I," the man hesitated, "touch her?"

I practically gasped with his words. *Touch me? My god—why?* A rush of panic pushed through me.

"No," Christian snapped. "I don't think that would be a good idea." He tightened his grip like armor, reaffirming my safety.

He wouldn't let anything happen to me—at least I hoped he wouldn't. I shifted my gaze upward toward the sky. The strange veined limbs of the trees were hardly any cover from the downpour. The rain was steady, unlike the beating of my heart. I listened as the water fell against the leaves. It was like music. Larger beads of rain harmonized with smaller trickles to the steady rhythm of the middling droplets. The melody was calming, and soon I almost lost interest in their conversation—almost.

"Are we allowed back in the house yet?" the man inquired.

"No," Christian replied.

I started shifting in his arms.

"She's stirring, Christian," the man said nervously.

Christian grasped me tighter. I stopped shifting.

"I have to go," Christian said. "I have to get her inside. Will you be okay for a little longer?"

"Do we have another choice?" The man laughed softly, and then his tone changed. "Eva wants new clothes."

"Forget Eva," Christian scolded. "It's *you* I'm concerned about."

"I told you not to worry about me," the man insisted. "We trust you, Christian. I trust you."

And then I heard the man starting to leave. His footfalls were hard at first before suddenly softening to a squashy slide. I wanted to look, but Christian cradled me close, and within an instant we bolted into the forest, through the frozen speckles of rain that hung in the air like a dew studded curtain.

"Hang on, Hope," he whispered as we soared. "You're almost home now."

Where was home? Was it the place where I was born? The place where I became an adult? Or maybe neither? Perhaps it was here—the place from my dreams, the place filled with foreign memories that now suddenly belonged to me again.

I brushed the wet hair away from my face and looked around. We were back at Ambrose House. It was dark, and we were nearing the porch just as Christian set me down.

"Are you okay?" he asked.

I nodded, wiping the rainwater from my face. I started walking up the front steps. I noticed that he didn't follow me—again. I turned back to face him, my brow furrowing and my eyes narrowing. "Who was that?"

He didn't answer.

"Christian," I persisted.

He took a deep breath and exhaled, but he still didn't respond.

I shook my head at him, disappointed with his silence. I tried to be mad, but he was just so damn beautiful standing there dripping in the moonlight.

"You should get some rest," he whispered. "You've been through a lot."

"I don't want to rest."

"Why not?"

"I don't know," I snapped. "I just don't."

"But your head must be overflowing with—"

"Memories?"

He ran his hands through his wet hair. "I just thought you might be exhausted is all."

"I'm not."

"What are you?"

"*What are you?*" I spit back.

His lips remained sealed.

"Never mind." I turned away. My dreams were the truth, and the truth was my reality. I knew this place because I had been here before. I knew Christian because I had known him before. I knew what he was. I didn't need him to tell me; I just wanted him to.

"But you don't know what *you* are," he said coolly, cutting the quiet between us.

He stepped closer, and I trembled with his nearness.

"There are things you need to understand," he said. "It's like you've put a puzzle together upside down and are finally ready to turn it over." He smiled. "You shouldn't be alone when you finally see the whole picture." He put his hand on my arm. "You're freezing. You should go inside."

"Alone?" I asked shrewdly.

"I think you know the answer to that question." His tone was sharp.

"You can't come in, can you?"

He shook his pretty face from side to side.

"Not without an invitation," I added.

He grinned.

"What else is real, Christian?"

"The way I feel about you."

I shook my head. "That's not what I—"

He placed his icy finger to my lips. "Shh," he whispered. "I know what you meant."

I pulled his hand away, grasping it within my own, and turned it over. I stroked the scar in the center of his palm with the tip of my finger. "Tell me," I urged. "Tell me what else is real."

"An invitation is real," he said, brushing the damp hair out of my eyes. "The burn of the sun is real." He ran the tips of his icy fingers along my face and down my jaw. "Strength is real, and heightened senses too." He inhaled as he traced the length of my neck. "Starvation makes a reflection fade, and knots will force you to the brink of insanity." He smiled, his voice smooth like satin. "But the urge to kill is real. And above all," his soft lips only a breath from mine, "the blood," he hissed. "The blood is *very* real."

I froze. My pulse beat with the weight of an anchor inside of my chest.

"Hope. You don't need me to tell you what you already know."

"But I want you too."

"Trust yourself." He dragged his icy fingers from my neck across my chest a little. "Search your heart for the answers."

"My heart," I groaned. "My slow and inelegant heart."

"But still a heart that beats."

"Would you like to come inside?" I whispered.

15-Ripe With Age

We stepped over the threshold together and entered the house. Christian flicked the light switch near the door, but nothing happened.

"The storm must have knocked out the power."

"Now what do we do?"

He chuckled as he rummaged through the antique sideboard. "You modern women with your electricity and other luxuries." He held up a box of matches and smiled before moving around the room, lighting the tall tapered candles. Soon the house was aglow with the soft radiance of candlelight.

"Wow," I said. It was undeniably romantic.

Christian grinned. "Dry clothes?" he asked before disappearing deeper into the darkness of the house. And then suddenly, he reappeared again. He was wearing a dry white T-shirt and a new pair of black jeans.

"Where'd you get dry clothes for yourself?" I said.

He shrugged before tossing some dry clothes at me. "Thought you'd look great in this."

"My jean skirt and tank top? You went through my stuff?" I said uneasily.

He ignored my question and held up a vintage wine bottle. "I've been saving this … for today."

"Good. I could use a drink." I retreated into the book room, nestling myself between *Lord of the Flies* and *Interview with the Vampire*. I laughed under my breath before peeling the wet clothes from my body.

"What's so funny?" he hollered across the house.

"Grandma's taste in books!" I put on the tank top, feeling the taut ribbing distend as it hugged my curves.

"Appropriate, don't you think?" he laughed in reply.

I slid the jean skirt over my toes and up to my hips and then crept back to face him, a ball of wet clothes hanging heavily in my hands.

"You look—"

"Dry," I said.

"Beautiful."

He handed me an old patchwork quilt.

"What's this?"

"Something to keep you warm," he replied, taking the ball of wet clothes from my hands and tossing it out through the front door onto the porch.

I wrapped the quilt around my shoulders. "Lavender," I said, inhaling the tender smell of the fabric.

"It was hers."

I grinned and closed my eyes. I inhaled again. "I can almost remember something." I opened my eyes. "Her hair … it smelled of lavender, didn't it?"

He nodded. I could tell he was pleased that my memories were finding their way back into my thoughts. He grabbed my hand and pulled me toward the velvet couch. We sat together. Close together. I watched as he blew a thick coating of filth off the wine bottle. The flecks of dust danced in the candlelight. Then he brought the old bottle up to his mouth. With a swift tug, he pried the cork from the neck with his sharp teeth.

I gasped.

A severe whiff of tin instantly sailed past my nose. It was more biting than the reek of a rusty car in the rain. I took a deep breath.

Christian poured the contents into two antique pressed glasses. He handed me a goblet. "Ladies first."

I took the glass from him and studied the contents.

"It's much better served warm."

I grimaced.

"But the power is out, so—"

"Chilled is fine," I said, bringing the glass to my mouth. But as the goblet neared my lips, my breathing suddenly quickened. I could feel my heart struggling to speed up. My mouth started salivating like an animal as beads of sweat seeped along my skin. The drink had triggered some visceral reaction within me. I wanted a taste of that drink. I needed a taste of it, and so I took one, savoring its oddly delectable sting as it slid down my throat. I licked my lips and exhaled after I swallowed. There was a blissful aftertaste, sharp and acerbic, like sucking on a coin as though it were a dinner mint.

"Another?" Christian inquired smoothly.

I nodded elatedly, every ache and pain in my body suddenly dissipating. The drink was making me fiery and full of fervor, and like a beautiful butterfly with new wings, I broke free from my quilted cocoon. The comforter fell to the couch, the soothing scent of lavender paling against the harsh metallic stench of the drink. *The drink. I want more.*

This time, we clinked our glasses together. I anticipated the sting going down and craved its bitter bite on my tongue. It was addictive.

"Savor it," Christian insisted. "It's not like I can go to the store and get another." His lips and cheeks were suddenly much rosier than before. He glowed with an indescribable vitality. "You don't remember what you're drinking, do you?" His voice had a peculiar pitch.

"An old vintage or something?" I shrugged. "I've never been much of a wine enthusiast."

"Hope," he said, "search your memories."

I took another sip and closed my eyes, letting the viscous beverage marinate in my mouth for a moment. I could feel its angry sting biting at my tongue like a wasp trapped in my mouth. It was exhilarating, both delicious and disgusting. And then suddenly a vision from my past flashed in my mind. I was sitting next to Christian at the foot of a gnarly rooted tree, my tiny hands occupied in crafting a daisy chain. I was a child, and yet he looked the same—*exactly* the same. I looked closer. His hand hovered above a bottle, a thick stream of blood flowing from his palm dripping into its mouth.

My eyes flew open. I spit out the pool of liquid that lingered near my lips.

"Ah, you remembered."

"This is your blood!"

"Yes," he said, laughing, "but don't forget, it's your blood too."

"What?" I shot back, my heart skipping a beat. I swished my tongue around in my mouth, tasting what was left of the drink. I closed my eyes again, eager to remember. Another memory flashed in my mind. Scarlet blood streamed from a thin cut in the center of my tiny palm, staining my hand. Fresh droplets entered the mouth of the bottle, dripping and dripping until finally fusing together with Christian's in a seamless mélange. I opened my eyes again.

"But it was already too late," Christian said as though he was somehow reading my thoughts. "I couldn't stop you."

"Why did we do it in the first place?"

"You."

"Me?"

He nodded. "I knew that you'd need it one day. That's why *I* did it. But you—so headstrong as a child, you thought it would be fun to mimic me or whatever it was you were doing."

"I'd need it? For what?"

"Strength."

"What—am I weak or something?"

"Not weak," he said, tugging on my right hand, turning it palm up and tracing my scar with the tip of his index finger. "But not fully human either."

"What?"

"It was all *your* brilliant idea," he insisted regretfully. "The blood pact." He dropped my hand and ran his fingers through his raven colored hair. "I was stupid. I knew better. But you wouldn't take no for an answer. Even if I had refused—you would have found another way."

"Another way? Another way to what?"

He stared into my eyes. "You were obsessed. Insatiably obsessed."

"With what?"

"Immortality. Ghost. Demons. *Vampires*." His words resonated like the verses of a morbid rhyme.

Vampires, I thought to myself. The word felt meager in my mouth, as though unworthy of defining the essence of my Tin Man. He was so much more than that. And even though I knew the undeniable paleness of his face, coldness of his skin, and sharpness of his teeth, I couldn't see him as anything other than the man in my dreams. My soul mate.

"Soul," he said. "The eternal damned don't have souls."

How did he know what I thinking? Had I spoken aloud?

"When you were a child," he said softly, "you weren't like other kids. You preferred ghost stories to fairy tales. Truth to fiction." He poured more drink into my glass as he spoke. "I knew that knowing you was wrong. But you needed someone and—"

"My mother just died," I said, interrupting him.

Christian nodded. "You were only a kid," he uttered with compassion. "The last thing I wanted to do was hurt you. You'd endured enough pain already." He hung his head low. "And yet by knowing you I *was* hurting you."

I took a deep breath and struggled to remember. "It wasn't like that, Christian," I said, shaking my head. "You fascinated me entirely. You were like a character from one of my storybooks come to life."

"Yeah," he said. "The monster."

"No. The savior."

His drew his eyes upward a little.

"You protected me. You let me live in this enchanted world with you—and it was like living in a fairy tale. You made the sadness bearable."

Christian nodded knowingly. "This wasn't the place for a child," he whispered under his breath. "Everyone was so preoccupied with the funeral and the—"

"But not you," I insisted. "You took care of me."

"Well someone had to."

"But it didn't have to be you." I stared at the scar on my palm. "You're a good person. Damned or not."

He smiled. "Clearly I didn't do a very good job taking care of you," he said sarcastically.

I laughed in reply.

He poured more into our glasses.

"What happened to me after the blood pact?" I took another sip of the sinful swill.

"You started the progression."

"Progression?"

"My blood in your veins was like a trigger, infecting you with my disease." He recoiled a little. "I tried to protect you from all this." He downed the contents of his glass. "I wouldn't have even considered that stupid blood pact if I thought it would have affected you the same way as a—"

"Taste?"

He nodded. "Yeah."

"Am I dying?"

"No. Quite the opposite actually." He laughed. "Your body is preparing for an eternal hibernation of sorts. It wants immortality, it's craving it, but you haven't completed the progression."

"What does that mean?"

"Well, you're stuck in a kind of limbo."

"Purgatory."

He laughed.

"How do I get out this purgatory?"

"Being brought to the point of death." He sighed. "And ingesting some of *my* blood. But that won't happen. You've got the best of both worlds," he said. "A longer life without the anguish of eternity."

My face furrowed.

"Think of it this way," he said. "While everyone you know is slowly dying, you're slowly living."

"That doesn't sound like the best of both worlds."

"Trust me; it is." He took my hand and placed his fingers across my wrist, feeling the sluggish rhythm of my pulse. "The beating of your heart, it's decelerating. Every year, every hour, minute, and second of your life, your body is slowing down. You won't age like your peers. You never will."

"You mean I won't grow old?"

"Not at the same rate as everyone around you."

"Like Peter Pan," I mumbled.

He smiled.

"Is that why you look the same? I mean … is that why you look exactly as you did when I was a child?"

"Yes. But I do age. *Very* slowly. It's nearly impossible to discern with human eyes."

"But …" I struggled to find the right words. "I mean, aren't you—"

"What—dead?" He took my hand and pressed it against the cold of his muscular chest. "Feel," he whispered.

My hand trembled nervously against the icy firmness of his body, but there, beneath the quivering, I could feel a beat. It was incredibly faint and barely palpable. "Your heart?" I said elatedly.

"Still beating."

"You're alive?" I said with awe.

"Immortal," he conceded while pouring a little more brew into our glasses. "Drink it. It's the antidote to our poison, the cure to our sickness."

I looked at the nearly empty bottle. The urge for more was impossible to ignore, especially considering the fact that I knew the reason why I craved it so badly. I longed for it, hungered for it. I needed it the way Christian did because I was like him, well almost. He said it himself—I wasn't fully human. I brought the glass to my mouth and indulged in yet another taste, my body exultant with a divine satisfaction as I swallowed.

"That's why I had to veil you," he explained. "There was no other choice. Otherwise your cravings might have taken over. I took all of your dark memories away. You deserved a chance to live. A chance to be normal."

"Normal?" I said feeling the burn of the blood on my tongue. "My life was a lie. I lived in my dreams, and you—you haunted them."

"Tin Man," he said, a smirk emerging.

"How did you—"

"We're connected. I can hear your thoughts."

"You know what I'm thinking?" I asked, mortification surging through me like a wave.

"Yes. Look, if it makes you feel any better, it seems to work both ways."

"You mean I can read your thoughts too?" I could feel myself starting to fade with dizziness. The drink was strong and its power undulating.

"With practice, I bet we could get really good at it." His voice was soft and sultry.

I stared into his eyes and smiled. And then I heard him—not his voice, but his words. They coursed to me with a feathery softness through my thoughts. It was as though he was still speaking, but gentler, more velvety and dulcet. I listened attentively, with ease, as he told me to stop trying so hard and just trust my instincts. I smiled. "I heard you," I said, slurring, the effects of the drink suddenly overwhelming me. "You just told me to—"

"Stop trying so hard and trust your instincts?" He laughed.

I laughed too, but I was fading fast. Unconsciousness was only a breath away. I could feel it, and there was no escaping its hold on me. I was perched on the brink of slumber, my senses swiftly anesthetized in an unexpected blissfulness. "Sleep," I said aloud or perhaps through my thoughts. "I need sleep." My eyes felt as though they were laden with iron mascara. I couldn't hold them open any longer. I took a deep breath and surrendered to the darkness.

16-Moment

When I awoke, I saw Christian's pretty face. He was radiant in the soft candlelight. His icy hand was pressed against my forehead. It felt good. *He* felt good. "Am I dreaming?" I asked, trying to sit up. But lightheadedness consumed me, and I fell back into the arms of the velvet couch.

"You drank too much," he said with a grin.

"What else is new?" I teased.

"I should have known better. The blood was far too rich for a system as pure as yours. Moira would have killed me if she knew I let you drink too much on your first bottle."

"Moira? You mean my grandmother knew?"

He nodded. "When your mother died, Moira made me promise that I would …"

"You would …"

"She wanted me to keep an eye on you."

"An eye on me?" I said, pulling myself up to a sitting position.

"I watched you, from afar, but I never interfered."

"You what?"

"We just wanted to make sure that you were okay."

I was silent.

"Say something, Hope."

"For how long?" I snapped.

He cocked his head to the side and smiled. "Since—" And then he exhaled. "Forever."

"What? My whole life?"

He nodded.

"Like a stalker. My own personal stalker."

"More like a protector," he stressed. "We all agreed that if your progression started intensifying—if your cravings started dominating—you'd need someone there to help you."

"And that someone was you?" I said bitterly.

He nodded again.

I stared into the vivid glow of his green eyes. "You're lying," I said.

"I'm not."

"I know you're lying. I can *see* your thoughts." I leaned closer to him and stared deeper into his electric eyes. A swirl of dark emotions suddenly filled my mind. There was anger, rage, a brooding resentfulness, and love—a deep, burning, unrequited love. "You watched me all these years because you loved me. And it killed you that you couldn't interfere." I took a breath. "It had nothing to do with my cravings dominating."

He sprung from the couch and moved toward the large window.

"Aren't I the one who should be angry?" I said.

He turned around, his face frazzled with fury. He looked as though the rage of a thousand warriors was pent up inside of him, just brimming to burst from within. "You can't imagine the torture of watching you!"

"A guilt trip, Christian? You can't be serious!"

"First there was your high school sweetheart … what was his name?" His voice was hard. "It was like a girl's name—Sally or Cindy or something."

"Sam?"

"Yeah," he growled. "Sam. I loathed that guy. He was an arrogant jerk."

"He was a teenager."

"*I'm* a …" He paused awkwardly. "I mean, I know teenagers."

I wanted to be mad. I tried—really tried. But there was something amazing about knowing that he had been there, invisibly woven through the fabric my life, as seamless as my own shadow. I was never alone. My Tin Man was always there, only a breath away.

"And your gawky college guy," he complained, bringing me back into the conversation. "The one with the crooked smirk. He was dreadful."

"Who?" I taunted, playing dumb.

"Oh right—Jonathan," he groaned, reading my thoughts. "Smug scooter-boy," he said scathingly, his lean body cringing as he spoke. "Your taste in men is—"

"Watch it," I snapped.

He took a deep breath. "I hope you know you made it insufferable for me."

"I—"

"Wait. Before you get angry, hear me out." He swallowed uneasily, the candlelight illuminating his sublime splendor. "I know I sound ridiculous, but you have no idea what it's been like all these years." His voice softened, his words slowing as he spoke. "Watching you become this unbelievable woman and still not being allowed to …"

"To what?" I whispered with anticipation.

He shook his head. "And your Bradley," he growled, changing the subject. "He's the worst of them all. The way he treats you is deplorable. He's not a man."

"And *you* are?"

"Yes," he replied resolutely, his damp hair dangling in front of his face as he spoke. "He's not what you need, Hope."

"What do you know about what I need?"

And then suddenly he was by my side on the couch, sitting next to me.

"You need to be loved the right way," he whispered, his breath tickling my skin. "You need a man that will respect the woman you've become. A man that believes in you—in everything you're capable of. You, Hope Havergale, you need to throw caution to the wind, forget your fears, and allow yourself to be loved in the way you deserve to be loved."

My lips quivered. I bit down on them. Hard. I swallowed and struggled to resume composure. 'That doesn't sound like Bradley," I teased.

Christian smirked, his pretty face alive with emotion. "And yet," he said, "*he* gets to be the one who holds you. *He* gets to be the one who kisses you."

I moved closer to him, and with the soft brush of my fingers, I swept the hair out of his eyes. "But it was *you,* Christian," I said tenderly, "you in my thoughts always." And as I stared at him, his agelessness mesmerized me with its ineffable truth; he was a fairy-tale character come to life, and he *was* real: every strand of hair, tissue of flesh, splinter of bone and drop of blood—real. I stroked his pale cheek with the side of my hand and smiled. "You look *exactly* as I remember."

"You've changed," he whispered.

"I got old."

"You became a woman."

My body trembled.

"I waited for you," he whispered.

"Most guys can't even wait five minutes," I joked.

"For you, Hope, I would have waited longer. As long as it took."

"You waited over twenty years to be with me again," I said, starry-eyed.

"It's nothing when you consider the span of eternity."

I sighed with bliss and looked into his thoughts. Cascades of emotions surged through my mind. His feelings were like a vast sensation filling me with the depth of his authenticity. "You knew that this would happen," I asserted. "You knew I would come back to you—didn't you?"

"Yes." He grabbed my right hand with a soft firmness and turned it palm up. He traced the scar with the tip of his cold finger.

I slipped my hand into the palm of his. Our fingers locked, our hands joined, his scar and my scar together again. He took me in his arms and moved his cold mouth across my neck. I heaved a sigh and stiffened my spine, raising my face to meet with his. *Kiss me already*, I urged in my thoughts. *Put your lips on mine.*

He laughed in response.

I flushed. "Fine then. Kiss me somewhere you probably shouldn't."

His beautiful eyes widened. "You're going to regret saying that."

He swept me off of my feet in a tight embrace and levitated us inches above the couch in mid-air. I trembled in his arms, but I was amazed, inspired even. I closed my eyes and allowed myself to surrender to him. A moment later, I felt the deceleration of warm wind against my face as we descended within shallow water. And when I opened my eyes again, I knew exactly where we were: the wiry tangle of mangrove roots from my dreams—from my memories. Christian set me down on the sandy floor. I sank to the ground and sighed. “This is where we first met,” I said. “Where you saved me.”

“You saved me far more that day.”

I smiled, feeling the awkward pound in my chest suddenly struggle to pick up pace. My heart swelled with the sound of his angelic tone. I looked around. Everything was the same, but different. Time had swept its tender hand upon this place too. The flora was wild, and the roots were thicker, but it was still the same wonderful place from my dreams—my memories—my childhood.

“It changed,” he said. “Like you.” He tugged on my fingers. “It's more beautiful now,” he said with a whisper.

I smiled bashfully and drew my eyes upward, into the distance. Beyond the trees was the most unbelievable moon I had ever seen. It was enormous, hanging like a balloon in the sky, its tawny light illuminating everything with incredible warmth. And then suddenly I felt Christian's icy hand upon my cheek. He was sitting next to me on the sand. I leaned my head against his shoulder and looked up at him, into his boyish face, just as I had when I was a child. He was beautiful—maybe even more beautiful than I remembered. And then a solitary tear emerged from my eye and slid down my cheek. Faster than speed itself, he caught my tear in his pale hand just as it was about to drop. He held it tightly, and when he opened his hand again, the tiny symbol of my profound love for him sat comfortably upon the scar in the center of his palm like a diamond, glittering in the bronze blaze of the moon.

“Hope,” he said softly without speaking aloud.

“Yes,” I replied, swelling with emotion.

“This is what you need,” he whispered through my thoughts, and then he leaned in close and pressed his beautiful lips to mine in a kiss. The fiery orange moon fueled our passion, and with everything static surrounding us, we were free to experience each other utterly and infinitely, moving in unison. It was the moment I'd been waiting for all of my life, and it belonged to us. It was our moment together—our moment of stolen time.

I wanted to stay forever in his arms, feeling him against me, tasting his sweetness, but suddenly we were torn asunder. Out of the stillness, a bitter gust of wind managed to blow, annihilating our idyllic instant with it swift swirls and forcing our lips to rescind with the relentlessness of its rage. A mere flutter of Christian's eyelashes seemingly reanimated everything again. The transition from our expanded moment to real time was as seamless as our embrace. *Christian,* I thought to myself, *you have set me free.* His blood in my veins made me strong. His kiss on my lips made me brave. I felt capable of everything. I felt the feeling of being loved the right way. But the wind persisted, and like a bird with new wings, I decided to follow the tempestuous gust as it led deeper into the scrawny pines.

"Hope—don't!" Christian yelled, tearing off after me.

But I couldn't stop myself. I had to run, darting deeper into the trees, sinking my feet into the sandy ground beneath me. The orange moonlight sparkled like citrine jewels on the water as I dashed past. It was breathtaking. I smiled to myself as I soared. *Oh, love,* I said in my thoughts, sprinting though the forest in a senseless effort to catch the wind, *you have made me drunk with happiness.*

17-Birthright

When I came upon them, they were huddled together by the side of a boathouse at the water's edge. Their pale faces reflected the brilliant orange glow of the moon. There were three of them, two men and a woman. I slowed my stride as I neared. A last gust of chilly wind pushed past me; I wobbled with its force and struggled to steady myself. And then suddenly the air was calm and the wind was gone.

Tin, I contemplated. I smelled tin. It was unmistakable. I looked around for Christian, but he wasn't behind me. He wasn't anywhere. And then I realized it wasn't Christian's smell at all—the smell belonged to them. My body quivered. I could feel my awkward heart struggling to race inside my chest. A burst of metallic tangs infused the air with a phenomenal robustness. Notes of copper, hints of iron, and traces of tin filled my senses like a metallic bouquet. I salivated, licked my lips, and stared over at them. Their eyes reflected with an animalistic shine in the moonlight. I swallowed hard. I knew what I smelled. *Vampires*, I thought to myself. They were definitely vampires.

I took a step closer toward them.

"Don't," Christian implored as he approached.

But like a moth to a flame, I couldn't stop myself. They intrigued me, and their smell—oh the harsh addictive tang of their smell—it was, well, delectable.

I continued slinking closer, my head filling with questions. Who were they? Why were they out here? And then suddenly, like my conscience, I could hear Christian in my head providing me with the answers. His telepathic explanation wasn't comprehensive, but it was definitely convenient.

"They're not dangerous," he explained firmly through my thoughts. *"But they can be."*

I stopped in my tracks.

"Don't be afraid, Hope," he whispered soundlessly. *"But don't let your guard down too easily either."*

I scanned their pale faces again. Of the three of them, the young man with the ear-length blond hair seemed the least threatening. He was withdrawn, his body language barely a whisper. His head was hung low, and his shoulders were hunched. And there was something familiar about him—his smell maybe.

"Henry," Christian told me. *"His name is Henry."*

"Henry," I said, but the man didn't respond. Embarrassment embraced me hard. I felt stupid for speaking, when suddenly a voice pulled my attention away.

"Hola chica," the low tone rumbled.

My eyes shot over to the brawny guy edging his way toward me. He had a sinister smirk on his scruffy face and a long piece of black licorice hanging from the corner of his mouth. And then he winked at me. He was wearing a dark baseball cap, black short-sleeved shirt, and jeans with a pair of worn-out military boots. He looked about my age, late twenties, and his complexion was pale despite the fact that it seemed as though it should have been swarthy. His skin was incredibly rough, scarred in places and covered in tattoos. Elaborate portraits (exquisite photorealistic imagery of people) hung upon his body like pieces in a museum or pages of a photo album. I shuddered as I stared at him. He was like a prison inmate with the physique of a gorilla, and he chewed on his piece of licorice the way a cow chews the cud. With each bite, he attempted to intimidate me, tearing it from his sharp teeth as though it were my flesh. I tried staying calm, but it wasn't easy.

"Baptiste is mostly all show," Christian whispered through my thoughts.

"Mostly?" I replied, my eyes glued to his enormous physique. And then I felt Christian nudging me in the arm.

"Relax," he whispered aloud.

“Yeah. Easy,” I said, moving my attention to the fiery, red-haired woman.

“That’s Eva. She’s crazy. Watch out for her.”

My eyes widened with his words. *Eva,* I thought to myself. Suddenly it came back to me. I remembered hearing her name in the forest—the man that Christian was talking to said something about Eva wanting new clothes. My thoughts raced when suddenly the prickly sound of Eva kissing her sharp, white teeth distracted me. I stiffened up a little but continued to stare. How could I resist? She was incredible.

“Careful,” Christian urged. *“Her bark is definitely worse than her bite—but that doesn’t mean she won’t try.”*

She draped herself over Baptiste like a python; her lovely, long arms and perfect, long legs coiled around him seductively. Eva was young, tall, and curvy with shoulder-length hair the color of blood. She was blowing and popping pink bubble gum and glaring at me with her pretty eyes. The red of her lipstick and fiery mane against the paleness of her skin were like the swirls on a candy cane. And like Baptiste, she proudly flaunted a collection of tattoos. Her long, slender neck was covered with an intricate ivy filigree pattern while her upper arms were tattooed with the images of two beautiful women; the right displayed the likeness of a classic forties-era pinup girl (that bore an eerie resemblance to herself) while the left boasted an old-fashioned mermaid. She was decidedly statuesque, picturesque, sexy, and tough. In short Eva was everything every woman ever dreamed they could be. I heaved a sigh of envy as I gazed at her when suddenly my senses filled with a most peculiar aroma; it was strong and feminine. *Iron,* I thought to myself, *and salty gardenias.* It was Eva’s scent, and it was as enchanting and peculiar as she was. I inhaled again, recalling the familiarity of the unique smell from the white room in Ambrose House. Why did the white room smell of Eva?

“Take a picture, blondie,” Eva suddenly snarled. “It’ll last longer.”

“Eva!” Christian barked. “Can’t you just behave for once?”

“Ugh,” she growled. “You’re so freakin’ protective.” Her voice was smooth and unexpectedly low.

Christian rolled his eyes while Eva flipped him the bird.

“Classy,” Christian said. “Real classy.” He grabbed my hand and squeezed it tightly.

"Oh how cute," she scorned.

Baptiste started laughing.

"What's so funny?" Eva asked, popping a pink bubblegum bubble in his face.

He shook his head, mumbling something to her in Spanish, and then he turned around to face me. He started moving closer, his slow prowl like an animal. He was frightening to look at and smelled of black licorice. *No one likes black licorice*, I thought to myself.

"Hold it, B," Christian said, pressing his hand against Baptiste's chest, stopping him mid-stride.

"What's the matter, *hombre*?" Baptiste replied in his thick Latin accent. "You don't trust me with her?" He drew the strand of licorice out of his mouth as though it were a cigar and winked.

I was paralyzed, petrified with fear, my eyes fixed on his tattoos. I couldn't get past the huge spider across his throat—the way it stared at me like it was preparing to leap out and poison me with its venom.

"Now that's what I'm talking about," he said with an inhale, his already enormous chest inflating like a balloon as he breathed in my scent. He moved a little closer, pushing against the resistance of Christian's hand with ease. *"Esperanza,"* he said, "do you taste as good as you smell?"

"C'mon," Christian ordered. "That's enough."

But it wasn't. Baptiste growled in response, showcasing his sharp fangs. "Put 'em up, put 'em up," he taunted with the bogus bravado of the cowardly lion. And then he inhaled again, deliberately devouring my scent.

Christian's eyes narrowed at Baptiste.

I quivered, my eyes jumping back to the spider tattooed across Baptiste's throat. Fear was only a breath away; I could smell its suffocating stench hanging in the air, readying to suffocate me.

"Stop!" Christian beseeched.

But Baptiste still refused. He inhaled once more and howled in reply, his sharp teeth dripping with saliva.

Christian sprang into action. He darted through the air like a blurry smudge and positioned himself behind Baptiste. With his sharp fangs exposed, he held his mouth just above the thin skin on Baptiste's neck, perched to penetrate. The tension between them was intense, and the smell of their blood in the air more heady than perspiration. My body suddenly kicked into gear; fear turned to fascination, rousing me with a ravenous hunger. My veins burned with a craving so incredible I thought I was going to ignite. I trembled with exhilaration, my eyes intensified, my face twisted, and my gums swelled with a strange soreness, my teeth abruptly much more sensitive and reactive. And suddenly it wasn't enough to simply smell their blood—I wanted to taste it too. I opened my mouth, baring my teeth, ready to attack one of them, either of them, or maybe even both of them, when all of a sudden *bang*—I was distracted by the unexpected feeling of someone restraining me from behind. "Christian," I growled. His icy hands firmly clenched my wrists, and his solid body pressed against my back.

"What the hell are you doing?" he whispered fearfully thorough my thoughts.

I exhaled, feeling the energetic crescendo of my pulse swiftly diminishing inside of me with the soothing sound of his feathery inner voice. What *was* I doing? Was I really going to attack them?

"Chica! You're scarier than I am," Baptiste teased.

I swallowed hard and tried to calm my breathing, and soon the craving began to quell.

"Hope?" Christian said, his eyes fixed on me.

"I'm fine," I assured him. "I don't know what came over me—okay?"

"It's okay, Esperanza," Baptiste said. "I like a woman with a little fire."

"Hey!" Eva shrieked, incensed with jealousy.

"You," Baptiste muttered softly, "you are an inferno!" He grabbed Eva by her tiny waist and spun her around in circles. She laughed, enlivening the forest with her obnoxious tone.

"Hope—" Christian said soundlessly.

"I told you," I replied, cutting him off. "I'm fine. It was nothing."

"That was not nothing."

"Well what about you and Baptiste? That was normal?"

"Boys will be boys," Eva piped in from across the way.

Christian shrugged with a grin.

"But you literally looked as though you were about to kill him!"

"So did you."

I bit my lip and stayed quiet for a moment.

"Are you—"

"Can we just forget about it?" I said.

He nodded.

I stared across at Eva and Batiste, watching the way they laughed and flirted with each other.

"They're both crazy," Christian said, trying to lighten the mood.

I nodded in agreement when suddenly Baptiste and Eva thrust themselves into us. I began falling to the ground with the force of their push. Christian grabbed me by the hand with lightning speed and caught me just in time.

"Guys," Christian said.

Eva laughed hysterically as Baptiste danced her around in circles in front of us.

"Let me formally introduce myself," Baptiste said, pulling Eva up from a deep tango inspired dip. "I am Baptiste," he said with the pride of a matador. I nearly expected to hear the strumming of a guitar accompanying him as he spoke. He extracted the piece of black licorice from his mouth for a moment to kiss my hand with his cold lips. He smiled and put the licorice back in his mouth again.

Baptiste was scary, but he was definitely charming.

Eva groaned and tugged on his hand. "Well now that you've finished trying to impress the new girl," she said, dragging him away from me, "will someone please tell her to get on with it already?"

I turned to Christian. "What is she talking about?"

"Honestly," Eva huffed. "Didn't you explain anything to her?" She slammed her thin, pale hand on her curvy hip and turned to face me. "Invite them back in the friggin' house already."

"What? What is she talking about, Christian?"

"See the thing is, when the house was bequeathed to you—so was the invitation." He sighed. "They live in the house."

"They do?"

He nodded.

"And Christian does too," Eva added with a smile.

My eyes narrowed as I stared at her. I could practically taste the chilly satisfaction she felt from imparting that tidbit of information.

"Hope," Christian said, "I know I should have—"

"Do you?" I said. "Do you really live in the house too?"

"Live in the house," Eva mocked. "Christian *buil—*"

"Yes," Christian said. "I live there too."

"Well why didn't you tell me?"

He heaved a sigh.

"Well she's already invited me in," Eva said.

"I did?"

"You did?" Christian asked.

"I didn't. I've never even seen her before," I insisted. "I swear."

Eva shrugged her slight shoulders and inflated a huge bubblegum bubble.

Christian stabbed the bubble with his index finger. It popped in her face. "I'll deal with you later," he said.

She stuck her tongue out at him like a rebellious child and moved closer to Baptiste.

"We've been trying to tough it out here in the boathouse." Christian's voice was gentle as he slipped his icy hand into the palm of mine. "It sucks. I'm not going to lie. I know it's too much to ask. I don't even know *how* to ask really."

Initially, the mere inheritance of the house seemed a heavy burden to bear, but now being obligated to decide the fate of the beings who resided in that house seemed entirely too much.

"What's the big deal?" Eva said.

"Woman, give her time." Baptiste reprimanded while running his tattooed hands through her shiny red hair. "You really are the most insensitive person I have ever met."

"But that's why you love me," she replied, placing a sloppy, wet kiss on his lips. They laughed together.

Christian shook his head, embarrassed. I smiled a little before shifting my eyes over to Henry. I had practically forgotten he was even there. He hadn't said a word the entire time. *"Why is he so quiet?"* I asked through my thoughts.

"Henry is, well, he's different."

He was leaning against the side of the boathouse with his arms folded neatly across his chest, and then suddenly he raised his face. I gasped. *"His eyes,"* I said inside my thoughts. They were unreal, reflecting with a radiant opalescent shine. *"What's wrong with him?"*

"He's ... different."

"I can see that."

"Hey, blondie," Eva interrupted, "you gonna invite them in or what?"

"Eva!" Baptiste sneered.

"Well it's getting dark out here, and some of us prefer beds to boathouses," she continued in her surly tone.

"Give her time," Christian said. "It's Hope's house now and—"

"It's okay," I said, cutting him off. "It was your house, too." I took a deep breath. "You can all come in." I wondered if a surge of regret would rush through my body the instant the invitation left my lips, but it didn't. I felt okay with my decision, confident even.

"Are you sure?" Christian whispered.

I nodded. "You were Moira's friends ... my grandmother's friends. I think she'd want it this way. Don't you?"

Christian slid his hands around my waist. "Thank you," he whispered.

I beamed.

Eva and Baptiste howled with excitement, and we all started our trek back toward the house, all of us except for one—Henry. I noticed that he was still leaning against the side of the boathouse. "Should we ...," I whispered. "I mean, does he need help or something?"

"No. He'll be fine," Christian said. "Just give me a second, will you?"

I nodded and watched him jolt through the air like a blurry streak of color toward Henry. When he reached him, he leaned in close and whispered something in Henry's ear. It was interesting seeing the way the two of them connected; they were obviously close, but the rapport didn't strike me as merely friendship alone—they seemed more like family. They two men smiled at each other, and within a fragment of an instant, Christian was standing by my side again.

"Everything okay?" I asked.

"Yeah. Henry will meet us back at the house."

I nodded. We turned around to face the moon. It was glorious. We started walking when suddenly Christian slid his hand in mine.

"He wants me to thank you."

"Henry?"

Christian nodded.

"For what?"

"For letting him come home again."

I smiled.

We were quiet for a while as we walked through the trees. The night didn't scare me anymore—not with Christian by my side, but then I suddenly I heard a rustling in the brush up ahead.

"It's okay," he said, tightening his grip on my hand. "Probably just a deer."

"Yeah," I replied, but I wasn't convinced. A strange chill ran down my spine. I could sense something out there—something much more menacing than just a deer.

"Don't be silly," Christian whispered in reply to my thoughts. "There's nothing to be afraid of. After all, *we're* the monsters."

I didn't feel like a monster, and I certainly didn't see Christian as one either. I took a deep breath and tried to clear my thoughts. I looked ahead through the trees, forcing myself to forget about whatever it was that was out here—watching us. The sky was alive with a gleaming luminosity. Eva and Baptiste were ahead of us in the distance. Their silhouettes moved like the flickering of a candle flame against the light of the moon as their laughter echoed through the trees.

"It's a blood moon," Christian said inside my thoughts.

"Blood moon," I uttered aloud, feeling the words roll off of my lips like thunder.

I thought about the many phases of the moon and felt a strange connection to it that I hadn't realized before. I too was changing, progressing into something different. I contemplated whether I would be as splendid as the moon while I phased, when suddenly I heard Christian's soft, feathery inner voice assuring me that I most undeniably would. And like a chorus of chimes humming through my thoughts, he continued amusing me with flattery as we made our way back to the house.

I relaxed myself to the rhythm of our stride with his hand in mine, my eyes flitting back to the moon every so often. *Blood moon*, I thought to myself, licking my lips, and suddenly I became thirsty again.

18-Secrets

When we reached Ambrose House, I was surprised to find that Eva and Baptiste had already let themselves inside. It didn't bother me as much as I thought it would have. I watched Eva skip across the front hall like an adolescent toward the massive wooden lady. She jumped up and planted a huge kiss on her timber mouth, staining it with crimson lipstick.

"Miss me, sugar?" she teased.

"You so loco, Eva," Baptiste bellowed, grabbing her by the waist and spinning her around.

"Nice candlelight," Eva purred, scanning the room. "You two in the middle of something?"

I could feel my face flushing. The candles were still burning, tall with strong flames, as though they hadn't even melted an inch since we left the house, and yet I was certain we had been gone awhile.

"The power is out," Christian said.

"Really," Eva said. "I thought it was just your lame seduction technique."

Christian shot her a dirty look.

"Is she always like this?" I asked.

"Ooh," Eva hissed, "blondie has a mouth."

"Ignore her," Christian said. "Want something to drink?"

Baptiste suddenly appeared out of the back room, cradling several wine bottles in his burly arms.

"Party time!" Eva hollered, skipping her way into the living room.

Christian and I trailed behind. We sat together on the Victorian couch. And when my eyes flitted over to the loveseat next to us, I nearly fainted. I couldn't believe what I saw. It was my friend Ryan! She was sitting there holding a wine bottle in her hand. My heart struggled to pound inside my chest. I sprang to my feet and stared at her, stupefied by her presence.

"Cut it out!" Christian barked at Ryan.

"What—what's going on?" I asked.

Baptiste walked over and sat down on the loveseat next to Ryan. "C'mon, Eva," he said nonchalantly. "Don't you think she's been through enough already?"

"Eva?" I asked, bewildered.

Suddenly Ryan started transforming. She was becoming Eva; her bony facial features slowly morphed into the roundness of Eva's visage, the deep black of her hair saturated with Eva's brilliant red, the slightness of Ryan's body fleshed out with Eva's meandering curves, and clothes appeared and disappeared with the simplicity of mixing watercolors. I stood speechless just watching the supernatural transmutation that was materializing before my eyes.

"You're such a showoff," Baptiste snorted while uncorking one of the bottles with his teeth.

It was the smell emanating from the bottle that finally shifted my attention. I watched as Baptiste slowly poured the syrupy contents into the glasses. It was blood. *More blood.* But this bottle was different. It didn't smell nearly as delicious as *our* bottle had.

"Will you two be joining us?" Baptiste asked.

Christian nodded and then tugged me by the hips. The force of his hands on my waist made me fall backward into his lap. I laughed as I landed, but I was embarrassed. I liked the feeling of him beneath me—almost too much, and so I quickly moved back to my position beside him on the couch. I could hear the sound of him cracking a smile. *Damn it,* I thought to myself. He was listening to my thoughts again. Quickly, I focused my attention on something other than his lap to save face. "Okay," I said, "what exactly was Eva doing?"

Christian grazed my cheek with his tender lips, kissing me softly, before leaning in to grab the two brimming glasses from Baptiste's hands.

"I'm a shifter," Eva said.

"You looked exactly like my friend Ryan."

"No biggie. I can shift into anyone." She grabbed her glass from Baptiste. "I was looking through your phone and saw a bunch of pictures of you and your friend acting like idiots."

"You looked through my phone?"

"Yeah—so?"

"Apologize, Eva," Baptiste insisted. "You can't just take her stuff."

"I didn't *take* her stuff—I was just *looking* through it."

Baptiste nudged her in the arm.

"Fine." Eva rolled her eyes and glared at me. "Sorry." She looked back at Baptiste. "There—you happy now?"

He nodded. "She's annoying, but believe me, her talents come in very handy."

"I'll bet," I said, unimpressed.

"I've got the Powers to control your mind," she teased, suddenly shifting into Shirley Powers the real estate agent.

"Stop it Eva!" Baptiste ordered.

"Wait!" I said. "That was *you*?"

She nodded.

"Eva, you didn't!" Christian implored with rage.

Eva shifted into herself again and shrugged. "So what? I just wanted back in the house. And you were taking too long to romance her—or whatever it was you were doing." She downed a swig of her drink, licking off the tiny droplets of blood that were left on her lips. "Mmm, smooth. It's well aged, but I can really taste the junkie in it."

"Don't change the subject," Christian said.

"Whose idea was it to ruin the virgin with a junkie?" Baptiste's voice was stern. I watched as he swished the drink around in his mouth before swallowing.

"Definitely *not* mine," Christian piped in defensively, taking another sip.

"Eva!" Baptiste said.

"Okay, okay, it was my idea. At least I'm adventurous. You two are so straight-laced. It's all notes of this and hints of that." She huffed. "It was 1978. Everyone was a junkie back then. Do you remember how hard it was to find clean blood?"

I eyed my glass. I wanted to taste it, but I wasn't sure what I was drinking.

"Christian," I whispered, "this isn't *us* in it—is it?"

He smiled. "No, of course not. *This* is what we do."

I cocked my head to the side and grimaced a little.

"Drink it and tell me what you taste," he urged.

I put the glass to my lips. It smelled good, but I didn't yearn for it the same way as I did with our brew. I could smell the subdued metallic scent immediately. I took some of the drink into my mouth, swishing it around briefly before swallowing. It was course and bitter, like drinking a vat of raw meat marinated in acetone. My face contorted with the awful flavor, but then suddenly my mouth tingled with the smoothest aftertaste. It was like a burst of softness on my tongue; I felt as though daisy petals were dancing in my mouth. The sensation was lighter than water and yet sweeter than sugar. It was the most wholesome flavor my mouth had ever experienced.

"Well?" Christian asked.

"The first part was terrible, like raw meat and nail polish remover." I could see Eva rolling her eyes. "But the second part," I smiled. "It was the purest thing I've ever tasted."

They all laughed.

"She's one of us all right," Eva said.

"No—she's not," Christian shot back.

"But what if I wanted to be?"

"See, Christian," Eva snarled. "She wants it."

"Well it's not happening." His tone was firm.

"He probably didn't even explain it to you—did he?" Eva asked.

"I did. I told her," Christian said.

"Yeah, you probably told her in your lame, Christian-sucks way." She rolled her eyes again and turned to stare at me. "Look," she said with a sinister grin. "The whole thing is quite simple really. All you have to do is convince Romeo to suck you nearly dry, and when you're stuck lingering in the excruciatingly painful darkness of misery with one foot in the grave ready to become food for maggots, lick the crap out of that gorgeous boy's blood until you feel the pound of your heart reduce to nothing more than an infinitesimal thump." She downed another sip of her drink. "And *that* my dear, that's when your real life begins."

Everyone was silent.

"Yeah," I said. "That's what he told me."

Christian and Baptiste broke out into laugher. I couldn't help but laugh along with them. Eva hissed at everyone. Baptiste mumbled something in her ear while uncorking a new bottle. A peculiar aroma filled the air, and I inhaled deeply, my body coming alive with a surge of exhilaration.

"He'll never do it," Eva asserted, distracting me. "He's way too obsessed with you to ever hurt you again. Even Henry could see that a mile away."

"Oh, Eva!" Christian shouted.

"Hombre," Baptiste said, changing the subject, "this bottle tastes like teen angst and old person." He took another sip. "Is that what you were going for?"

Christian's eyes glimmered with a silvery shine. Eva knew how to get under his skin. I grabbed his hand and squeezed it, feeling him relax a little with the warmth of my touch.

"Lighten up, you two," Baptiste said. "Have a drink with me." His face curled into a vile expression. "Spring break," he spoke slowly, "fun in the sun," he closed his eyes, "mothballs … roast beef … and um, arthritis medicine?"

Everyone started laughing and tried a taste of the new bottle. With each sip, I noticed their faces suddenly flushing with hints of color. They were revitalized. Nourished. They laughed as they drank, as though the more blood they imbibed the more intoxicated they became. I listened to the happy hum of their laughter.

"What exactly is this?" I whispered in Christian's ear, gesturing to the blood in my glass.

"It's our sole sustenance." He smiled. "Obviously, murdering for blood was wrong, and over the years, we learned to curb our craving to kill."

"Speak for yourself, fancy lad," Eva interrupted. "Some of us actually enjoyed those dark days—you know, when evil was still cool."

"Oh, Eva, you're so full of it," Baptiste said. "I remember your face light up the first time you had a taste of the Stromboli."

Christian leaned over to me and whispered in my ear. "Stromboli was the first bottle Baptiste ever corked." He laughed quietly. "He compares *everything* to it."

"Was Stromboli the name of the guy in the drink … the blood?" I asked.

"No, no. It's a reference to Pinocchio actually." He looked toward Baptiste. "Something about him being the wooden puppet on a string and finally having the courage to outsmart the slave driver."

"You're kidding?" I grinned. "I didn't take him for a big cartoon buff."

Christian shook his head. "Baptiste was the son of an amazing winemaker in his old life—his mother was Cuban, his father was French. When I first met him he was nothing like he is today. He was insecure and cowardly, ripe from living in the shadow of his overbearing father. Even after he changed—even a hundred years after his father died—there was still a part of him that stayed meek." He shrugged. "Maybe he'll never feel differently."

"Meek? I can't imagine anyone overshadowing *him*." I eyeballed the gargantuan size of Baptiste's body.

Christian laughed. "He's actually extremely talented. The whole blood corking thing didn't happen until Baptiste finally discovered a way to preserve it infinitely."

"Infinitely? How? I mean doesn't blood spoil or something?"

"Yes, but Baptiste applied old-fashioned principles of winemaking to human blood and then combined that with our own blood. He discovered a way of slowing the coagulation." He smiled. "And suddenly a whole new world of feeding opened up to us. A safer world with less death."

"Vampire vintner." I laughed with a nod. "It's impressive."

Christian explained, "As time went on, we actually got quite good at it. We learned how to infuse different ingredients to make better blood, just like they do with wine. Imagine middle-aged tourist mixed with hints of teenager on Spring Break. Or weekend warrior with notes of lonely, single mother."

"If you don't kill people, then how do you get their blood?"

"We have our ways," Baptiste interjected, his tone vaguely reminiscent of old monster movies. I half expected him to say bru-ha-ha and tap the tips of his fingers together.

"Is this what all vampires do?"

"Don't know," Christian admitted.

"We don't know any—other than each other of course," Baptiste added.

I stared at them with confusion.

"Oh c'mon, blondie," Eva barked. "Don't you get it? We're the only ones. There's no big underworld full of vamps in tight Lycra or sparkly skinned bloodsuckers playing together in meadows."

"But, what about—"

"Crap," she said. "All crap."

"In all my living," Christian said, "I've never come across anyone else like us."

"Then how did you all become …"

"It's rather incestuous really," Christian whispered.

"I made Eva," Baptiste explained. "William made me, and Christian made Henry."

"Who is William?"

"He—um—he died. It's a long story." Christian's tone was uneasy.

"Well who made you?" I asked.

"Now *that* is a great story," he said, "for another time."

I pursed my lips tightly and glowered.

"Hi, Henry," Christian suddenly said, turning around. "I'm sorry—I didn't notice you standing there."

He was standing in the hallway near the staircase as though he had just miraculously appeared.

"Let me get you something to drink," Christian said, filling a glass and taking it over to him.

"Is everything okay?" Henry asked.

"Everything is fine," Christian assured him, handing him the drink.

"Did you tell her?"

Christian shook his head. "Not yet."

I froze. I knew that voice. I recognized it from the woods in the rain. It was Henry who wanted to touch me. But why? A sinking feeling grew in the pit of my stomach. I stared over at him, watching the way his eyes roamed around the room aimlessly, and then suddenly it struck me: Henry was blind.

Christian returned to the couch and sat next to me.

"Doesn't he ever get tired of you cuddling him like that?" Eva snapped.

"He's not *cuddling* him, you imbecile, he's *coddling* him," Baptiste said.

"Same diff," she replied.

"He's blind?" I asked.

"Only in his human form," Christian replied.

"You see, honey," Eva piped in, "when you change, yeah sure, you get amazing superhuman abilities like speed, strength, and maybe even the uber-fabulous potential to shape shift like myself, but just like in life, it all comes at a cost."

"A cost? What kind of cost?"

She laughed. "How about your fundamental senses."

"What—like smell, sight, and stuff?" I asked.

Christian took my hand and placed it in the palm of his. "It's not as bad as it sounds. For Henry, it was his sight. But for Baptiste, it was his threshold for pain, which is kind of a good thing."

"And you?" I asked.

"Taste."

"Taste?"

"Taste is a tricky thing for me." He swallowed. "I can't tell the difference between salt and sweet or sour and spice. Corking is …," he laughed, "a challenge. Unless everything is labeled, I'm at a loss."

"But that's sad! You're a connoisseur of this blood winemaking thing you've got going, and you can't really enjoy it?"

"It's not so bad. I can still taste—it's just that everything tastes like metal to me. Tin mostly."

"Tin?" I said with a grin.

"And those candies," Eva said. "I hate those things."

"They're your candies?" I asked.

He nodded. "For some reason, the taste of cinnamon I'm certain of—the sweet sharpness of its flavor, I guess."

Eva cleared her throat. "But that's not all he has a taste for…"

"What does that mean?" I could feel my face beginning to flush.

"He's got a taste for you, sweetheart." Eva winked. "Your blood."

"Well," he shot back, "I guess it's easy to see what fundamental sense Eva lost. Her mind."

"Ha!" Baptiste hollered.

"Sometimes you are so seventeen," Eva barked.

"Seventeen?" I muttered, mortified.

"Don't tell me you didn't know how old your little piece of eye candy was?" she razzed.

Christian looked at me with an awkward smile and ran his fingers through his hair.

"She's been parading around with him like some freakin' prom queen reliving the best years of her life, and she didn't even realize how old he was?" Eva's voice was theatrical.

"Eva," Baptiste snapped. "Christian is more than two hundred years her senior when you think about it."

Eva paused, a hint of embarrassment streaking her pretty, pale face. "Yeah, I know. But it doesn't look like it."

I shook my head at Christian.

"Oh don't," he said before I could get a word in edgewise.

"Don't what?" I replied. "I'm not sure whether to be bothered by the fact that you're more than two hundred years old or the fact that you *look* seventeen?"

"Hope," he said, taking my chin into the palms of his hands. "Why be bothered by either?" He smiled. "I'm still just me." And then his voice went soundless while his words continued inside my thoughts. "*You've known me all along, from your dreams—your childhood. It's still just me.*"

I stared into his beautiful, electric green eyes. He was perfect—the soul of an old gentleman and the body of a young one. It was a perfect moment, until I suddenly heard my phone start to ring.

"It's yours," Eva said. "Some guy named Richard. See, Christian, she's cheating on you already." And then she threw the phone at me with the force of a rocket.

Christian shot his hand out in mid-air and caught it just before it hit me in the face. "That's her father, you moron."

I scowled at Eva as I sprang from the couch and sauntered into the hallway to take the call. "Hello, Richard," I said. "I know, I know, it's taking longer than expected." His voice was hard and cold. "She left this house to me. It's *my* estate to deal with, not yours." Through the corner of my eye, I noticed Christian edging his way closer. He moved with a delicate poise. I loved to watch him; he made me forget about all the nonsense in my life. "I'm doing my best, Richard." Christian reached me and started tracing my spine with his long fingers. His touch was what I needed. "Look, Richard, can I call you back?" I giggled a little as Christian continued to tease me. "*Yes,* I'm still going to be at your wedding." I rolled my eyes and then froze. "What did you just say?" My body stiffened. "W-well," I stuttered uneasily, "he gave me a ring, but—what exactly did that pig tell you?" I pressed my lips together. "I *didn't* say yes to him." I groaned with rage, my blood boiling inside of my veins. "Forget it. Just forget it. You are impossible to talk to." I threw the phone to the floor with incredible force, shattering it upon impact.

Christian ran his hands around my waist and pulled me close.

"He's nothing but an arrogant—"

"Shh," Christian urged, pressing his icy fingers to my lips.

"Tell me something that will make me forget about that. *Please.*" I was desperate for another tryst in mid-air or a moment against the milieu of the enigmatic moon, but he didn't resort to any mystical tricks. Instead he simply leaned in close and uttered three of the most powerful words in the world.

"I love you," he whispered. "I always have."

And then he kissed me again.

19-Truth or Dare

Dawn turned into dusk. Time with my new friends seemed to vanish like steam on a mirror. It was immeasurable for some reason, like they had the power to manipulate the feeling of an hour or an instant and make it seem the same. I already knew Christian's capacity for slowing time to a lingering stagnancy, but collectively as a group they seemed to possess an even greater power like a kind of mind control. Maybe this was how they could bear spending eternity together: by convincing each other that time didn't exist!

I stroked the jewels on my necklace as I stared out the window, playing with the tiny pendant between my fingers. Something about wearing it—having it against my chest close to my heart—made me feel strong, as though Ryan was protecting me.

Outside, a breadth of sinister hues saturated the surroundings. The murky blues of the deep sea and the black of the cosmos materialized like the arms of night unfurling across the yard. The blazing auburn of the huge moon had returned again too, along with my brood of vampires.

The sound of Christian's motorcycle was accompanied by the revving of two other engines as well. I figured I must have slept the day away. I was still wearing the tank top and jean skirt from the other night and honestly hadn't even noticed when any of them even left the house. I felt a little nauseous too—like a hangover, only worse. My head swirled with dizziness like a posy of ribbons rippling in the wind. I attributed it to the mishmash of blood I'd imbibed. I imagined the pool of crimson deep inside me, sitting heavily in my stomach, sickening me with gut rot, and suddenly I wanted to puke. I swallowed hard and took a deep breath, and after a moment, the nausea faded and I felt fine again. "This is definitely going to take some getting used to," I said under my breath. My stomach was tender and yet somehow replete. I smiled a little at the thought of how the blood both disgusted and delighted me. I recalled the viscous liquid touching my lips, entering my mouth, and sitting on my tongue. I remembered the way it filled me with an inexplicable fullness.

Suddenly the front door swung open. A robust bouquet of smells imbued the stagnant air. I inhaled. It was them. Their strong, familiar metallic scents filled the air, making me salivate like a hungry animal. Baptiste and Eva were the first to enter. Their clothes were soaked with water, ruining the Persian carpets as they cavorted.

"Is it raining outside?" I asked.

"No," Eva replied with a smirk.

"Then why are you wet?"

She didn't answer. Just then, Henry sauntered through the door. He nodded at me before ascending the staircase. I assumed that he could smell my presence. He was wet too. His clothes were drenched and his honey blond hair was spiked out in a tangle of prickles. I smiled as I stared. He was cute—slow and awkward, but cute.

Then finally Christian arrived. His smell alone was enough to drive me wild, but when he appeared through the front door, I could feel my stomach fluttering with excitement. His black hair dripped with beads of water that tenderly fell against his fair skin.

"Hi," he said softly.

"Why are you guys all wet?"

"It's a long story."

My face furrowed. "Still keeping secrets?"

He laughed, running his fingers through his hair like usual. "Are you just waking up?"

"Yeah, what time is it?"

"Nighttime. I guess it sucked you in too."

"Now what would that be?"

"The vortex."

"The what?" I asked.

Eva and Baptiste returned to the living room, dressed in dry clothes and cradling a selection of bottles in their arms.

"Dinner time," Eva hissed, happily arranging the collection of bottles on the glass table. She was wearing a tight red shirt, tiny red shorts, black fishnet stockings, and incredibly high red heels. Her silky, scarlet locks hung snugly aside her neck, teasing the tips of her thin shoulders with their ends. She was beautiful. She was always beautiful.

"Did I hear someone talking about the vortex?" Baptiste said. He looked disheveled, as though he just threw on his jeans, T-shirt, and baseball cap.

"Yeah," I said. "What's this vortex?"

"It's this weird thing that seems to happen when we're all together," Christian explained.

"I'll tell her," Eva interrupted. "Picture it like a fire. One little bonfire is no big deal, can't do much harm. But when that fire unites with other fires, it becomes a serious force to reckon with."

"Together we can move mountains," Baptiste interjected. "Realign the stars or even tweak the whole time-space continuum."

I nodded.

"Do you even realize how long eternity is?" Eva snapped.

"No," I retorted. "Why? Do you?"

Baptiste and Christian laughed. Eva glowered at me.

"The vortex makes our infinite lives more bearable," Christian whispered in my ear. "Especially with Eva around."

"I heard that Christian," Eva snapped.

"Don't you want to change, bro?" Baptiste asked, motioning to Christian's wet clothes.

"Right," he replied. "Won't be a second." He vanished into thin air. Within a fragment of an instant, he returned wearing dry clothes.

"Oh my—"

"Yeah, yeah," Eva sneered, cutting me off, "he's fast. Whoopee!"

Christian grabbed my hand and pulled me over to the couch. I nestled myself within the cradle of his arm. His dry, white T-shirt smelled of fresh laundry and his skin of its usual mouthwatering tin-cinnamon. I inhaled deeply and smiled. A moment later, the succulent stench of blood distracted me. I perked up, eyeing the bottle that Eva was letting breathe. I watched as she poured out the thick glutinous contents. The liquid oozed like molasses as it entered our glasses. A tangy burst of something bold, shallow, and tough tickled my nose.

"Nineteen seventy-five—good year," Eva said while reading the label. "A shot of college frat boy, a hint of prom queen, and a dash of biker."

"Who corked it?" Baptiste asked.

Eva searched the label again. "Um, you actually."

Baptiste smiled. "Esperanza," he whispered, leaning closer to me, his voice rumbling like a sleeping dragon, "you'll like this one."

I smiled nervously, and we clinked glassed before ingesting the warm drink. Baptiste was right. I did like it. I nearly downed the entire glass in one gulp. *"So good,"* I said through my thoughts.

Christian laughed.

My body panged for more.

"It's the hints of *our* blood in the drink that you're craving," Christian whispered.

I nodded, embarrassed.

"Your body wants our blood. It's trying to persuade you to turn—to become one of us."

A chill ran up my spine. I looked away and swallowed nervously. Maybe he was right. My mouth *did* water every time they entered the room. Even the nearness of Christian's body was making me thirst for a taste of him.

"Stay strong," he urged through my thoughts. *"The blood will make you powerful, but it will test you."*

"Hey, I've got a brilliant idea," Eva cackled. "Let's play a game of truth or dare."

"No," Baptiste said.

"Forget it," Christian agreed.

"Well, I'll play," I declared confidently.

Eva laughed.

"You will?" Christian said.

"Yeah. How bad can it possibly be?"

"She's a vampire, Hope. And she's … she's Eva!"

I turned to her. She smiled unevenly, the edges of her mouth like the teeth of a jigsaw. "It'll be fine," I said, half-smiling. "I think."

"Well I'm impressed," Eva admitted. "I didn't think blondie would be so eager."

Christian rolled his eyes and slipped deeper into the fold of the couch.

"Do we *have* to do this?" Baptiste grunted.

"Yes." Eva barked. She grabbed the open bottle and poured what remained into our glasses. "Okay, here's how we'll play." She ran her finger around the rim of the empty bottle, licked the remnants, and placed it on its side in the center of the table. "Spin the bottle."

"Chica, I think we're all a little past kissing in the closet for five minutes," Baptiste teased.

"That's not what I mean, you idiot. You," she said, pointing her long, red fingernail at me. "You go first."

I gave the bottle a hard twist. It twirled like a spinning top before stopping in front of Baptiste. "Truth or dare?" I asked awkwardly.

"Truth," he said, eyeballing me with a menacing stare.

"The tattoos," I mumbled. "You have so many … and you'll have them *forever.* How do you choose?"

The room was silent, dead silent. I should have asked him how many people he killed. Guys like him probably enjoyed bragging about that kind of stuff, I thought to myself.

Then suddenly he moved, extending his arms forward. "These are the faces of *mi familia*. My ancestors." His voice was swollen with emotion. "This is my way of remembering who I was."

His answer was unexpected and beautiful. I nodded my head and smiled. "But—"

"That's it, blondie. One question only," Eva ordered.

Baptiste nudged her in the arm. "It's okay. Let her ask." He took off his baseball cap and ran his fingers against his bald head, caressing the tattoos of an angel and a devil on either side of his skull.

"Your skin … why doesn't your skin burn in the sunlight?"

His fingers tickled the intricate black and gray wings of both the angel and the devil as he scratched his head. And then he leaned in close; the shadows under his pale green eyes were dark and sinister. His mouth opened. "Who says it doesn't burn?"

Christian grabbed my hand. "The top couple of layers continually burn and regenerate. It's grueling at first, but in moderation, you get used to it. So why live in the sunshine state?" he joked.

"Yeah," I said. "Why not Canada or something?"

Christian smiled. "Here is just where we ended up."

"Okay, I'm bored of this," Eva said before spinning the bottle again.

This time, the bottle stopped at Christian.

Eva whispered something into Baptiste's ear. An evil smile crept across his rugged face. "Okay, hombre, truth or dare?" he said.

"Dare."

"Okay then, I dare you to the absinthe bottle."

"You can't be serious!" Christian said.

Baptiste slowly nodded his head.

"What's the absinthe bottle?" I interjected.

"It's probably the riskiest Baptiste ever corked." Christian's voice was fiery. "It's our blood infused with absinthe."

"What's absinthe?"

"It's an old drink," Christian continued.

"You should know, Christian," Eva teased. "You're old." She laughed.

He glared at her before moving his eyes back to me. "It was a very popular drink in the late eighteen hundreds. It's made with wormwood. It has hallucinogenic properties. It wasn't legal here for a long time."

"Oh," I said, intrigued.

"I know you danced with the green fairy back then, Christian," Eva said. "And don't even try to deny it."

"Green fairy?" I said with a giggle, but through the corner of my eye, I noticed Eva disappear, morphing into an emptiness that seemed like darkness, and when she rematerialized, she was holding a wooden case. It looked hand carved. It was adorned with intricate filigree and accented with metal studs. She unlatched the sturdy fastener and raised the lid. The box creaked with the yelp of an old door in a haunted house.

"Voila," she said.

"Is that it?" I asked. "The absinthe?"

"No, doll, its kryptonite," she spit back with sarcasm.

I rolled my eyes at her before studying the contents of the case.

Flanking the aged green bottle was a strange slatted spoon and small box with cubes of sugar. "It looks, um, complicated? What are the sugar cubes for?" I asked.

"Watch and learn, blondie." Eva extracted the green bottle from its velvet cradle and tugged the cork free with her sharp teeth. A robust burst of licorice, mint, and metal suddenly filled the air.

I closed my eyes and inhaled, letting the curious smell satiate my senses.

"Still remember how to do it, Eva?" Christian taunted.

"Duh." She placed a raw sugar cube on the flat, perforated spoon that sat across the opening to her glass.

"It's no Stromboli," Baptiste said while pouring the drink over the cube and into the glass.

Christian leaned in with a lit match, touching the tip of the flame to the sugar cube. A tiny inferno raged atop the glass, bubbling until the sugar caramelized into a pool of russet colored pulp. When the flame died out, Eva doused the cube with a shot of water and stirred the sugary goop into the drink with the flat spoon. They were like a finely tuned machine, working together to create one flawless concoction.

"It's Christian's dare," Eva said. "Make him drink it first."

"Give it to me," he said, leaning across and reaching for the glass. He flashed me a wink before bringing the glass to his lips. Then, in one quick gulp, he downed the drink.

"Well," I said, "how is it?"

"Lethal," he replied with a raspy voice. "Even *I* can taste that." He smiled and then leaned in to kiss me.

"Mmm," I purred as we parted, tasting the minty sharpness that lingered on his lips.

Christian handed me a glass. I stared at its strange cloudy greenness before bringing it to my mouth. And then I took a sip. Like liquid fire, it burned my throat, stinging like a hornet as I swallowed. It left me breathless. I liked it.

"Nice, blondie," Eva said. "I didn't think you'd have the guts."

"Oh she has the guts all right," Christian said.

I leaned in close to him and sighed. "Why do you believe in me so much?"

"You're kidding, right? What's not to believe in? The real question is—why don't you believe in yourself?" He traced the arc of my lip with his finger.

He made everything sound incredibly easy. I wanted to respond, but I couldn't. I didn't have the answer. Why *didn't* I believe in myself? The question sat heavily as I struggled to unearth a reason. But after two glasses of the absinthe, I could feel myself fading in and out of consciousness, as though I was asleep and awake simultaneously. Every so often, a surge of energy rushed through my veins like a shot of adrenaline. And soon I was numb—frozen in a wonderful state of bliss.

Eva spun the bottle again. The green glass whirled around and around with the tremendous force of her spin. Finally after several swift passes, it stopped. This time, the opening pointed directly at me.

Eva cleared her throat. "Truth or dare?"

"Dare," I said boldly, liquid confidence flowing through my feeble mortal veins as the word left my lips.

"I'm starting to like this girl, Christian," she joked.

"Play nice," he said.

A surge of their blood in the absinthe suddenly rushed through my body with the force of a freight train. I exhaled hard, letting its vigor strengthen me.

"I dare you to the Devil's Tongue," Eva said.

"No!" Christian yelled.

"No!" Baptiste agreed.

"Wait a second—what is it?" I asked.

"It doesn't matter," Christian growled. "It's *not* happening."

"It's a place," Eva answered, "where we race." She licked her red lips. "It'll be fun. Nothing will happen if you're with Christian. He won't let it. Because he sucks."

I turned to Christian and shrugged. "C'mon. It sounds pretty harmless."

"But we're intoxicated," Christian reminded me.

"Buzz-killer," Eva snubbed.

"He does have a point," Baptiste agreed, downing another absinthe shot.

"Oh c'mon," Eva pleaded. "If it was 1959, both of you would have been in your cars already."

"But it's not the fifties, Eva," Christian retorted.

"Uh duh. Honestly, you two are getting so lame in your old age." Eva shot her fierce blue eyes over at me. "So, blondie. You wanna do it or what?"

I shifted uneasily and bit my lip.

"What? You afraid a cop might pull us over? We barely have a pulse—let alone a legal license." She stood up and tugged on Baptiste's arm, pulling him to his feet. "C'mon. It's the middle of the night. No one will be around, and it's not even a real road." She slammed her slight hand on her hip. "Christian, it's an abandoned stretch of highway, barely even a fishing pier for crying out loud."

I nudged Christian in the arm. "I wanna do it."

Christian shook his head. "I don't know why I'm letting you talk me into this. It's a bad idea." He heaved a sigh and shifted his eyes over to Eva. "She drives with me," he insisted.

"As if you'd have it any other way," she replied.

"And no funny business," he warned.

"Cross my heart and hope to die," she teased.

And then with the drink coursing through our bloodstreams, we headed out the door and into the moonlight toward the Devil's Tongue.

20-Time

I revved the engine on Christian's '69 Boss. It was a car with more power than I was used to. Each time I pressed on the gas, it rumbled like the growl of a bear. It was sleek, black, and perfect.

"Careful with her," he sighed in his thoughts.

"You don't mind that I'm driving?"

"I trust you," he whispered.

I looked over to my left and saw Eva behind the wheel of her seventies Chevelle. The car was silver with black rally stripes. She revved the engine hard and then leaned out of the window.

"Let's do this, blondie," she snarled, her fiery red hair blowing in the cool night breeze.

Baptiste was sitting beside her in the passenger seat. He looked more nervous than excited. His tattooed fingers gripped the side of the car.

"You okay?" I shouted over to him.

"You've never seen Eva drive," he said with a half-smile.

"Hey," Christian said, placing his cold hand on my thigh. "You don't have to do this. You don't have to prove anything."

"I know," I said, revving the engine. "I just want to do this."

"Brave girl," he cooed with pride.

I stared at the road. The moon was huge. It was dead ahead in the distance, sitting at the end of the highway like the jaws of an enormous jack-o-lantern waiting to swallow us whole. The air was cool. I shivered as the breeze graced my skin with its wintry wheeze. I looked up into the rich sapphire sky. A strange blur swooped overhead. Like a wispy haze, the peculiar night cloud zipped across the sky at an unnatural pace. I leaned closer to the windshield to get a better look, but it was gone.

"What's the matter?" Christian asked.

"Nothing. I just thought I saw … I don't know."

"There's nothing out here, but us," he assured me.

I nodded, listening to the ocean water breaking against the support beams beneath us. It was a quiet stretch of road on an old bridge high above the ocean, with only a frail guardrail to stop us from ending up in the drink. "Why do they call this place the Devil's Tongue?" I asked.

"Because of the tip. It's this huge incline at the end of the road. We call it the tip of the Devil's Tongue. And … a section of the bridge is missing."

"What! This is *that* bridge? The one at Bahia Honda?"

"Look, if you drive the stretch hard enough, you'll launch, slipping off the tip to the other side."

My heart struggled to kick into gear. I was speechless and terrified.

Christian laughed. "Just keep tight to the guardrail and you'll be fine."

"Hey!" Eva howled. "You're not chickening out, are you, blondie?"

I took a deep breath and pursed my lips. I squeezed the wheel with both hands and revved the engine again.

"Good. Let's do this," she hollered.

Baptiste counted us down in Spanish, and we were off. I pressed on the pedal, thrusting us ahead into the darkness. The engine roared with muscle as we accelerated. I could taste the salty breeze against my lips as we flew down the road toward the mouth of the moon, the torque twisting the car's frame as our speed increased.

"Careful here," Christian coached from the passenger seat.

Eva cackled like a crazy witch as our cars lingered within inches of each other. "C'mon, blondie!" she yelled. "I know you haven't got the guts to slip the tip!"

We were neck and neck when suddenly I saw it again: the strange swooping night cloud. This time it was close.

"Did you just see that?" Christian asked.

Then suddenly, in the distance, the blurry cloud imploded into the manifestation of a man standing at the edge of the road. I gasped. The huge moon silhouetted the tall, dark figure. His eyes glowed bright white with the intensity of the sun. Everyone saw it. I could hear Eva's shrilling shriek and Baptiste's outburst of profanities.

Christian grabbed my arm tightly, nearly shattering it with the force of his hold. "Brake!" he hollered.

Eva and I immediately hit the brakes. Our cars collided as we charged the pavement with the power of stampeding rhinos. The impact attached our front bumpers together in a steadfast bind. We tried everything to unlock the cars. Every second counted, every fraction of a second significant. The wind raged through the window as we cranked our wheels as far as possible.

"We're not going to make the tip," Christian said anxiously. "The end of the road … we're coming at it too quickly."

I stared ahead into the brightness that radiated from the figure's eyes when suddenly he raised his nose to the sky and inhaled. "Leechers," he moaned with the swell of a megaphone.

"What do I do, Christian?" I shrieked. "I'm going to hit him!"

Within a moment before impact, the over cranking of our wheels finally gave way and freed our cars. We shot off in different directions, silently parting as we soared through the cool, dark night air. Christian and I broke through the guardrail as though it was made of paper and hung like a balloon high above the ocean. Thoughts of drowning consumed me. Fear devoured my body like a sickness. My eyes swelled with tears, when suddenly I realized that the wind no longer whistled and the water no longer lapped. I looked to my right. The night shine was fiery in Christian's eyes. Everything was at a standstill *except* for us. I heaved a sigh of optimism, watching the moment linger.

"Listen to me," Christian said, "I can't keep us here forever, but I can at least try to give you the strength to get out of this alive."

Reality hit me like a fist. *I could die here*, I thought.

"Not if I have anything to do with it," he avowed, eavesdropping on my thoughts. He pulled a switchblade from the glove box and extended the knife. He ran its razor sharp edge down the center of his tongue. The deep sever oozed immediately with his blood.

I gasped. The smell of his sweet tin cinnamon taste suffused the air with a suffocating succulence. A jolt of excitement coursed through my veins as I inhaled.

He pulled me close, his hands grabbing at my back with enough force to leave marks, and with his lips to mine, we embraced in a kiss. His icy tongue entered my mouth, pleasing me with the sweet taste of his blood, and soon I could feel him in my veins invigorating me with an indescribable strength.

I breathed him in wholly and completely when unexpectedly my body started to tremble, gently at first before becoming severe. Then suddenly an unspeakable force fought to tear me away from him. Helpless as a butterfly in a windstorm, I struggled uselessly to resist its might. Eventually I was forced to surrender, and when I finally gave in to its fierce coercion, my body stopped shaking. Christian moved back to his side of the car, the blood on his tongue began to disappear, and the blade of the knife resealed his cut. He retracted the knife and returned it to the glove box.

I couldn't believe my eyes. Everything that had just transpired was taking place again—only in reverse.

Then suddenly I was tossed against the side of the car as it propelled itself through the air and back onto the road. I looked around amid the reversal and noticed the Chevelle moving beside me. In unison, the two cars moved away from the dark figure at an incredible speed, our bumpers unlocking and freeing as we drove.

And then it stopped. Everything stopped.

A thunderous blow accompanied by a flash of white instantly halted the rewind. For a moment, everything was silent. There was no wind, no ocean, no engines, only the subdued sounds of my quickened breath as it struggled to escape from my fragile body.

21-Realization

"Just keep tight to the guardrail and you'll be fine," Christian coached from the passenger seat.

It was as though nothing had happened—a grand déjà vu that only I was aware of, as if the devastating events of only moments prior had yet to unfold.

"Hey!" Eva howled. "You're not chickening out, are you, blondie?"

I turned back to stare at Christian.

"What's wrong?" he asked.

"Everything." And with a quick flick, I killed the ignition and pulled out the keys.

"What are you doing?"

I tossed the keys into his lap, opened the car door, and jumped outside.

"Chickening out! I knew it!" Eva shouted, jumping out of the Chevelle.

I stared ahead into the moonlight. There was nothing but black pavement and a stretch of empty road. I was mesmerized by the bareness. "Baptiste counted us down in Spanish," I said. "We took off fast. We were having fun until something happened."

"What is she talking about?" Eva complained.

I pointed ahead, toward the giant moon. "We all watched as a strange cloud turned into a man. He was standing in the middle of the road at the tip of the Devil's Tongue."

"She's crazy," Eva exclaimed.

I turned to Eva. "We slammed on our breaks, but our cars collided and our front bumpers locked together."

"Why are you telling us this?" Baptiste asked.

"Let her finish," Christian insisted.

"We cranked our wheels, unlocking our bumpers, and swerved off the road into the guardrail," I looked toward the dark sky, "through the air."

"Go on," Christian said.

"It would have been fatal," I continued.

"What do you mean, Esperanza," Baptiste asked nervously. "What would have been fatal?"

I shifted my eyes away from the road and over to the three of them. "I turned it back. *Time.* I turned back time."

"It's true," Christian said. "I read her thoughts. I saw it all, as though I was seeing it myself."

"Wait," Eva growled. "You can read her thoughts?"

Christian nodded. "And she can read mine."

"That's so not fair," Eva whined.

Baptiste moved closer to me. "Esperanza," he mumbled in his low voice. "You can reverse time? Is this true?"

I nodded. "Christian gave me some of his blood when he thought we weren't going to make it."

"It must have motivated a latent ability," Christian uttered under his breath. He turned to me. "Did you have control of it, or was it controlling you?"

"When I stopped fighting against it, everything was strangely natural." I sighed. "As easy as breathing."

"Okay, congratufrickalations on your new ability," Eva barked. "Now what the hell was this cloud-man you said you saw?"

I shrugged. "It was a patch of fog like a cloud at the end of the road, and then it just imploded into a man. I couldn't see much except for his eyes. They were incredibly bright. He sniffed into the air the way a wolf howls at the moon. And then he said something."

"What did he say?" Baptiste asked.

"Only one thing. *Leechers.*"

A gust of cool wind swept past, sending shivers along my skin.

"Impossible!" Eva said. "No one even knows we exist."

"Apparently someone does," Christian said.

"How do we handle this?" Baptiste slammed his fist into the palm of his hand.

"We need to call Henry. He'll know what to do," Christian replied.

I watched Eva reach for her phone and make the call. Her voice was loud and dramatic as she relayed the events to Henry.

Christian put his arms around me. "Time manipulation," he whispered. "Somehow you never fail to impress me, Hope."

I was still a little uneasy with the acquisition of this new ability. "Henry," I said, changing the subject. "Why would Henry know what to do? I mean he seems so ..." I shrugged.

Christian laughed. "Henry and I trained together in the Second World War."

"You did?"

"Yeah. He's very perceptive and a great fighter too."

"Even though he's—"

"Blind? It's a transient thing. When he shifts, he kicks ass."

"What exactly happened to him?" I asked. "I mean, how did he become like you?"

"Mugged in a back alley." He shook his head. "Imagine having the training of US Special Forces only to be blindsided by some stupid hooligan one night."

"So, is that why you turned him? Out of mercy?"

"No." He stroked my hair with his hand. "It was his wife's idea. She *begged* me. To her, it was better than losing him forever."

"A wife?"

Christian smiled. "Yes, a wife. She stayed human, and they loved each other until she died."

"You mean he didn't turn her?"

He shook his head. "No. She didn't want that."

"So he stayed young, and she grew into an old woman?"

Christian nodded. "Once, he told me that losing his sight let him remember his wife's face just as he left it. To him, it was as if they grew old together."

"Hey, love birds," Eva hollered, summoning us like children.

"So?" Christian asked. "What did Henry say?"

Baptiste's lips curled into a sinister smirk. "Know thy self, know thy enemy."

Christian nodded.

"*The Art of War*," I said. "Why is he quoting *The Art of War*?"

"Because, sweetheart," Eva chimed in, "it's time to strap on your armor. We're heading into battle."

"What?" I said.

"Henry thinks we should do it again," Baptiste clarified.

"Oh I don't know about that," I said, my heart thumping in my chest like a lazy hammer.

"Hope," Christian said, "forget fear. That's not part of who you are anymore."

"But what if—"

"He'll keep coming," Christian interjected. "If not here, then somewhere else—when we're *not* expecting him."

I sighed.

"Right now," he smiled, "we know where to find him. All we need is a closer look." He cupped my chin between his hands.

"Let's do this!" Eva shouted, hopping into the Chevelle and revving the engine.

"Just a closer look," Christian promised.

I nodded nervously. "But Baptiste rides with me. You and I need to be in separate cars. We need to be able to *hear* each other."

"But what if something happens to you? What if you need my—"

"Don't even say it. As long as I can hear you, nothing will happen." I took the keys from his pocket and jumped into the Boss. "It's just a closer look you need, right?"

Christian nodded.

"Then if we brake in time, nothing will happen." I bit my lip, nervous exhilaration pushing me onward.

"I've got her," Baptiste said, sliding into the passenger seat beside me.

Christian kissed me one last time before retreating to the other car. I watched as he casually evicted Eva from the driver's seat and made himself comfortable at the wheel.

I ran my fingers across my mouth feeling the coldness left from his lips and forced my eyes on the road ahead. The moon at the end of the road blazed like a fire in the sky. I inhaled and let the scent of darkness fill my senses like fuel for the ride ahead.

22-Residual

Baptiste counted us down in Spanish, and we were off—again.

"Hope," Christian called through my thoughts as we sailed down the road.

"I'm listening."

"Tell me when he's near."

"I will."

The wind picked up as we drove. Baptiste's sharp metallic scent sailed toward me on the breeze, the deliciousness of its dark licorice-like iron tang empowering my fury.

"Did you see that?" Baptiste said, watching the smoky cloud swirl past us at an incomprehensible speed.

"Yeah. It's him," I said both aloud and through my thoughts.

Christian drove tight to my side. We continued our internal line of communication as we flew along the pavement. He told me when to veer and when to accelerate, and I told him where the hazy cloud was moving and when to anticipate the implosion.

Then suddenly, just as predicted, the cloud hovered above the road at the tip of the Devil's Tongue. A moment later, it transformed into the dark figure with the bright eyes, sniffing the air.

"Do you see him, Christian?"

"I see him all right. Just keep driving. I'll fall in behind and stretch the moment to get a closer look."

And so I continued driving, the figure's gleaming white eyes practically blinding me as I approached.

"Esperanza!" Baptiste suddenly roared. "Slow down. You're going much too fast!"

I ignored his words of warning and pressed on, listening to Christian inside my thoughts counting us down.

"Four, three, two, one."

I stared into my rearview mirror, watching as the Chevelle fell in behind. Everything was falling into place just as planned.

"My god, you're going to hit him!" Baptiste hollered. "Brake!"

A fraction of a moment before approaching the tip, the dark figure suddenly disappeared, vanishing into thin air like a puff of smoke. I slammed on the brakes, and we skidded sideways to a screeching halt.

I struggled to catch my breath and turned to stare out the window. I saw the Chevelle in the distance and the wispy cloud creeping toward it. "No! No!" I shouted, fumbling with the door handle and struggling to get out of the car. Through the corner of my eye, I watched the cloud move in like an octopus, wrapping its wiry tentacles around the Chevelle, swallowing it entirely within the breadth of its haze.

"Christian!" I called anxiously through my thoughts, shoving the car door open and rushing along the pavement. But he didn't answer. There was nothing, only the whistling of the wind and the sound of ocean water breaking against the beams beneath the highway. I stopped, my body frozen with fear.

The cloud suddenly bolted away from the Chevelle, upheaving it with a colossal spin. The car flew through the air before crashing upside down on the road behind us.

A moment later, Eva's haunting scream cut the stillness like a sword.

"Eva!" Baptiste hollered, tearing from our car and storming the pavement toward the wreckage, his huge body nearly shattering the ground with the force of his feet.

Shivers ran down my spine. I swallowed hard. Fear wasn't a part of who I was anymore, I tried convincing myself as I tore off toward the sound of her cry.

Just as we approached, Christian emerged from the wreckage. I rushed toward him and threw my arms around him. "You're okay! Thank god." I withdrew a little to examine him, my hands roaming his strong frame. He seemed perfect, unscathed by the incident, and yet when I searched his mind, his thoughts were ghastly and terrifying.

"Eva's not okay," Christian said. "She's stuck."

But Baptiste was already on it, shredding the Chevelle to pieces in a frantic effort to extract his beloved. He yanked the door open, tearing it from the hinges, tossing it to the side as though it was made of cardboard. And there, inverted and wedged between the dashboard and the seat, Eva hung suspended in the air like a bat in a cave.

"No, baby," Baptiste whispered. "You have to come out of there. Shift into darkness and free yourself from this."

"I … I can't," she wailed.

"I'll get you out," he avowed. And with a bellowing roar, Baptiste peeled back the floor of the car with his burly hands, ripping and tearing through the metal as though it was a sheet of newspaper.

When Eva was finally within reach, he gracefully slipped her past the sharp metal shards and carried her away from the wreckage. The dreadful sounds of her wincing in pain resounded as he laid her down on the pavement.

"Shh, baby, shh," he purred, his baritone voice soothing and comforting.

"Sorry about the Chevelle, B," Eva mumbled, tears streaming down her pale cheeks.

A bittersweet laugh emerged from Baptiste's lips. "I don't care about the car. It's you I care about." He plastered her face with kisses.

Eva started flickering like a weak signal on a television station, her slight body fading in and out of nothingness.

"I don't feel so good," she groaned, grabbing hold of her stomach with both hands and doubling over in the fetal position.

"What's wrong with her?" I asked nervously, my eyes flitting back to Christian. And then I froze. A trail of blood streamed down his forehead, staining his pristine pale flesh. "What's wrong with you?"

He touched his face with his hand. "What is this?" Christian muttered, confused.

I inhaled the unavoidable delectableness of his tin-cinnamon scent as it imbued the air. I turned away from him, embarrassed by how much I desired the smell of his fresh blood. I trembled with a thirst for a taste of him when suddenly a heady whiff of even more blood dominated my senses. It was like a drug, and I was immediately inebriated by the delightful harmony of the fresh metallic tangs that unexpectedly filled the night air.

Eva yelped with pain. I turned to her, immediately noticing the deep sever on her abdomen. Her blood spilled out in a steady stream down her skin, across her clothes, and along the road. I dropped to my knees. I was like a wild animal inside, fighting to repress the voracious compulsion I had to lunge at her. Thirst controlled my sensibilities. My breathing quickened, my heart hammered, and my head ached. I inhaled deeply, letting the overwhelming sweet stink of Eva's fresh blood tease me with its succulence. Bloodlust gripped me hard.

"We have to get Eva home!" Baptiste shouted.

"La Fuente is closer," Christian said, yanking my hand with a swift tug. He pulled me along the pavement away from Eva. "C'mon," he insisted harshly. "It's testing you again—don't let it control you, Hope."

I rose to my feet and swallowed hard, fighting to hold my breath. If I couldn't smell it—then I wouldn't crave it.

"I know you can control it," he said sternly. "You just have to believe in your strength—in yourself."

"I am trying, Christian," I pleaded desperately through my thoughts.

"Try harder," he replied, pulling me along the road toward the Boss.

We all piled in the car. Christian and I got in the front while Baptiste and Eva spread out in the back. The salty scent of her blood permeated the air with a biting severity. I rolled down the window to breathe, but it didn't help much. Being trapped with Eva, with the smell of her blood so close to me, was unbearable.

"I'm cold," Eva moaned weakly. "Make it stop, B. Just make it stop."

I trembled with thirst as I listened to her, grasping myself with my arms and biting my lips. A moment later, I leaned my head outside of the window where the air was fresh.

"Get in here, Hope," Christian barked, tugging at my shirt to bring me back inside.

"No!" I shouted. "I can't breathe in the car with her damn blood spewing everywhere."

Christian pulled me hard, and I fell back into the seat. I turned to glare at him when suddenly I noticed that he was bleeding again too. "Oh my god," I muttered through gritted teeth, the steady flow of his sweet, deep crimson fluid practically driving me to the brink of insanity.

"I can't do this, Christian!"

"Oh, Hope!" he complained, wiping his forehead with his hand. "Look, if you can't control it—then just satisfy it." He extended his blood soaked fingers to me. "Take it."

I stared at his electric eyes for a moment before shifting my gaze to his hand. His sweet, syrupy blood oozed down his long, white fingers. My heart thumped excitedly as I stared. I took hold of him and brought him to my lips, pulling his fingers into my mouth. My body quivered with delight the moment his blood touched my tongue. I reveled in the sick pleasure I took from ingesting his divine taste. I moaned as I continued to imbibe him when suddenly my body began trembling, gently at first before becoming more relentless. It was the same force as before, vigorous in its effort to pull me away. But this time I surrendered to its lure without struggle, letting it draw me away from Christian's fingers, away from the window and through the night air, pushing us along the road and back to the wreckage.

I watched as our world put itself back together again, Baptiste assembling the car instead of tearing it apart, the Chevelle spinning through the air and landing back on its wheels. And then, like a voyeur in my own reality, I watched as the hazy cloud transformed into the dark figure once more.

I exhaled, and suddenly everything stopped moving. A thunderous blow like a sonic boom shook my eardrums, and a flash of white blinded my eyes, halting the rewind entirely.

When I focused my eyes, I realized I was back inside the Boss, sitting next to Batiste and driving toward the tip of the Devil's Tongue. I stared out the window and saw the sinister cloud as it hovered above the road in the distance. And just like before, we all watched as it transformed into the dark figure with the bright eyes. I hit the brakes, thrusting Baptiste and I toward the windshield and then back against the seats.

"Stop now!" I yelled, desperate for Christian to hear me either internally or aloud. And with my eyes on the rearview mirror, I watched as he screeched to a halt just behind me.

I jumped out of the Boss and hurried toward the Chevelle. "Are you okay?" I asked.

Christian and Eva bolted from the car and stared up the road at the dark figure.

"You guys okay?" I repeated.

"Yeah," Eva replied. "Why?"

"What happens?" Christian asked.

I shook my head, afraid to vocalize what I had seen—what we had endured.

"Look," Baptiste said, pointing ahead to the tip of the Devil's Tongue.

We watched as the dark figure suddenly transformed into the hazy cloud, twisting away like a ferocious tornado into the blackness of the night.

"It's gone!" Baptiste said.

I moved my eyes back to Christian and froze. Blood trailed down his pale face from the wound on his head.

"Why am I bleeding?" Christian asked, perplexed.

"There was an accident," I said. "It was the dark figure."

"I don't feel so good," Eva suddenly cried out before doubling over in pain and letting out a huge moan.

"No!" Baptiste exclaimed, catching her in his arms before she fell to the ground.

Blood seeped through Eva's clothes.

"La Fuente!" Christian yelled. "Take her there. It's not far. We'll meet you."

Baptiste nodded and rushed toward the Chevelle with Eva draped lifelessly across his arms. Christian and I jumped into the Boss. Engines revved like the hungry rumble of thunder as our cars came to life.

"But the accident never happened," I said, confused.

"And yet we bleed," Christian replied, blood still streaming down the side of his face.

With a screeching soar, we sped away from the moon, distancing ourselves from everything that happened.

23-Oz

La Fuente, I thought to myself. I knew where I was. The strange smell of disinfectant and metal emanating from behind the heavy velvet curtain intrigued me. Christian pulled me by the hand, pushed back the curtain, and took me with him this time.

"Ready to meet the wizard?" he whispered as we slid through to the other side.

And there it was, the central hub of their operation in all its glory. The steady buzzing resonated like a choir of cicadas. It was clean, organized, stylish, and intimidating. It was exactly as I had always imagined a tattoo shop to be.

Christian smiled. "This is how we get the blood without killing. Two sets of needles. One goes in with ink while the other extracts the blood. We use special machines." He laughed a little under his icy breath. "And we freely veil unruly customers." He sighed. "It's certainly not the most ethical practice …"

"But it sure as hell beats murdering the innocent," I added, impressed. "It's ingenious."

Christian grinned. "Time gave us a chance to hone our skills. Don't get me wrong. We're good at what we do. Some people really do come because they appreciate our artistry. Others come because they're addicted to the thrill—or the pain."

"Really?"

"Sure. Tattooing is like anything a little risqué. It can be fun, a rush, therapeutic even. It's actually become quite mainstream. Which has been *great* for corking. C'mon." He pulled me through the shop.

"La Fuente," I muttered. "What does it mean?"

"The fountain."

"Fountain?"

"The fountain of youth," he said with a smile.

"The blood. The blood is your fountain—isn't it?"

He nodded. "And in here, it flows freely."

I took a deep breath, and there beneath the stench of antiseptic was the smell of blood. I sighed aloud.

"Keep moving," Christian urged, tugging me by the hand deeper into the shop.

I eyeballed a pretty young girl draped across a white, vinyl tattooing table as we passed by. The outline of a rose had been etched into the tender flesh on her abdomen. The skin surrounding the tattoo was red, swollen, and oozing with a fresh crimson smear. I smiled as I stared, scrutinizing the way she flinched the second the sharp needles penetrated her skin. I was fueled by her vulnerability and watched her like prey, imagining what she'd be like to taste.

"Tempting, isn't it?" Christian whispered. "It's like grocery shopping on an empty stomach."

"So this is what you call a *speakeasy*," I teased as he pulled me along. "More like a smorgasbord."

Christian laughed.

"So what about the other tattooers?" I whispered. "Do they know?"

"Naw," Christian said. "We've been at this a *long* time … since the days of sailors and sparrows. We've perfected our ways. Besides, humans are easily deceived and persuaded. And if that fails—"

"You veil them."

A burst of scent suddenly filled me with its potency. "Eva," I moaned, my mouth salivating from the salty metallic smell of her blood.

"Will you be okay in there with her?" Christian asked.

"I'll try."

He unlocked the door, and we went inside. It was a small room, like a storage area, dimly lit and filled with an assortment of boxes and locked refrigerators. There was a makeshift bed in the middle of the room, and Eva was propped up on it. She was hooked up to a hospital IV and connected to a bag of blood like a patient in a ward. Her skin was pale, but it was always pale. She didn't seem like she was in any pain, and she didn't seem to be flickering anymore either, which I figured was a good thing. The smell of blood was strong, but nothing compared to what it had been on the road.

"Well?" Christian asked.

Baptiste was sitting next to Eva, squeezing her hand while Henry meticulously tended to her wounds.

"Is she okay?" I asked.

"Yeah, *she's* okay," Eva said.

I rolled my eyes.

"Nice to see the experience humbled you, Eva," Christian jibed.

"Shut up, Christian."

"Eva regenerated from the wound," Henry explained, his voice smooth and calming. "She's healed now, but she's still very weak. The steady stream of blood will help to restore her back to normal."

"Normal?" Christian teased.

I laughed.

"Esperanza, what happened out there?" Baptiste asked.

I took a deep breath. The room was quiet except for the steady hum of Eva's IV and the periodic beeping of the machine.

"Tell us, blondie," Eva snapped. "You're the only one who really knows."

"Go on, Hope," Christian encouraged soundlessly. *"Tell them."*

I nodded at him before turning my attention to the others. "The dark figure turned back into the hazy cloud and swarmed the Chevelle." I stared at Eva. "You and Christian were powerless. The cloud, it seemed to incapacitate you … your abilities."

"That's ridiculous," Eva snarled, running her hands along her bare stomach.

I shifted my eyes to her abdomen and stared at the faint scar. It was about the size of penknife. I was struck by the swiftness with which the gash had healed. It looked as though it was years old instead of minutes old. It was remarkable—they were remarkable, all of them. Their ability to regenerate from injuries and heal with effortlessness mesmerized me. They seemed indestructible, impermeable to everything.

"But not death," Christian added through my thoughts. *"We are as defenseless against death as anyone."*

My eyes flitted over to him.

"We are just as fragile as you." He took hold of my hand. "Hope, you have the ability to turn back time. You have the power to change things. Tell us what you saw out there, what we all experienced, so we can understand these things that are happening to us."

I looked into Christian's electric green eyes. He was young, unchanged, perfect, and beautiful. *They all were.* And suddenly I felt like Wendy in Neverland standing before an audience of lost boys. It was their story too, I realized, and despite the fact they couldn't remember experiencing any of the events, they deserved to know what happened. I cleared my throat. "The hazy cloud tore off with the force of a tornado," I said. "It was fierce and volatile. It spun the Chevelle through the air until it crashed upside down on the road. It was horrible. In all honesty, you were lucky it didn't kill you."

Henry took a deep breath. "So you changed the outcome the second time around." He folded his arms across his chest. "And yet you were affected by what happened in the *initial* incident."

"What does it mean?" Christian asked.

"It means we've got to kill it," Baptiste growled.

"But, the Chevelle" I said. "The car. It wasn't affected. The second time, the car was fine—no wreckage at all."

"Yes, of course." Henry tapped his index finger on his chin. "Your ability, Hope, it mustn't affect the inanimate, inorganic … the lifeless … the dead." He started moving toward us, running his hands along the wall to help him find his way.

"But look at me!" Eva exclaimed. "How can you argue that it didn't affect me?"

"I can't." Henry said.

"I don't understand," she hissed. "I was apparently ripped apart by that *thing,* and you're going to tell me that her ability doesn't affect the inanimate?"

"It's because we're not dead," Christian explained.

"Now is not the time for theories," Eva said.

"I'm *not* theorizing," Christian shot back. "Eva, every time you drink—every time the blood of a human courses through your veins—

you know you've felt your pulse quicken. You are alive again when you drink. *Immortal.*"

Eva stared at him and grimaced. "Blah. Blah. Blah."

Christian shook his head while Baptiste's laughter filled the room.

Henry leaned close to me. "When our hearts stopped beating at a normal rate, our human life was over. But we didn't die. We changed—the way a mutation or disease changes people. At least we think that's how it works."

"Okay, Einstein," Eva jabbed.

Christian grabbed my hand. "Like hibernation, our pulse slowed, but it didn't stop. And when we drink blood, our pulse pounds with a steadfast beat and we feel human again—the essence of how alive we really are."

"And how dead you could have been had Hope not reversed time," Henry insisted.

"Big deal!" Eva barked. "It's not like she can *stop* us from getting killed."

Suddenly the room silenced. I watched as all of their eyes glimmered. They inhaled in unison, aiming their noses into the air just like the dark figure on the road.

"What's going on?" I whispered to Christian through my thoughts.

"Breathe in."

And so I inhaled with them. There, past the succulent smell of Christian's mouth-watering essence, past the harsh reek of disinfectant, and beyond the robust scent of human blood, I could smell exactly what they could smell: another vampire.

Suddenly the shrilling ring of tiny bells cut the quiet like the sound of shattering glass as the front door to La Fuente opened.

"It's *him*," Baptiste declared. "I'm going out there."

"Wait!" Henry implored. "This man—this *thing*, he entered through the front door. It's not like he forced his way in. We can't assume we know why he's here."

"Have you all gone mad?" Eva hollered, ripping the IV from her arm. "Kill that son of a—"

"Stop!" Henry snarled.

I looked back at Eva. She was straddling the table, licking the remaining drops of blood from the tube that she pulled from her arm.

"Aren't you even the least bit intrigued?" Christian said. "He might have answers. He might know things about us—what we are."

Eva glanced up at him, her face pale and her mouth stained with crimson. "He tried to kill us, Christian! If we ain't corking him—I say crush him."

"Oh right, shoot first—ask questions later," Christian retorted.

"Look, he was drawn to the shop by the smell of blood. *Our blood*," Henry said. "He'll find the house just as easily."

"Eva and I will take care of the house," Baptiste said. "But promise me, if this turns out the way I think it will, you'll let *me* kill him." He slammed his enormous fists together. "He hurt Eva. He *will* pay for that."

"Fine, but be careful." Henry's voice was hard. He leaned in close to Christian. "You should be the one to address him."

"I'm going with him," I interjected.

"No!" Christian snapped.

"I wasn't asking your permission."

"Good. Because I wasn't giving it."

I glared at him and pulled away.

"Wait," he said, stopping me, his cold hands firmly looped around my wrists like handcuffs. "It's too dangerous for you."

"I like dangerous," I replied with a smirk.

"Since when?"

"Since you told me to keep telling myself that fear is not a part of who I am anymore."

"You two better get going," Henry interrupted. "He knows we're here. He can *smell* it. It's probably best if we don't keep him waiting."

Christian shook his head and glared at me. "I sure hope you believe what you're saying, because it's about to get really dangerous." He grabbed me by the hand and pulled me toward the front of the shop with him.

"Thanks," I sighed through my thoughts.

"Don't thank me for this," he replied aloud, his voice harsher than normal. "Thank me when it's over and we're not dead."

A flagrant burst of scent suddenly imbued the air. It was bitter and disgusting, like a foul blend of corroding metal and decomposing flesh. The vile stench nauseated me. I struggled to keep from gagging.

"Are you sure you're ready for this?" Christian asked.

"I guess," I uttered nervously.

Christian shook his head, and we turned the corner together. The melodious buzzing of a tattoo machine harmonized with the droning of a local news broadcast on the radio. I listened as the anchor's voice carried on about the continuing rise in missing cruise ship passengers when suddenly I spotted him—the figure from the road. He was leaning back in a chair with a foot propped up on a vacant tattooing table. He was thin, blond, and pale, with the clearest eyes I'd ever seen. His clothes were white and expensive looking.

"Tourists just don't taste like the others," he said in a deep, broken-English accent. "So full of carbohydrates and saturated in alcohol."

"Something tells me you're not here for a tattoo," Christian said.

The man laughed, his eyes fixed on me the entire time.

I swallowed and tried to look away, but his gaze was intensely persuasive—practically paralyzing.

"What can we do for you?" Christian asked coolly.

"What can *you* do for *me*?" he repeated, his voice far too deep for his youthful appearance. "Hum. Well you can introduce yourselves for starters."

"I'm Christian."

"And the girl," he hissed, his eyes pouring over me. "Who is the girl?"

Fear reared its vile head the longer I stared at him. I was captivated by the translucence of his eyes. They were empty: lucid domes sheathing the hollowness of his ocular cavities. If eyes were meant to be the windows to the soul, then obviously he didn't have one.

"I am Maxim," the man expressed, dramatically whipping his foot off of the table to stand up. He was tall and imposing.

Christian tugged on my hand, pulling me rearward a little.

"Is she yours?" Maxim inquired.

"Excuse me?" Christian snapped.

"Is she yours?" Maxim repeated, moving closer, stepping lightly as though he was floating on air.

"I don't think I understand the question," Christian snarled in reply.

"Oh, I think you do," Maxim countered as he neared.

I held my breath in a desperate effort to keep from inhaling his sickening stench. Death. He reeked of it. I could actually smell the blood of the dead as it coursed through his veins. That's what made his scent different from Christian and the others, I realized. Maxim fed upon humans. He drained them dry and left them for dead. He was a murderer.

Maxim moaned and then moved in close, dragging his icy cheek along my warm face, and when he reached my ear, he nestled himself within the tangles of my hair. He inhaled my scent. "I love the smell of a half-breed," he purred in my ear. "So pure and corruptible." He took another deep breath of me and then recoiled a little. "Your heart," he said, perplexed. "It's old. You're an *aged* mongrel?" He cocked his head to the side and scrutinized me with a peculiar abhorrence. "How long have you been like this?"

I didn't answer. I couldn't. My lifeless lips were locked, petrified in a strange state of paralysis. Only my thoughts could speak, but that was futile because he couldn't hear me. My inelegant heart pounded while I let fear control me with its grasp. Christian was right—I shouldn't have come. It was dangerous, and I was helpless.

"Why do you let them torture you like this?" Maxim inquired repulsion on his face and loathing in his voice. He turned to Christian. "What perverted pleasure do you get from making her suffer this way?" He shifted his hollow gaze back to me again when suddenly his clear eyes began filling with a vaporous mist.

The mist, I realized. He was controlling us with it the same way he controlled the Chevelle at the Devil's Tongue. We were powerless—wooden puppets on strings, weak and defenseless against him. He had control over our bodies, I realized, but not our minds. *"Christian,"* I urged soundlessly through my thoughts. *"He's coercing us with the mist, but you're stronger than he is. You have to find a way to stop him. Please..."*

Suddenly the room started trembling as the space between Christian and Maxim vibrated with thousands of tiny shock waves. A ghostly black mist materialized, exuding from Christian's body and funneling like a tornado as it returned into Maxim's eyes. I looked around the room; everything was static, hanging in a motionless suspension. A mosquito hovered in mid-air while the tattooer's needle was frozen in position on the blond girl's skin. Time was standing still. Christian was fighting back. And a moment later, we were free.

"What do you want from us?" Christian raged, tearing me away from Maxim.

"I am not here to make trouble, my friend," Maxim replied.

"You're *not* my friend," Christian snarled.

Maxim smiled. "We are all comrades in arms. What legion have you fled?"

"What do you mean?"

Maxim laughed wickedly and abruptly changed the subject. "My girlfriend and I have arrived here … on vacation. To … soak up the sun. Forgive me if I have," he hesitated, "troubled you in any way." And then he bowed like an actor after a performance before vaporizing back into a wispy haze again. We watched as he seeped through the seams of the front door, disappearing like a ghost.

With his departure, Christian unfroze time and suddenly the world resumed normal speed again. I looked around the shop. The tattooer and his client were mindless of the incident.

"Are you all right?" Christian asked, wrapping his arms around me.

"He could have killed me. He's a murderer. I could smell death on him. But he didn't. Why didn't he kill me?"

"You're not his type. He came here to feed. Its untainted human blood he's after. This isn't good." His beautiful face was rigid like a statue. He shook his head. "He could jeopardize our life here. He could ruin everything."

24-New World

Christian drove fast. We soared along the pavement in the Boss. The early morning dew that slicked the highway like a light rain swiftly vanished with the intense blaze of the rising sun. As the scorching beams met with the coolness of the pavement, a strange low-lying fog transpired, covering the road like a blanket.

We rushed through the mist, sending wafts of airy tendrils spiraling through the residual dark of night. I imagined it was Maxim and with every wisp we struck, we weakened him.

I gazed outside at the sunrise. Suddenly my picture of paradise seemed to have been painted with a rusted brush.

I watched the rays of the sun as they touched Christian's arm, tenderly searing him. He brushed the thin layer of ashes away with a gentle sweep of his hand, as routinely as scratching an itch despite the fact that it probably hurt like hell. A strange sorrow overwhelmed me as I stared at him. Christian had conditioned himself to accept the burn of the sun as a part of his survival, learning to endure it, building a tolerance to it. And as I watched his ashes blow into the wind, soaring through the air and dispersing back into the world, suddenly everything became clear to me. I realized why Maxim's presence was so devastating: Christian, Henry, Baptiste, and Eva had struggled for some time to make a home for themselves here—a life—and Maxim was about to eradicate that life with a single breath of his soulless vapor.

"Don't worry," Christian said.

His voice startled me.

"Blood *is* thicker than water," he muttered with an ominous grin. "Our family comes first."

I smiled and leaned back in the seat. *Our family*, I thought to myself. He included me as part of that family. We were connected like a family, connected by blood.

My eyes flitted back to him. The beauty of his immortality and the tragedy of his struggle captivated me. To drink of his very blood was to drink of the mythical fountain, the legendary spring that restores youthfulness, and yet it came with consequences, weaknesses—some more tolerable than others.

I sighed at my Tin Man, mesmerized by how alive our love really was. And then my thoughts turned dark again. How was it that I should love an immortal? What ungodly act allowed our love to even exist? Destiny may have brought us together, but something other than destiny, something much more sinister, gave my beloved the power to defy time and death in the first place.

"Christian," I said gently, "I want to know how you became what you are. No more secrets."

He slowly nodded and then began. "Imagine the darkest night you've ever seen and then soak it in sable ink. That's how it looked on the night I was changed. It was a long haul from the New World back to England, especially in those days. Things were nothing like today. They were much simpler, crude even. They were different. *Very different.*"

I listened intently. He spoke of the crew, his mates, and the captain of the ship as though he sailed with them only yesterday. He described the blue of the sea as seamless from the sky; he never knew which way was up. He talked of how he sweltered in his heavy woolen waistcoat and breeches the farther south they sailed and complained about the rank smells aboard the ship—their perspiration mixing with the salt-soaked air and how it nauseated him. And then he told me of the number of sleepless nights he spent staring into the sky, wishing on the brightest star for love to find its way into his heart.

I could picture it. I could feel myself in his past, walking in his shoes, tasting the air, and enduring the restless nights.

"The weather was treacherous. Whitecaps and sea squalls heaved us from port to starboard as the heavens unleashed a most angry deluge upon us that fateful night."

I was captivated by his words, watching as he bowed his head when he alluded to the tempest as atonement for their sins and wrongdoings. His sense of morality was practically romantic. When he spoke of the morning after the storm, he likened that first awe-inspiring sunrise to the way he felt about my beauty. My eyes welled with tears. I'd never known a man capable of such compassion.

Listening to Christian was like history coming alive in a way I had never seen or heard before. His firsthand accounts were heartfelt and saturated in authenticity. I was a voyeur within his thoughts, treading like a ghost among his everlasting memories.

"The people were primitive," he explained, "living in lands rich with natural beauty beyond anything I had ever imagined. Once, the sky ignited like molten gold as the sun set behind the mountains. There's nothing quite like sunset in South America."

"Why were you traveling so far from home?"

"My benefactor. He was obsessed with Sir Walter Raleigh."

"Sir Walter Raleigh … why?"

"The lost city of gold. The voyage was basically a glorified treasure hunt, guised as a naval mission."

"Guised?"

He ran his long fingers along the wheel of the car. "I was a kid and desperately wanted off of the Island. Little did I know that I'd never return. 'Over the mountains of the moon, down the valley of the shadows.' It's Edgar Allan Poe. He didn't write that until nearly fifty years after our voyage." A little laugh escaped his pretty lips.

"I don't get it. Why is that funny?"

"It was a shrewd guess."

"You're not implying that you actually found the fabled lost city of gold?" My eyes widened. "Are you?"

"No—not the city."

"But the gold?" I laughed. "You mean to tell me that you found the gold?"

"I've been selling it on the black market in small quantities for the last two centuries. Only the bits and pieces that can't be linked to the lost city of course. I didn't want fame—that was the last thing I wanted. I just needed something to get me settled."

"Get you settled?" I said, taken aback.

"I was immortal and sitting on a gold mine! What was I supposed to do?"

I shook my head, confused.

"Say something," he pleaded.

My brow furrowed. "So how did you become immortal?"

He laughed. "I tell you that I've been salvaging the mother-load of all treasure finds for the last two hundred years in a hidden wreck a mile off shore, and you're still more fascinated by my immortality?"

I blushed. "Look, the treasure thing blows my mind—don't get me wrong—but the fact that you're old enough to have been aboard the ship that actually found the treasure, well that astounds me!"

He beamed. "We've tried so hard to fit in for so long that sometimes I forget how different we really are."

"Tell me your story," I said, snuggling up in my seat.

He took a deep breath. "The ship was ravaged. All I could see was smoke. Hazy smoke. I knew we were ruined."

"Were you on your way back?"

He nodded.

"With treasure in tow?"

"Stuffed in the mouths of cannons and stashed in the beds of livestock."

"And you were a military ship?" I asked, confused.

"We were *guised* as a military ship, the HMS *Ambrose*. But we were ill prepared to defend against any actual adversary … especially a demonic one."

"Wait a second. Did you say your ship's name was the HMS *Ambrose*?"

He nodded.

"But that's the name of the house."

Christian glanced over at me. "The house *is* the ship. I built her from the wood of the wreck. It was a painstaking process. But I had time on my hands." He grinned playfully.

"Tell me more," I pleaded. "More about what happened to *you*."

"At first I thought we were being attacked by another ship, but there was nothing out there but darkness and haze. Then I considered that we must have run the ship aground, hitting a reef."

"Had you?"

"Yes, and she was taking on water rather quickly as I remember." Suddenly his brow furrowed. "And that's when it all started happening."

"What did you see?" I asked anxiously.

"It wasn't so much what I saw as it was what I heard. Their atrocious song of agony filled the night air. Their screams harmonized with one another as they sang the last verse to their own demise."

I could hear the pain in his voice as he spoke.

"The screaming, the howling, and the snapping. I had no idea what was going on. The smoky haze that surrounded the ship seemed to grow thicker incredibly quickly. I couldn't see anything. All I could do was listen, listen to them dying all around me. When I scoured the deck, all I found were the lifeless corpses of the crew. They were white like ghosts with dark hollows beneath their eyes. I could barely make out their faces. Anguish couldn't even begin to describe the wretchedness of seeing them like that." He shook his head and pressed harder on the gas pedal. "The more bodies I looked at, the more I realized that they all had something in common; section of their flesh had been torn from their throats. Then suddenly there were no more screams. It was silent except for a strange rhythmic sucking sound that pervaded the air like a metronome."

"What did you do?"

"I followed the sound through the smoky haze."

"And?"

"I found a man, a monster, a demon—I don't know." He swallowed. "He was huge like a bear, his skin dirty and badly scarred. He had long, dark, untamed hair that hung down his back in shafts. His clothes were dirty too, tattered and drenched with blood. He was hunched over William, my close friend, feeding on him."

I shook my head, apperceiving the absolute anguish he was feeling by reliving the memory of that night.

"Then instinct took over. I had to save William. I wasn't trying to be a hero; I simply had to stop the monster from desecrating the only other sole left alive on the ship."

"What did you do?"

"I jumped on the monster's back and started thrashing. He immediately stopped feeding and swatted me away like a fly. I smashed into the side of the ship, breaking several ribs. And as I was contorting in pain, the beast grabbed me by the leg and dug his sharp fangs into my flesh. He started to feed on me. It was the worst pain I had ever felt in my life, and yet I continued to fight. I wasn't about to just give in and die." He pressed harder on the gas pedal. We soared along the road like an arrow in flight. "What I remember most about approaching the threshold of death was feeling like I wasn't done yet—as though it wasn't my destiny to die at that moment."

I sighed, captivated by his story.

"And the pain was a small price to pay for saving William," he asserted.

"He didn't die?"

"When I looked over the monster's beastly shoulder, I noticed that William had joined me in the fight for our lives. William could have jumped ship—but he didn't. He stayed to save me."

I smiled.

"William wouldn't give up easily either. He was limping, bleeding, and in very bad shape, but he still had some fight left in him.

"We signaled each other before making our attack. We had no weapons—only ourselves. While the monster continued to bleed me dry, I stretched my body as far forward as I could until I was close enough to reach him. He had a huge scar across his forearm that looked like the teeth of a jigsaw. I used it as my target. I dug my teeth into the monster's cold flesh as did William in a desperate effort to slaughter him with our pitiful vengeance. At first, I don't even think the beast noticed our assault, but after a few moments, he finally stopped feeding and stared at me with a frightening shine in his eyes. And then," Christian hesitated awkwardly, "then he vaporized into a smoky haze and vanished into nothingness."

"Like Maxim," I said, my lips trembling.

Christian shook his head. "It's *not* him. The monster that did this to me had a massive scar across his right cheek. I'd know him if I ever laid eyes upon him again."

"And have you?"

"No. Not yet," he replied, a menacing quality in his voice.

His story was bloodcurdling and tragic. It was as though Christian had been orphaned, spit out of a demonic machine born of necromancy, and turned loose on the world. Surely he'd wondered whether the monster that created him would ever return.

"For the first hundred years, I was preoccupied with it," he said in response to my thoughts. "I tried to prepare myself for his return, training and devising a plan to kill him."

"But he never came—did he?"

Christian shook his head.

"What happened to your friend?"

"William," he sighed, his eyes still fixed on the road.

A sharp pain suddenly shot through my head. I closed my eyes. My thoughts raced with a peculiar montage of images. I saw Perish, Ambrose House, a woman with long hair waving her hand, and blood on the sharp fangs of a blond man I didn't recognize. And then I saw my father, Richard; his face was young and his expression irate. Suddenly the images disappeared. I gasped, tearing my eyes open.

"Sorry," Christian apologized. "Some thoughts are harder than others to contain."

"Those were *your* thoughts?"

He nodded.

"But, my father—why were you thinking about my father?"

Christian shrugged but didn't answer.

"There was a man," I said. "A young man with blood on his teeth."

"That was William." Christian squeezed the wheel tighter.

"Well where is he?"

"He died." Christian sighed. "Life—death, it's all so tragic and so incredibly confusing." The rigid expression on his face eased. He turned to me and smiled. "And yet when one life ends, another begins again." He reached over and stroked my cheek. "You want to know the real day I changed? It was the day I found you."

He had a way of soothing my soul and melting my heart. I breathed him in, letting him fill every part of me with euphoric bliss when suddenly something darted out in front of us on the road. Christian slammed on the brakes. The car screeched to a soaring stop.

"My god!" I shrieked. "What is it?"

25-Fight or Flight

We stormed the pavement to reach the tiny deer. Just as we approached, he arched his back. The pretty reddish-brown animal raised his slender face to us. His eyes glimmered with a reflective shine. They were opalescent and unmistakably familiar. I knew those eyes—they belonged to Henry.

"Don't be afraid, Hope," Christian whispered.

The deer turned and limped away, his white tail swaying behind him. He crossed the road and hurried into the cover of the trees, a fresh trail of blood spilling from his side as he moved.

"Did we hit him?" I asked frantically.

"No. *We* didn't touch him."

Just then, the deer sprinted off deeper into the woods.

"It's Henry—isn't it?" I said as we hurried toward the trees, following after him.

"He wouldn't have taken this form unless he felt it was absolutely necessary." Christian's tone was as steady as his pace.

"What do you mean *necessary*?"

"It's incredibly dangerous for him. This stretch of road is very exposed; anyone could have hit him."

"Do you think that's what happened?" I asked, stumbling over the thick tropical ground covering. "Do you think a car hit him?"

"I doubt it." He stopped walking for a moment and smelled the air. A warm breeze sailed past like the breath of an angel. "C'mon. Henry's just up ahead."

The sun peeked through the canopy of pines, illuminating Christian in spots of sunlight. His shaded flesh looked like ivory while his exposed skin smoldered with a gentle rage. He swept his hand along his arms, freeing himself from his own ashes again. I loved watching the way he made his suffering look sublime.

"C'mon," Christian said, grabbing me by the hand. "Let me take you. It'll be faster."

He led me through the brush on the wings of the wind. At first it was hard trying to make sense of the static surroundings at such speeds, but soon I learned to see it the way he did, by fracturing the moment. "What is Henry doing out here?" I asked, as we shot through the brush, darting in and out of columns of sunlight at a hypersonic pace.

"He's been waiting for us. Maybe he was trying to catch us before we reached the house." Christian stopped moving, and the world suddenly resumed normal speed again.

I looked ahead into the distance. Henry was doubled over on the ground, half hidden by some low-lying palmettos. There was blood on the undergrowth next to him. He was barefoot and naked. His flesh was badly severed around his ribcage, blood pooling within the recesses. I bit my lip and struggled to keep my cool; the sight and smell of his blood triggered my craving again.

"Henry," Christian said, kneeling down beside him. He started sopping up the blood with his hands. "What happened?"

Henry whimpered with pain as Christian touched him. "Stop," he said, grabbing hold of Christian's arm with tremendous force.

"Shh," he urged. "Don't waste your breath."

I watched in awe as suddenly the thin skin that surrounded the gashes on Henry's ribcage started to shift. Like two fabrics coming together, his skin traversed to repair itself.

"Stop them," Henry muttered between groans before closing his eyes and collapsing in Christian's arms.

"C'mon, old friend," he urged. "Don't give up on me."

"What's wrong with him?" I asked. "The wounds look healed."

"Healing is the easy part. The pain takes longer to disappear."

I knelt down beside them. Henry's gashes were gone; only the faintest trace of scarring remained. "Would it help if he had *my* blood?" I moved my arm close to his lips, offering my wrist to him.

Henry opened his eyes. He pushed my wrist away with a gentle nudge. "No," he sighed. "A generous offer, my dear, but not one I would ever dream of taking from you."

"What the hell happened, Henry?" Christian asked.

"You must get to the house and stop them," he replied.

"Stop Maxim?" Christian asked.

Henry staggered to sit up a little, much of his naked body still hidden by the palmettos. "Yes." He heaved a sigh. "And the other one too."

"What other one?" I asked.

"The one with Medusa eyes." He hesitated. "She kept trying to entrance me the same way she entranced Eva and Baptiste."

"What!" Christian exploded.

"She didn't realize I was blind. Her ability didn't affect me."

"Who is she?" I asked.

"His girlfriend. He called her Sakura."

"How did you get out of there?" Christian inquired.

"By the skin of my teeth." Henry took a deep breath. "It was a struggle to escape them." He grabbed his ribs. "I nearly *didn't* get away."

A column of sunlight gracefully illuminated Henry within the scope of its splendor. He was transcendent, a sightless prophet sent by the tender hand of destiny like the black butterfly—a harbinger of death. Tiny insects danced through the air like fairies while Henry's pale skin radiated.

"You must work together to save each other," Henry whispered, brushing the ashes from his skin. He grabbed hold of our hands. "If Maxim turns to vapor, he'll render you both powerless. And no matter what happens, *don't* look into his girlfriend's eyes." He put our hands together. "Now go and save our family."

And with his blessing, we disappeared through the trees at the speed of light.

26-The House

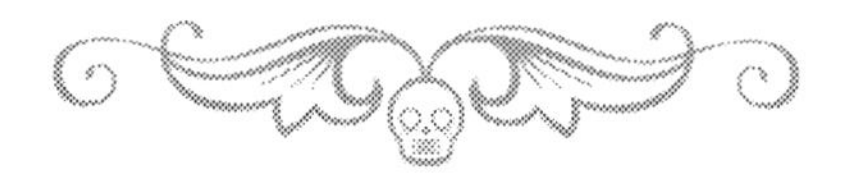

The sun was bright and the air was hot when we reached Ambrose House.

"Hope," Christian whispered as we hid beneath the shade of the banyan tree at the end of the estate. "You don't have to do this."

"But I do. Let this be my fight too."

"It's dangerous."

"Fear is no longer a part of who I am," I asserted.

Christian shook his head. "I really wish you actually believed that." There was a sorrow buried deep within his savage stare. He brought his wrist to his mouth, closed his eyes, and dug his sharp teeth into his flesh. The deep red of his blood dripped from his bite, sliding down his arm.

"What—"

"For you."

I watched with hungry eyes, trying to tame the frenzy beneath my skin. I inhaled a little. His sweet smell was like air to my lungs. "Me?" I whispered, struggling to restrain myself.

"To give you strength. Now drink." He moved his wrist to my mouth.

I reached for his arm and pressed him to my warm lips. And then I drank from him, his sweet blood intoxicating me.

"Stop," he moaned after a few moments.

But I couldn't stop, and my grip was unyielding as I continued to swallow his sweet savor. To drink from Christian was like drinking from the purest glacial spring: invigorating and restorative.

"Hope. Enough," he insisted, his tone growing in severity.

"Don't deny me," I uttered, my lips still pressed to his wrist.

"I have to," he moaned, pushing me away.

"Change me," I begged. "Make me strong like you."

"Not now," he said, his wrist healing over as though nothing happened. "Not out of convenience."

"I don't understand," I said, wiping his blood from my lips with my tongue.

"Hope, when I do it, I want it to be because it's perfect. When I change you, it will be because you have decided that you want nothing more from the life you have now." He touched my cheek with the palm of his hand. "You should want—"

"What?" I snapped. "Fireworks?"

"At the very least, you should want the sun to be near setting, the wind light on your warm skin as the smell of fresh flowers fills your senses for the very last time." He smiled, his eyes glowing green again. "You deserve perfection. And today is not that day."

I could feel my heart breaking, and without the steady stream of his curative blood in my veins, the murmur returned. I touched my lips with my fingers and licked the last drops of his blood that remained. I wanted more. These brief swells of potency would suffice, but things would change. It was inevitable. Eventually he *would* turn me. The perfect moment was there, I could feel it, already scribed by the hand of fate; I was simply yet to catch up to it.

And then suddenly I became numb. My body started trembling uncontrollably.

"It's happening again, isn't it?" Christian asked.

I fought to nod.

"You must try to control it. Breathe."

Breathe, I thought to myself. *Just breathe.* But the force was powerful, and I struggled to catch even a single breath. When finally I inhaled, the shaking ceased. Everything started moving in reverse. My actions, although controlled, were graceful as I was being led through the events of just moments earlier. I exhaled. Everything stopped. A thunderous blow like a sonic boom shook my eardrums and a flash of white blinded my eyes halting the rewind.

"I stopped it!"

"You controlled it." He smiled. "What's your spark?" he asked, reading my thoughts. "Your trigger—the thing that sets off your ability. We've all got one."

"Breathing."

He nodded.

"What's yours?"

He ran his fingers through his hair. "Blinking."

I grinned, recalling the countless times I watched him flutter his beautiful long eyelashes. I couldn't believe he could stretch time so casually.

"That's good. Really good." He pressed his lips to my forehead and kissed me, his eyelashes fluttering as he withdrew, and then suddenly he was gone.

I stayed by the tree, inhaling the dampness that hung in the air. The sound of thunder rumbled in the distance. A storm was on its way. The blue sky deepened with tones of gray while the clouds changed shape more swiftly than the flickering of a flame.

Then suddenly there was a loud crash followed by the shrill shattering of glass. I hurried across the lawn to the front of the house. The door was ajar. I skulked along the porch and peered inside. Glass and blood covered the floor. The waste was outright deplorable. At that moment, the rain pounding against the roof of the porch distracted me. I turned away, and suddenly Christian appeared crouched at my feet.

"What are you doing here?" I asked uneasily. Something was wrong. I could feel it. My stomach sank as I stared into the silvery shine of his eyes.

"It's much worse than I thought. The girlfriend is stronger than he is. I need to shift her focus."

"What has she done?" I asked nervously.

"She's killing them."

My skin crawled with his words.

"I have to break her stare," he said. "I need to distract her."

"Forget her," I said. "Distract *them* instead. Remember La Fuente? You were able to release yourself from Maxim's control."

He nodded.

"Well this is no different. Maybe you can release Eva and Baptiste the same way."

"Come with me. If I can't—you can turn it all back."

"I don't know that I'm ready for this."

He pressed his hand to my cheek. "This is *your* fight too," he whispered. "You said so yourself."

I nodded.

He took my hand, and we entered the house. We roamed the rooms like ghosts, lingering in one of Christian's static moments. He pulled me deeper into the living room with him, and then I saw Maxim. He was tossing a bottle. The green glass hung suspended in mid-air moments from being destroyed. I wanted to reach out and grab the pristine bottle, liberate it from smashing to smithereens. I stretched out my hand to catch it.

"Don't," Christian snapped, pushing my hand away. "Focus on what we came for."

I watched the inert bottle as it hung suspended in the air, saddened that its fate was so inevitable when I had the power to change it, save it—but I didn't.

An instant later, I spotted Sakura. I was careful not to look directly into her eyes, but from what I could see, she was tiny and young like a teenage schoolgirl. She was very pale like a geisha, with shiny black hair that sat against the sides of her face in two long braids. A thick globule of blood frozen in a drip hung at the corner of her mouth. I didn't look for long. It was far too risky.

"Brace yourself," Christian warned before turning to face Eva and Baptiste.

I nearly fainted at the sight of them. It was ghastly. They were propped up next to each other on the couch like mannequins. They were riddled with bite marks, ravaged with flesh wounds, and smothered in their own blood, their souls literally sucked from them. They were limp like rag dolls, their faces vapid and their eyes hauntingly empty. They were cadaverous encasements of themselves.

"Stay strong, Hope," Christian urged.

"My god," I whispered. I could smell death in the room—their death. "Are they—"

"Not yet. Hold on to me," Christian ordered.

I pressed myself against his back and placed my hands over his nearly silent heart. We moved to Baptiste, positioning ourselves between him and Sakura.

"C'mon, B," Christian said sternly. Then suddenly every muscle in Christian's body came to life with an indescribable vigorousness as he fought against the pull of Sakura's manipulation. With his hands on either side of Baptiste's head, mere fractions of an inch away from touching him, his thin fingers vibrated with the slightest severity as he fought to bend Baptiste's gaze. After a few moments, the struggle intensified. The slight vibrating became full-on shakes. It was working. With great determination, he was awakening Baptiste from the trance. A spectral darkness secreted from Baptiste's body like smoke. It followed the pull of Christian's hands until finally it disappeared, vanishing into nothingness. Baptiste was free. Christian heaved a loud sigh and dropped to the floor with the cessation of the pull.

Instantaneously everything sped back to real time.

Baptiste gasped for air, the wheeze of his deep breath terrifying.

I crouched down beside Christian. The inelegant beating of my heart filled the room like a calamitous cacophony. I ran my hand along his arm. He didn't flinch. His body stayed inert. He was weak. I had to get him out before Sakura had the chance to entrance him too.

Just then, a low rumble resonated as Baptiste's voice boomed. He was terrifying, more monster than man at that moment. I watched as he scanned the room with acerbic eyes. He saw the blood and the glass, and then he saw Eva. He sprang from the couch, turned to Maxim, and charged him. He struck Maxim with his iron fists, each hit vaporizing Maxim into fragments of nothingness. A blow to the jaw briefly dissolved Maxim's face, a bash to the ribs dispersed a chunk of his torso, and a strike to the throat atomized him perilously.

The deep hum of Maxim's wail distracted Sakura, and finally she broke her gaze with Eva. The nimble vampire swung her agile body over the couch and jumped onto Baptiste's back, shrieking, thrashing, and biting him like a rabid animal.

Suddenly, a screech devastated my eardrums. *Eva*, I thought to myself. After seeing what was left of her ravaged body, she shifted into what looked like death incarnate: a combination of black smoke, smoldering ash, and flames with an arsenal for arms. She was vexed beyond belief and ready for retribution.

Christian squeezed my hand. *"Maxim and the girlfriend, they're staring at us,"* he whispered inside my thoughts.

I peeked over my shoulder. "I'm not afraid," I said under my breath as my eyes swept across Maxim and Sakura's long shadows on the bloodstained hardwood floor. Christian was right. They were focused in our direction. And at that moment, I knew they had traded their meager assault on Baptiste and Eva to wage war with us.

"Look away, Hope!" Christian warned me.

But I already had. I had seen the bloodshed Sakura was capable of. I wasn't taking any chances.

A warm, wet breeze suddenly blew in through the front door, and with it came the earthy reek of rain. The room went silent. Maxim and Sakura abruptly darted through the door at a speed nearly immeasurable with human eyes. And then they were gone.

27-Water

The rain streamed from the sky like a curtain, obscuring everything beyond the porch. Suddenly the most beautiful butterfly whisked its way into the house on the edge of a breeze. The slight creature was studded with tiny droplets of rainwater. I was fascinated by the grace with which it floated, flaunting its remarkable black wings as it soared. I blinked; the butterfly vanished, and suddenly Henry appeared in its place, crouched behind the settee, wet and naked. There were no words to describe how strange it was watching the ease with which both Henry and Eva could move in and out of body—it was surreal to say the least.

"Henry," Christian called out, rushing toward him. "Are you okay?" He grabbed a jacket that was hanging on a nearby peg and draped it around him.

"I'm fine," Henry replied quietly.

I took my grandmother's quilt from the cabinet in the hallway and handed it to Henry. I trembled as I neared him, still feeling a little uncomfortable being so close to his nakedness. It was clear that Henry was in great shape and obviously felt comfortable with himself, but that didn't do much to ease the awkwardness I felt. Likewise, it seemed as though Christian went to painstaking efforts to shield me from Henry's nudity.

"Thank you," Henry whispered with a smile, taking the quilt from my hand. He breathed in the heady scent of lavender that fragranced the comforter. "It was very thoughtful of you, Hope." He wrapped himself in the quilt.

A smile graced my face as I peeked over my shoulder, seeing the way he had comfortably cocooned himself within the fabric. Henry really was a beautiful butterfly, shrouded in his quilted chrysalis, waiting to emerge in some new form.

A harmony of sounds distracted me. Whispers, giggles, and sighs flooded the room with cascades of cheerfulness. It was love in the air, the sweet sounds of love overwhelming the brutal bloodshed that Maxim and Sakura had left behind in their wake. My eyes flitted over to Eva and Baptiste. They were across the room, sitting together on the blood-soaked couch. The vivid red velvet of the Victorian settee was spattered in blood, and shards of broken glass glimmered like thousands of tiny jewels upon the wooden frame, and yet they were absorbed in the most beautiful embrace. Eva was draped across Baptiste's lap with her head nestled beside his massive chest. Her ear was pressed to his heart, listening to the familiarity of its unhurried beat. Their love flourished the way a ghost flower blooms in the desert—against all odds. I smiled as I stared, recalling the haunting image of their cadaverous position together upon that same couch only moments earlier.

I took a deep breath, the smell of Christian's body drawing my focus back to him. "Tin Man," I sighed to myself. He had more heart than anyone I'd ever known and yet his own barely made a sound.

"What are you thinking?" he purred in my ear, interlocking his fingers with mine.

I smiled bashfully, knowing that he already knew, but pleased that he had the very courtesy to ask.

"Heart," he whispered with a wink.

"Love," I amended with a smile. I closed my eyes for a moment, marinating in the sweet scent of him. *Love,* I thought to myself. It was as fixed a concept as eating or breathing and yet wholly magical and unpredictable. *"Fate let me find you,"* I said without speaking.

"Fate had nothing to do with it," Christian replied aloud.

I opened my eyes, startled with his brusque tone.

"We write our own destiny," he continued.

"You really believe that?"

"You don't agree with me?" he teased.

I shook my head.

"Well then Fate must be a cruel woman."

"Why would you say that?"

"Because no one is intended to see as much as I have. No one is meant to experience the kind of suffering I have." His voice deepened to a billowy whisper. "No one should be destined to live forever."

I stared into the iridescent shine of his eyes. His face was rigid like a statue. Then suddenly he smiled, his mischievous grin melting away the rigidity.

"Lighten up!" he teased with a laugh.

I exhaled a little, feeling the scent of fear escape from my body with my breath. "You were only joking?"

"Love," he whispered in my ear. "Love is *why* I can live forever." He grinned, pulling away.

The staccato sounds of talking interrupted us. Eva and Baptiste were in a heated discussion with Henry. Their voices were loud. The tension was high.

"Why did they leave the house then?" Henry said.

"Um, I don't know," Eva snapped. "I was too busy *dying* to analyze it."

"Ease up, Eva," Baptiste ordered. "Henry is only trying to make some sense of what happened."

"I know!" she said.

"Well someone has to remember something about what happened in here!" Henry's voice was desperate.

"I remember the breeze," I interjected timidly.

"The breeze?" Henry pressed.

I nodded. "It was the smell of rain that caught my attention. It was strong, and it swept through the house with the breeze."

"The smell of rain?" Henry asked. "You know, I was nearby when they came outside. I could overhear them taking about the rain. Something about how even the very smell of it unnerved them."

"You mean they left because of the rain?" Eva asked.

Henry shrugged.

"It's not over, you know," Christian warned us all.

"Damn right, it's not," Baptiste barked. "Look what they did to my Eva—again!"

"Not to mention the fact that they destroyed nearly every bottle we had in our vault," Eva added.

The vault, I thought to myself. It was here in the house like a wine cellar. It was where they stored the bottles they corked. It must have been the room that smelled so good in the narrow corridor.

Baptiste slammed his fists together. I jumped with the sound.

"Retribution," he threatened under his breath.

Christian nodded in agreement.

"If water weakens them, then we need to take it to the water," Henry said.

"Your ship!" I exclaimed. "The *Ambrose*!"

"*My* ship?" Christian asked.

I nodded. "You'll have the upper hand."

Henry smiled. "Not a bad idea. They'll be lost in what's left of her."

"And if we're right about the rain, the water will weaken them," I added.

"How can we get them down there?" Henry asked. "They won't go willingly."

"I'm already on it," Eva piped in, suddenly transforming into Maxim's likeness. She giggled strangely before shifting into the image of Sakura and then transforming back into herself with the effortlessness of a chameleon changing color.

"Your talents will be useful, but they won't lure them down to the *Ambrose*," Henry insisted.

"Blood will," Christian said. "Lots and lots of human blood."

28-Vats

The gentle morning light had been replaced by a scorching midday blaze. My body tingled as the radiant beams swept over my skin. The rain was gone, and there were no signs of darkness in the teal blue sky above. Today was a beautiful day—too beautiful a day to die.

I helped Christian haul the last rusty barrel onto the boat before I took a second to catch my breath.

"Climb aboard," he said, his hand extended toward me.

I could sense fear in the air, its darkness swirling together with sunbeams like yin and yang. I swallowed hard, gritting my teeth. *"Water,"* I groaned in my thoughts. *"Why did it have to be the water?"* I slipped my sweaty palm into the familiar icy smoothness of his.

Christian smiled in reply, escorting me aboard. "Stay strong, my love. Don't let your fears control your life."

The wind was warm on my face as we skimmed along the surface of the ocean in the speedboat. The faster we drove, the better I seemed to feel. The cerulean blue of the water and sky was interchangeable, and for a moment I felt like Christian aboard the *Ambrose* all those years ago, never knowing which way was up.

Eventually, he cut the engine. I peered over the edge of the boat, and there, through the crystal clear water, I could see the outline of what was left of his ship just beneath the surface. Even the tip of the *Ambrose*'s coral encrusted mast was close, just below only inches away. A strange sense of peace suddenly overwhelmed me. I looked around. "It's … beautiful out here," I muttered.

"Yeah," Christian replied.

"Pretty dead though," I joked.

He laughed.

"Seriously," I said, "why doesn't anybody come here?"

"The old myths about ghosts. It still manages to keep 'em away."

"What *myths*? Clearly they have every reason to be afraid."

"I suppose you're right." A sudden sorrow swelled in his beautiful green eyes as though my words disheartened him with the weight of their truth.

I moved closer and ran my hand along the side of his face. His thoughts filled my mind with their fury. "Tell me in your words," I pleaded.

He sighed. "When you returned, finally returned to me, I wanted nothing more than to show you the beauty of being here—the wonderful place that Perish is to me. Time means nothing to me. But for *you*, it's the essence of your humanity." He shook his head. "I waited for you to become a woman—death and bloodshed wasn't exactly the kind of wooing I had in mind for our reunion."

"Christian, you *have* shown me the beauty of being here, and I love that you waited for me." I took his hand. "Nothing's perfect." I traced the faint scar in the center of his palm. "There will always be death and probably bloodshed too, but we'll have *forever* to fall in love with each other."

He pulled me into his arms, and we bobbed with the rhythm of the water. When he pressed his icy lips to mine, we merged in a kiss and indulged in each other for a while—maybe a minute, maybe an hour. With him, time didn't exist.

Suddenly the hum of another boat engine resonated. An old, dilapidated trawler slowly approached in the distance with Baptiste at the helm. Eva was hanging from a beam, her leg wrapped around the pole like a snake.

"How come you guys got the greyhound and we got the mutt?" she yelled across the water.

"Where's Henry?" Christian hollered, ignoring her comment.

"Said he'd meet up later," Baptiste replied, driving the trawler in close and cutting its engine.

Eva hopped up on the side of the trawler and leaped across the water over to our boat. I watched her soar; she was like a bird in flight, agile and elegant. I nearly thought she was going to puncture the floor of the speedboat with her sharp stiletto heels when she landed.

"Wow. That smell!" she exclaimed. "How did you two manage not tearing those barrels to bits?"

I inhaled. The smell was rather luscious. Under the searing southern sun, even the sturdy metal vats weren't strong enough to contain the smell of their contents.

"Such a waste," Eva lamented as she stared at the vats.

"Maybe," Christian replied, "but we can replenish our loss—we can't replenish our lives."

Baptiste jumped aboard. Our small speedboat heaved like a rubber duck in a bathtub with his not so elegant entrance.

"You ready?" Christian asked, nudging Baptiste in the arm.

Baptiste nodded before tearing off the top of the first barrel with his huge fist. The robust smell instantly infused the ocean air with a startling strength. We all inhaled the succulent smell of human blood, sighing in harmony like a choir of ravenous songbirds.

"God I hope it's worth it," Eva said, eyeballing the full vat of blood as it sloshed around with the heaving of the waves.

"Keeping our life here is worth it, Eva," Christian said.

A moment later, Baptiste hoisted the vat onto his burly shoulder before tossing it like a skipping stone into the blue ocean. The rusty barrel splash-landed along the surface, bobbing for an instant before beginning its rapid descent. It fell incredibly fast, leaving a substantial trail of blood in its path.

"Now watch," Baptiste's said.

I kept my eyes on the water, watching with fascination as the blood hung in inky clusters as it sank. It was beautiful, like an abstract oil painting, and then suddenly they appeared—not our enemies, something even more feral. My eyes followed their fins as they scuffled just below the surface. They were gray like angry storm clouds and fierce like brooding tempests as they swarmed. I watched anxiously as their bodies shot up out of the water bursting with bloodlust.

"Not quite Sea World, is it, Cinderella?" Eva said, jabbing me in the arm with her cold, pointy elbow.

"It's a good sign," Christian insisted. "If it lured the sharks, then surely the others won't be far behind."

"Let's sink the other barrel," Baptiste suggested. "They'll never be able to resist *that* much blood."

"But it's our last vat," Christian said. "Maybe we should save it for ourselves."

"This is more important," Baptiste said. "We can replenish our stash; you said so yourself." He moved closer to the second vat and put his big, tattooed hand on it. "They've made this personal," he said. "I'd sink a boat-load of blood if it means I'll get the chance to bury them."

"Revenge," Christian scorned.

"I can't forgive what they did to my Eva."

"I understand that, but, B, we have to be smart about this."

"This *is* being smart," he replied, his voice hard.

"You just want to fight," Christian said.

"I just want to win."

The sun was hot, and the tension was high. The sharks swarmed the streaky water with a mounting hunger while we waited for our enemies to appear. I was standing beside the second vat when Baptiste gripped the top with his fingers. He was enraged, primed for vengeance. I quickly shuffled out of his way and continued watching as he grabbed the vat like it was a can of soup and effortlessly tore open its rusty lid.

"Wait!" Eva shouted. "They're here."

I looked out at the water, and there beyond the sharks, I noticed Sakura, her dark hair and pale face bobbing only inches above the surface.

"Don't look into her eyes," Christian reminded me.

I turned away.

"I'm going in," Eva said. She kissed Baptiste on the mouth before diving off the boat and into the water. Her thin body shot through the melee of enraged sharks. Just as she disappeared beneath the blue, Baptiste tossed the second vat into the water. The fresh blood streamed like a river as it fell, and then he too lunged off the side of the speedboat and into ocean, dropping like a lead weight through the shiver of vicious sharks.

At that moment, something gripped my ankle like a hangman's noose and yanked me to the floor. I slammed against the side of the boat with a crude tug, my breath knocked out of me. I was tangled in rope—rope that was attached to the second vat that Baptiste had just tossed overboard.

Breathe, I reminded myself, but I couldn't. The roped jerked me again with an excruciating yank, burning the thin skin on my ankle as it dragged me across the floor of the speedboat. I was an instant from being pulled overboard into the water when suddenly I felt Christian's hand on me, squeezing my wrist. His grip was strong and firm, and with his touch, everything immediately became motionless.

"Hold on, Hope," he said, his face straining with exertion as he struggled to keep his grasp on me. "Don't let go … I'm losing you," he said, his eyes glimmering with a fierce night shine.

My eyes swelled with tears as I watched him struggle, but his rescue was ill fated. A wispy cloud loomed above him, and the familiar hazy vapor was assaulting us with its silent attack. I knew it was Maxim immobilizing us with the magnitude of his power. Wispy tendrils swept across Christian's pale skin, weakening him, overwhelming him, until finally his grip eased with a most tragic reluctance. "No!" I pleaded, staring into the panic-stricken silvery iridescence of his stare. A moment later, the rope yanked me over the side of the boat, hurling me hard into the bloodied, shark-infested water.

29-One Down

Drowning was my greatest fear. I could feel the water closing in on me, suffocating me with its hold, but somehow I wasn't scared like in my dreams. It was though the years of reoccurring nightmares had somehow readied me for this very moment. *Fear isn't a part of who I am any longer,* I tried convincing myself as the bloodstained water saturated my skin. If this was death, then I knew I had to welcome it with open eyes.

The sharks were close. The rubbery skin of their bodies heaved against me, thrusting me deeper into the ocean as they fought for a taste of the inky blood that hung in the water. I looked up to the surface, watching the sharks block out the sun like a gray cloud as I descended. I lowered my gaze. Then suddenly the sun sliced through the water, bathing Christian's ship in a divine circle of light. I struggled to hold in the last trickle of air that lingered in my lungs long enough to lay my eyes upon the *Ambrose.*

The ship's shattered skeleton was exposed, the hull remarkably intact after decades of slumber on the seabed floor. Its position next to the reef was perfect, preserving it for centuries while concealing it from a passerby above. And with the sunlight illuminating my view, the ocean floor lit up like a match. I could see everything with clarity. The scattered remains of other fallen ships lined the ocean floor in the distance. Old anchors and planks jutted from the ground like tombstones in a mass undersea graveyard. It was rather peaceful and yet haunting at the same time.

An eerie presence surrounded me; the water seemed soiled with spirits, undulating and churning with sorrow. I shifted my gaze back to the *Ambrose*. There were fragments of wood like little spikes lining what remained of the bow and a spectacular entangled web of coral netting the stern. Crustaceans and other growth had taken refuge within the sunken abode. The kelp-covered iron anchor was wedged into the sandy floor while an old cannon was laid to rest next to it. The masts were striking, unbelievably tall, and encrusted with coral after years of submergence. It was history, real history—it was Christian's history.

A convoy of colossal bubbles zipped past, nearly forcing me to lose my last breath of air. The tubes of displaced water soared at an incredible speed, sheathing Eva and Baptiste within their hollows. An instant later, another tube rushed along, encasing Sakura. Then suddenly something brushed against my arm. It was gray, menacing, and cut through the water like lightning as it approached. A shark. With hunger in its eyes, the predator opened its jaws like a gate, inviting me in. Rows of sharp teeth lined the inside of its mouth like gnarled thorns. I tried to reverse time. *Breathe*, I told myself, but all I inhaled was water, and soon my lungs began to fill with it. I was drowning, dying, when suddenly another shark came into sight. It slammed my sharp-toothed attacker out of the way with a single, hostile blow. I panicked as the rescue shark neared, and then I noticed his eyes. They were familiar: strange and opalescent. *Henry*, I sighed in my thoughts—my last lucid thought before slipping smoothly into unconsciousness.

When I opened my eyes again, I was onboard the trawler. The sun was bright and blinding me with its radiance. I could taste the salty ocean air on my lips as Christian's beautiful eyes graced me with their compelling gaze. *Heaven*, I contemplated.

"Not even close," Christian replied with a kiss.

I sprang to a sitting position. "Henry," I uttered. "He was the shark. He saved me."

Christian nodded.

I smiled, running my fingers along the chain of my necklace, stroking the jewel encrusted pendant like a rosary.

"It's not safe here," Christian whispered, motioning to the sky.

I looked to the horizon and saw the hazy cloud looming just above the surface of the water. "Maxim! What is he doing out there?"

"He's watching what's going on below."

"How closely do you think he's watching us?"

Christian shrugged. "Not that closely, I suppose. He's more concerned with his girlfriend. She's under there with Eva and B."

I nodded. "I have an idea. Do something for me."

"Anything."

"Suspend the moment," I whispered. "Go down and get Eva."

"What for?"

I smiled, feeling him inside my head reading my thoughts.

Christian nodded. "It's a bold plan," he warned, kissing my cheek. "Be careful." He batted his long eyelashes, and within an instant, he was gone.

My eyes flitted back to the horizon. I watched as Maxim's wispy tendrils swayed with the cool current of the ocean breeze. A moment later, I felt a burst of cold air tickling the back of my neck. I gasped. I knew instantly it was her and that she was standing right behind me. I didn't turn around—it was much too risky.

Just then, a huge thud heaved the boat as someone else boarded. I looked ahead to the horizon for Maxim, but the wispy haze was gone. The foul smell of death saturated my senses. It was him, Maxim; he was here on the trawler in his form as a man.

"Sakura!" Maxim called out in his low tone.

My body shuddered as I stood with my back to them.

"What's happening down there? Did you finish them yet?" His voice was sharp. "I haven't seen fighters like them since the ignorant colonists of the early days!"

The tiny hairs on my arms stood on end as I listened. His voice grew louder as did his footsteps. He was nearing. I could almost feel his smug stare upon my back. I closed my eyes.

"You've captured the mongrel!" Maxim laughed, taking notice of me. "My sweet Sakura. Do you realize how rare it is to have found a half-breed like this one?" His voice smoothed to a silky slur. "She's so old and yet still so incredibly wholesome."

Half-breed, I thought to myself. The word unnerved me insufferably.

"Let's drink her!" he uttered gleefully. "You know what they say about the blood of a mature mongrel—an aphrodisiac of the gods!"

"Oh, Sakura," Maxim wooed. "Why aren't you speaking to me?"

The sickly sweet conceit in his tone enraged me with an anger I could barely contain. I was an instant away from driving my fist through his dark heart when suddenly I heard the hint of something uncertain in his voice—the sound of doubt.

"Sakura," Maxim implored, "say something!"

I gnashed my teeth in silence listening to the thumping of my heartbeat as it pounded through my chest.

"Sakura?" Maxim repeated apprehensively.

I swallowed nervously before peering over my shoulder, and then it happened. Sakura lunged at Maxim, her sharp, pointy fingernails impaling him through the chest. Blood splattered across the boat as she drove her nails deeper into his flesh. Her attack on him was incredibly fast, impeding his potential to vaporize into smoke. I watched wide-eyed as he struggled to atomize while she ripped her claws from his bloody torso.

"Why?" he fought to ask, blood pouring from the ten finger-sized gashes in his chest.

A corkscrew smile slithered its way across Sakura's doll-like face when suddenly her image began to wane, shifting back into Eva's likeness.

"No!" Maxim moaned, his arrogant, empty eyes enlarging with fear.

Eva let out a most thunderous battle cry before kicking him in the midsection. Her stiletto was sharp, and the force of her kick pierced what was left of his bloodied, fleshy torso. She extracted her shoe with a hard tug, jerking it free from his meaty middle, and watched as he tumbled overboard and into the water.

"Payback's a bitch," she jeered, her fingers dripping with Maxim's fresh blood.

I smiled a little, watching Maxim's remains infuse with the water like a steeping tea bag, and within moments there was nothing left of him apart from trails of blood and tendrils of vapor. He was dead.

A brisk wind tore through the boat, blowing past Eva's fingers, carrying the fresh scent of Maxim's blood toward me. I trembled with the smell—the disturbingly delightful stink.

"Blondie," Eva barked, startling me. "I'm going in." She motioned to the water. "Christian and B can't do it alone. They'll need help with the girlfriend."

I nodded in reply, watching as Eva dove into the water, snapping a fishing rod mount on the side of the trawler as she jumped. As she vanished beneath the surface, I became entranced by the hypnotic swaying of the waves when suddenly something appeared. With my eyes to the ocean, I spotted the outline of a body slowly rising to the surface. "Christian!" His lifeless body floated through the water. My heart pounded like a clumsy drum while saliva pooled in my mouth. "No!" I cried with a deep inhale, and suddenly everything started moving in reverse—I'd accidently triggered my ability. Instantaneously, Christian descended beneath the water, and Eva emerged again.

I heaved a sigh. A flash of white blinded my vision as the reversal abruptly stopped.

"I'm going in," Eva said just as she did only moments before.

"Wait!" I grabbed her arm.

"Look!" Eva said, staring out at the water.

I peered over the edge of the boat. It was Christian again, his motionless body floating along the surface of the sea.

"We have to help him," Eva said, eyeballing the bloodthirsty sharks. "They're going to devour him!"

"I know," I answered, panicked. My thoughts raced as I stared, watching as Eva ran her fingers along the fishing rod mount at the side of the boat—and then suddenly everything became clear to me. "The mount," I said, grabbing her arm with an intense grip. "The mount isn't broken!"

"What?" she barked.

"Henry was right!" I shouted. "Inanimate objects aren't being affected."

"Let go of me!" Eva demanded. "I have to get in there. They're moving in on him."

"Is Maxim dead?"

"Yeah," she snarled.

"But the mount isn't broken."

"No," Eva snapped, "your mount isn't broken, but Christian *is* going to die if you don't let go of my arm!"

I stared at the fiery, red iridescent shine in Eva's eyes. She was frightening and full of ferocity, and in a moment of clarity, I let go of her, watching her dive off the side of the boat and into the water in a vain effort to save my Tin Man. I touched the in-tact fishing rod mount with my fingers when suddenly my thoughts filled with the most sorrowful sound. It was Christian.

"Hope," he uttered, his inner voice no louder than a weak whisper. *"Help me."*

"I will," I avowed soundlessly. *"I know how to fix this."* And then I closed my eyes and inhaled again.

I exhaled. A flash of white blinded my vision. When my eyes focused, I knew I was aboard the trawler, dripping and breathless. I felt Christian pressing his cold lips against mine in a kiss.

"It's not safe here," he uttered, pulling away. He motioned to the sky.

I looked up and saw the hazy cloud hanging several feet above the ocean. It was Maxim. I remembered this moment. I hadn't gone far enough back in time.

"You're leaving again," Christian said nervously, struggling to read through my busy thoughts.

I nodded, my eyes filling with sorrow. "And I won't stop until it's done."

"Done? What are you doing?"

"Keeping *you* alive. Keeping all of us alive."

He smiled.

I smiled back, and then I inhaled again.

I was learning how to control it now. The more I moved through time, the easier it became. I was realizing that a shallow breath slowed the reverse just enough for me to cut in at specific moments while a deep breath raced me back like a rocket. I could whiz through the nonsense and get right to where I needed to be on a dime. I was pushing myself beyond anything I even knew I was capable of, and that's when I discovered a new skill: forwarding. With deep exhales, I had the power to return to the present as fast as inhaling could take me to the past. And suddenly I was skipping through time with a casual effortlessness.

Maxim was dead—gone permanently, but Sakura was still alive. She was clever and possessed the ability to weaken any one of us individually with the force of her gaze. We needed to work together to destroy her; using all of our skills in unison was our only hope.

The telepathic connection between Christian and me served as a direct line for relaying strategies. His ability to stretch time let us rework ideas and test things while my ability to move through time let us start from scratch when our attempts failed.

Eva's wrath was unparalleled. She was always ready. It was the chase that drove her wild. Her face lit up every time she stalked Sakura through the skeleton of the *Ambrose.* The primitive ferociousness of the hunt seemed to stimulate her repressed visceral impulses. She was an untamed animal, raging like a roaring fire beneath the ocean, seething with determination to catch her prey.

Baptiste's strength was incredible. He rearranged the remains of the *Ambrose* with ease in an effort to crush Sakura. Whether hurling the coral encrusted cannon, heaving planks of the ship's ancient wood, or spinning the iron anchor like a lariat, Baptiste was resolved to seek his retribution by any means necessary.

Henry brought in the reinforcements. As a shark, he was fast, menacing, and had the influence to recruit other sharks to join our small yet militant offensive line. The rubbery skinned army of killers grew quite substantial, and like a storm cloud, they lurked from above, their slick bodies fiercely weaving back and forth, keeping tabs on the events below. With mouths full of blades and hunger in their eyes, Henry managed to mobilize them with his riveting persuasion.

We tested tactics over and over again until we found what worked. We had strength in numbers and weren't about to be defeated by the likes of an agile, vampire schoolgirl. And with time, we found Sakura's weaknesses. We stayed out of her line of sight, hiding in the dark recesses of the *Ambrose.* We realized that surprise attacks caught her off guard and that distractions worked best. And soon Sakura didn't seem so fast. With the home court advantage, Christian was always right on her spry heels. He was the only one who could actually catch up to her. The injuries he continued sustaining were ghastly—but not deadly. It was a dangerous price to pay, but a worthy one if it meant protecting our home, our family.

We were getting close, and with practice, we were perfecting a recipe for Sakura's death. We were reacting like lightning and skirmishing with the power of pure vengeance. And then finally we were ready. The pieces of our elaborate puzzle had been put into place, and all of our practice had led us to this one last confrontation.

I exhaled.

A burst of white blinded me, and when I opened my eyes, I was back beneath the water in the *Ambrose*. It was the final act, and I was front row and center in the theatre of war. I scanned the surroundings. The disturbances were volatile. Convoys of bubbles zipped past. Algae blasted around in clumps while chunks of coral shattered apart. Dead and wounded sharks dropped to the ocean floor like lead weights. *It's working*, I thought to myself. It's affecting the living. We were carrying our damage forward; the disturbance was proof of the residual effects from our previous attempts. The more I moved through time, the larger the footprint I left behind, but this would be the last. The *very* last.

Everything was falling into place. Every note was being hit, and every mark was being met. I had memorized the perfect sequence of events like lyrics of a song. I held my breath and watched as nature took its course, waiting to see if my hand in destiny would ultimately influence the outcome. And I was certain that it would.

"Christian," I called through my thoughts, and with a shockwave of water, he materialized before my eyes. He pressed his soft lips to mine like a kiss, only more vital. And there at the bottom of the seabed, I inhaled, drawing in his icy breath as though it were a piece of his soul, letting it fill my lungs and pull me back to the beginning of the end of our fight.

A familiar flash of white blinded me. I opened my eyes and was once again aboard the trawler. I was dripping with water and shivering in the cool breeze. I turned around. "Christian!" I called out, rushing toward him.

"You shouldn't be up here," he warned me, his wet clothes clinging to his beautiful body as he neared.

I threw my arms around him and smiled.

"She's still out there," he said.

"I know. And she'll be here in a moment."

"I don't understand ...," he mumbled, sifting through my thoughts. "My god," he said, his eyes bulging with knowledge. He'd seen all that we had accomplished, and now he knew what was coming. "This is crazy," he said. "It could never work."

"But it already has. C'mon. The real show is about to begin." I grabbed his pale hand and pulled him across the boat.

"Glad you made it, hombre," Baptiste grunted as we approached, his huge body hovering protectively over Eva.

"Are you hurt?" Henry asked, shifting a ratty blanket around his naked body.

"No," Christian said. "I don't think so."

"What the hell is going on?" Eva snapped. "Blondie says jump, and we all jump? Aren't we in the middle of a fight?"

"Not anymore," I said. "Our fighting is finished."

"What's that supposed to mean?" Eva snarled.

I didn't reply. The biting scent of blood suddenly distracted me. It quickly suffused the air with its sharp stench. It was vampire blood, and it was fresh and succulent. I held my breath in a desperate effort to keep control.

"I'm bleeding!" Eva suddenly hollered with a horrified panic. Blood streamed along her neck and down her pallid chest, trickling though the tangle of ivy tattoos along the length of her jugular.

Baptiste exploded with rage. "My arm," he bellowed. "What's happened to me?" His arm was lacerated with rows of slits as though he had run against the narrow teeth of a thousand cheese graters. Blood trailed down his arm, streaking the tattooed faces of his ancestors.

"Don't panic," I said, when suddenly the sweet stink of Christian's blood tickled my nostrils. I turned to him. He was incapacitated on the cruddy floor of the trawler; deep wounds covered his chest and oozed with blood.

"Oh, Christian," Henry lamented, inhaling the scent of blood in the air. He moved close and touched Christian's chest. "The hand of death weakens in the face of love. He's fighting to stay alive, Hope. He's fighting for you. But he needs—"

"Blood," I said. "I already know." I moved my warm wrist to Christian's mouth and nudged his lips with my skin. "You need it," I whispered, pushing harder, feeling the razor sharp edges of his teeth brushing up against me. But he didn't bite. "Do it," I implored. "Now is not the time for humility." I thrust my skin against his mouth hard when suddenly I felt his lips begin to part. He opened his mouth and pierced my flesh. I groaned a little to stop myself from screaming. The pain of his bite was excruciating.

"That's good, Hope," Henry said, listening to the hushed sounds of Christian's sucking. "He shouldn't need much more."

And he was right; a moment later, Christian withdrew. He licked my blood from his lips and suddenly was glorious again, aglow with a transformed vitality like an adolescent after a first kiss.

"Blondie!" Eva shouted, distracting me, her voice strange and anxious. "Your arm ..."

I looked down at my arm. Dozens of bite marks suddenly appeared along my wrist like train tracks. Blood streamed along my hand, falling from my fingertips to the floor of the boat like trickles of rainwater.

"What happened? Who did that to you?" Eva's voice was sympathetic, compassionate even.

"I did," Christian admitted, shamefully rising to his feet.

"It's okay," I said, trying to push through the pain. "It's *not* the first time."

"Esperanza," Baptiste said, "how many times have we done this?" His eyes lingered on my wounds, counting the number of bite marks as though they were tallies of our attempts.

"Enough times to perfect it."

Just then I spotted Sakura's sinewy fingers creeping over the side of the boat.

"She's here," I announced.

Everyone watched as she pulled herself up from the depths of the *Ambrose*.

"Her eyes!" Eva warned. "Don't look at her."

"No!" I insisted. "It's okay. This time you *must* look."

"She's right," Christian said. "I've a feeling we don't want to miss this."

Eva and Baptiste cautiously shifted their eyes toward Sakura, and as they stared, they were stupefied by the sudden futility of her gaze.

"Unbelievable," Eva uttered.

Sakura's eyes were dark, and she was outright haggard. Her clothes were wet and sodden with blood, her hair was jagged and messy, and her porcelain like face was gaunt and lifeless. The sunlight on her wet, bloodied, white skin glimmered with a remarkable luminosity. She was a subtle firestorm of brightness, her soft tissue singing in the scorching blaze of the sun.

"What happened to her?" Eva asked.

"Keep watching," I said.

And suddenly several finger-sized lacerations abruptly materialized across Sakura's doll-like face. Blood spewed from the slashes, cascading crudely across her dainty features.

"My god!" Eva gasped.

A moment later, it looked as though Sakura's eye sockets were being mashed and crushed as fingernail-shaped depressions suddenly appeared, leaving nothing but blackened hollows.

"How is this happening?" Eva said. "Who—"

"You, Eva," I explained.

"Me?" She stared at the sudden materialization of Sakura's blood on her fingertips. "But I didn't even touch her!"

"Not this time," I said. "Before—in one of our attempts, you got her, Eva. You got your payback."

Eva smiled pensively. I knew she had no recollection of her preceding actions, but the truth was irrefutable; it was manifesting in a gruesome display before our very eyes.

Then suddenly a shrill crack cut the silence. We all focused our attention back to Sakura. Her right arm abruptly dislocated just below the shoulder blade. Sharp splinters of bone pushed through her fair skin like a toothpick driving through a rubber band.

"Lord," Baptiste groaned.

I turned to him and nodded. "Revenge. It's not pretty."

His eyes lit up. "Revenge," he mumbled, "but I don't remember …"

I grinned. "That doesn't mean it didn't happen."

Sakura let out a deafening shriek. A chunk of her midsection suddenly detached from the side of her body, falling to the floor of the boat. Rows of teeth marks bordered the fleshy cavity in her bloody side like a frame.

"That's a shark bite," Eva asserted.

"Yeah," Christian replied. "It is."

Henry sighed.

The sharp snapping of Sakura's spinal cord filled the air with an unsettling resonance.

"I finally caught her," Christian said, making sense of his actions.

I nodded at him before turning to watch as Sakura's neck twisted around, breaking like a twig before falling against the trunk of her torso. She was a living cadaver staggering before us: soundless, useless, and virtually lifeless.

"Now she's finished," Eva said.

"No," I said, "not yet." With all my might, I lunged at Sakura, shoving her overboard and into the water. She landed upon the sharp, coral encrusted tip of the *Ambrose*'s mast, which impaled her through the chest. "Now she's finished," I said with certainty, my body trembling.

"You did it," Christian said.

A surge of serenity washed over me. I turned to him. He was beautiful, smoldering sublimely in the sunlight. I sighed as he wrapped his arms around me, his icy breath running down my back like a necklace sprung free from its clasp. I pressed myself against him. "We," I whispered softly, a sudden pride swelling inside me, "we all did it."

31-Friend

There weren't any boisterous cheers as we glided along the ocean in the trawler. Eva, Baptiste, and Henry had left earlier in the speedboat, and we were all a little overwhelmed by the experience. It was a win cloaked in secrecy. Everything about the fight was well concealed from the outside world. Maxim had long since vaporized into nothingness, and the sharks happily finished off Sakura's body, leaving little more than scraps of clothes and splinters of bone to join an already crowded graveyard beneath the sea. Christian and Baptiste took some time to recover the empty vats from the ocean floor, and soon there was nothing left to show that anything had happened at all. The injuries we sustained seemed our only proof that the fighting actually did take place. The wounds had healed, but the scars remained, and like crude medals of merit, we'd wear them with pride, remembering the day we defended Perish in a bold effort to keep our secret safe.

"Thank you," Christian said, tracing his fingers along the rows of bite marks that adorned my wrist.

"You're welcome," I said. We interlocked fingers and maneuvered the trawler together. It was perfect: the wind was warm, the waves were calm, and we were together. Paradise *was* found, and we were finally unrestrained to indulge in our rightful freedom.

Then suddenly Christian stiffened up and extended his gaze toward the shoreline.

"What's the matter?" I asked.

"There's someone on the beach standing next to Eva."

"Maybe its Henry or B," I suggested.

"No. It's not them."

Christian pushed on the throttle, and within moments, we were docked. I disembarked and flew across the sand the second my toes touched land. I looked ahead and saw Eva in the distance standing next to a woman. "Ryan?" I hurried toward them.

"Hope, don't," Christian insisted through my thoughts.

Had Eva not been standing there beside Ryan, I would have easily guessed that she was playing another trick on me with her ability to shape-shift—but this was no trick. It was real. "I can't believe you're here," I said, throwing my arms around her. "Why did you come? How did you find me?"

Ryan didn't respond.

"Be careful," Christian cautioned. *"Something's not right."*

I withdrew a little. The fact that she didn't reciprocate my welcome made me nervous.

"Hello, Hope," Ryan greeted icily, pushing her sunglasses up over her forehead. She was clearly overdressed for the Florida heat; long sleeves, long pants, and tall boots. She seemed entirely out of place.

"What's wrong?" I asked. "Is it my father?"

She shook her head, her black ear length hair swaying as she moved. She was grasping a wide, red parasol with a beautiful painting of a Chinese dragon on it.

"I'm outta here," Eva suddenly piped in.

Ryan smiled. "Well it was nice to meet you, Eva."

Eva nodded. "Yeah, you too." She turned to Christian and me. "Guess I'll see you back at the house then?"

"Yeah," Christian said, watching as Eva hurried along the beach to join up with Baptiste and Henry.

Ryan turned to stare at Christian. "It's a pleasure finally meeting you."

"And you," he replied.

"You are *exactly* as Hope described. The beautiful stranger from her dreams."

"Ryan!" I said, embarrassed.

"What?" she said, extending her thin hand to him. "He *is* beautiful."

Christian laughed and offered his hand to her. Ryan grabbed it and turned it over to stare at the scar in the center of his palm.

"Ryan!" I exclaimed.

"I'm sorry." Her voice was as smooth as silk as she spoke. "Hope has told me so much about you. I just wanted to see the scar for myself." She released his hand.

"What's gotten into you?" I demanded.

She took a deep breath and sighed. "Actually, I'm here to tell you good-bye. It's better for all of us if I leave."

"What?"

"You don't need me anymore." Her eyes flitted to Christian. "You've found him."

"Ryan, don't be ridic—"

"Did you come with them?" Christian asked abruptly.

An awkward silence filled the air between us. Ryan's face hardened. She licked her red lips.

"Did you?" Christian pressed.

"By *them*," she said slowly, "do you mean the bloodsucking Bonnie and Clyde?"

He nodded.

She grinned. "No."

"But you knew them," Christian said.

"Not personally of course. But then it wasn't my job to know *them*."

"What the hell is going on?" I said.

Ryan shuddered, her dark eyes flitting back to me. "Hope," she purred in her low, sultry tone, "do you remember how we first met?"

"Of course. It was … um," I hesitated, "we … um." But I couldn't remember. My recollections of Ryan were little more than a jumbled mess of thoughts and images—nothing concrete was coming to mind.

"You have no memory of meeting me because we never actually met." Her voice was harsh.

"That's ridiculous!"

"Search your memories," Christian urged me. *"Could she be telling you the truth?"*

"No," I countered. *"It's impossible."* I searched my recollections again, this time determined to find that one specific memory: meeting Ryan

for the first time. I remembered as far back as I could. I recalled places I'd been with her and events I'd attended with her, but no actual memories of first meeting with her. I swallowed hard.

"She veiled you," Christian said, reading my thoughts. *"I'm certain of it."*

"But she couldn't have, unless …" I gasped. "Vampire," I said aloud.

"That's one way to put it," Ryan replied with a hiss.

"But I thought I was your—"

"Assignment," she said, interrupting. "Case number 312, savage mixed creation. The child half-breed."

"No … you can't be serious."

"They were fascinated with how you managed to survive so long unchanged with our blood in your veins. I was to observe and report on you." She stepped closer and grabbed my hand.

"Don't," I said, recoiling from her icy touch, it all making sense now: the coldness of her skin, the gauntness of her stature, and the shimmer in her dark, sapphire eyes. How had I overlooked it?

"There came a point when I just couldn't do my job anymore. Hope, I saw you as more than my work. I saw you as my friend." She swallowed uneasily. "And I haven't had a friend in a very long time."

"How can I believe you?" I asked, tears welling in my eyes.

"You can't. I've lied to you for so long." She stared over at Christian. "It seems we all have in our own ways."

"I did it to protect her," Christian said.

"I know," she replied. "I'm not arguing your intentions. In fact, I rather admire what you did for her. A weaker man wouldn't have had the strength to let her go. She was just a girl when you met, and yet you waited for her. That's love. I barely remember love. They took those memories from me. Our lives are predetermined even before we are born into them. We don't have the luxury of …" She stopped herself and sighed. "Many things have been outlawed. They've written them off as trivial and convoluted. It's been that way for eons."

"A life without love," Christian said. "I can't imagine it."

"Apparently neither could Maxim and Sakura," Ryan said. "The thing is, if you've never known something, you simply *don't* imagine it." Her dark eyes narrowed. "But once you've had a taste of the forbidden fruit, like Maxim and Sakura did, well, then suddenly the sanctity of certain solemnities becomes incredibly stifling."

"Maxim asked me what legion I fled," Christian said.

"He must have assumed that you and Hope were on the run, just as they were." She smiled. "Rebels for love."

I was confused. "They were considered fugitives just because they fell in love with each other?"

Ryan nodded.

"That's crazy!" I exclaimed. "It actually makes me feel kind of sorry for—"

"Don't," Ryan interrupted. "They went rogue. They cut out their implants and went off the meds. They were in withdrawal. Bloodlust tested them and won. They killed innocent humans and nearly killed all of you! Sorry is the last thing you should feel for them."

"Implants? Meds?" Christian said.

She bit her lip. "I haven't ingested pure blood in my nearly two hundred years."

"How do you survive?" he asked.

"A small, rechargeable implant," she explained. "It was inserted under my skin at my wrist after I changed. It contains a concentrated blend of ersatz plasma, cells, and platelets and releases slowly."

"And that does it?"

"Not entirely. A progressive intake of pills represses our more *visceral* urges."

"Sounds complicated," he replied.

"Not complicated. Clinical," she corrected. "It's sophisticated and sanitary and has enabled us to live among you virtually unnoticed for centuries." She hesitated. "Look, the less you know, the better. You've remained undiscovered for a very long time." She smiled warmly. "You should feel proud—nothing ever eludes them."

"Who are they?" Christian asked.

"*They* are everyone." Ryan smiled ominously.

"How did they find me?" I asked.

"Richard," she replied "Your father. He led them to you, not intentionally of course." She smiled. "He protected you very well for many years, but he's only human after all. You ought to understand that half-breeds usually die if they're not turned shortly after being infected. Throughout history, there have only been a few other cases as interesting as yours."

"Really?" Christian said.

"The fact that Hope survived in this transitional state while becoming even stronger," she laughed, "well, my dear, that intrigued them to no avail."

"Half-breeds usually die?" I asked apprehensively.

She nodded. "A normal, run of the mill half-breed will die if they're not brought to the point of death and fed the blood of their creator."

"Why didn't I die then? I mean, what makes me so different?"

"I'm not sure really," Ryan said. "All I know is that sniffing out a half-breed is easy; the human odor is still very redolent. But you don't smell like a half-breed. You're very different, like a finely aged vintage."

"And now they know about us?" Christian's voice was bitter.

"No," Ryan snapped. "I didn't tell them anything. I didn't report on Hope's inheritance. They don't know about Perish."

"What about Maxim and his girlfriend?" I added. "Would they have told anyone?"

"Unlikely. They were wanted felons." She smiled. "Relax. No one is looking for our kind this close to the equator." She straightened the cuffs on her shirt. "The sun is far too intense, and none of them are ambitious enough to endure it the way you all do."

"Will you tell them about us?" Christian inquired.

"And poison your Garden of Eden?" She shook her head. "Look, just because we've evolved doesn't mean we've improved upon anything. You can strip the fangs from a snake, but it still wants to bite."

"So you won't tell them," I pressed.

"No. Take this paradise you've found and treasure it." She transferred the parasol to her other hand, her shirt creeping up her arm as she moved.

"My god!" I said, eyeballing the freshly healed scar that suddenly became visible across her wrist. "Your implant …"

"I had to cut it out," she said, concealing her scar with her sleeve. "There was no other choice for me." She took a deep breath. "I'm *not* like Maxim and Sakura. I have no illusions as to how difficult this is going to be. I just couldn't stay like that anymore. I couldn't unsee the things I'd seen—the beautiful, unbelievable things that life still had to offer. I just couldn't be like them anymore. I remembered what living was like." She grinned at me. "I remembered because of you."

Ryan reached for my hand. My eyes welled with tears.

"What can we do to help you?" Christian asked. "I'd offer you something from our collection to keep you strong, but …"

"That's very generous, but you needn't worry about me." She leaned in close and ran her cool fingers along my collarbone until she met with the chain of my necklace. She gently pulled the pendant out from beneath my shirt and gazed upon the array of sparkling rubies and diamonds. "I told you this thing had special powers." She winked. "Three generations of women in my family found the loves of their lives wearing this necklace. Me included. You look good wearing my past."

"*Your* past," I said, perplexed.

She smiled. "This was all I had left. Most of my memories were taken away after they changed me, but because I hid this—kept it from them—I kept the memories it held too." She paused for a moment. "That was a long time ago. Another life." She placed the necklace back beneath my shirt before turning to Christian. "Take care of her. She's very special."

"I will," he promised.

"Where will you go?" I asked.

"Somewhere they won't find me—at least for a while anyway. Maybe I'll discover my own little piece of paradise." She shrugged her slight shoulders, the glint in her dark eyes gleaming with an iridescence I'd never noticed before. "Be nice to Eva," she pleaded. "When that baby arrives, she'll need all the help she can get."

"What baby?" Christian asked.

"She's pregnant, about six years, I would guess … nearly halfway there, but I'm no expert." Ryan searched the ridiculous expressions on our faces and laughed. "We've got a pulse. Granted not a very strong or steady one, but we do have a pulse. We can reproduce like humans; it just takes a lot longer. Your friend is lucky she didn't lose her baby with all the injuries she sustained."

"Does she know?" I asked.

"Yeah, Eva knows. I told her—whether or not she actually believes me is another story." She tucked her hair behind her ear. "One last thing," she said, her tone growing more serious as she moved her eyes to Christian. "For Hope's safety—for the protection of your perfect paradise—you really should consider making her one of us. If she stays like this, they *will* find you."

Christian heaved a sigh.

"No rush, but promise me you will consider it."

He nodded.

"I know you'll make the right choice, Christian, because you love her." Ryan pulled me into the cold embrace of her bony frame. "I'm so sorry," she whispered. "Maybe one day I can find a way to make it up to you." She withdrew from me. "Good-bye, Hope. See ya … ciao … until we meet again."

I blinked away tears, and when I opened my eyes again, she was gone; she'd vanished from my life as wondrously as she had been inserted into it in the first place. A stream of sadness spilled down my face as I stared at the empty beach ahead.

32-Skeletons in the Closet

When we reached Ambrose House, I knew that things would never be the same. Ryan's presence had changed everything. The line between my old reality and my new one blended together like watercolors. I had no reason to go back to my old life. Ryan wouldn't be there, I had no job, no fiancé, and absolutely no interest in revisiting my relationship with my father. But even more importantly was the fact that Christian didn't exist in that life. He lived here, and here was where I wanted to stay.

"Everything will be fine," Christian whispered, wrapping his arms around me.

"You're in my head again."

He nodded with a grin. "Life has a funny way of working itself out. You'll see." He laughed. "If you've been around as long as I have, then—"

"Then you're really old?" I teased.

He smirked, his pretty face like a ray of sunlight after a storm.

I stared around the living room and sighed. It was a mess. The place looked as though it had been coated with a macabre merlot splattering of paint.

"It can be fixed," Christian said. "Everything can be fixed."

"Even me?" I muttered, half-joking.

"I didn't realize you were broken," he purred softly in my ear before kissing the side of my face.

"I'm actually much better now—because of you."

"And so am I," he replied, and then he pulled away. "There's something I want to show you."

"Oh really," I said with a laugh.

He grinned before moving into the hallway. He pulled out a stack of stuff from the cabinet. "Come sit with me," he said, perching himself on the bottom step of the staircase at the base of wooden lady.

"What is all this?" I asked, parking myself next to him.

"Your grandmother's things. You should have them before they end up getting lost in the mess around here."

I sifted through some of the sheets. My grandmother's nearly illegible handwriting was scrawled across the pages.

"These must be from her journals," he said. "She was always scribbling in these." He handed me more of her stuff.

I smiled. Books and pages were filled with her writing. It was exhilarating knowing that these were her words, her thoughts, and that I was going to have a chance to know her through them.

"These too," Christian said, staring at an old photo album. "Here, look at this." He laughed, pointing to a black and white photograph of himself and my grandmother standing in front of a brand-new 1950s model Studebaker.

"That's you," I said. "You look *exactly* the same—except for the hair!"

"It was called the pompadour, and it was quite the rage back then."

"I'm not insulting you. You were hot—James Dean hot!"

"That photo was taken over sixty years ago. Am I still …"

"Incredibly," I insisted. "And you aren't just hot—you smolder. Now stop fishing for compliments and show me more of my grandmother's things."

Christian beamed.

I turned my attention back to the photo album. "Is that Eva?" I asked, pointing to a black and white picture. The woman in the center of the photo was dressed in fancy, turn-of-the-century lingerie and sprawled across two men in dark tailcoats, trousers, and black top hats.

"Yeah," Christian said, "same old Eva."

I studied the photograph a little closer. "And that's B, isn't it?" I asked, noticing Eva's head in his lap.

Christian nodded.

"But who is that?" I pointed to the attractive man in the picture that appeared to be stroking Eva's legs.

"That's William."

"William?"

"You sound surprised."

"I am. I mean, when you told me about him sailing with you on the *Ambrose* … when I saw him in your thoughts—he didn't look like this."

"That's because you were seeing him the way I saw him—through my eyes, not as he was in reality."

"I guess you didn't like him very much."

"It wasn't always that way. In fact, William was my closest friend. He and I built Ambrose House together with our bare hands."

"Really?"

He nodded. "We made this life here on Perish by convincing each other that we could survive without becoming savages." He leaned back, lost in thought.

"So what happened? I mean, why did your friendship change?"

"William changed." He took a deep breath. "I guess we all changed." He ran his hand along the carved scales of the wooden lady. "After a while, immortality does funny things to your mind."

"Like what?"

"Like make you feel invincible."

"That doesn't sound so—"

"It's worse than bad," he interrupted. "When time *isn't* of the essence, hopelessness eats away at you." He was quiet for a moment before his expression finally eased. "But I found my Hope," he whispered, nudging me in the arm.

"What really happened between you and William? You said he was your closest friend. What did he do?"

"He fell in love."

I laughed. "Love? That's not what I expected you to say. A heated brawl, a violent massacre, or even an indiscreet bloodbath, but not …"

"Let's face it," he said, "it's always about love, isn't it?"

I nodded.

"It was a human woman."

"Really?"

"I'd never seen a love like theirs before. They would do anything for each other—die even. But his love for her eventually drove him mad. He was convinced that he could somehow reverse his condition—become human again to be with her and live a normal life. He wanted to marry her and have a wedding here at Ambrose House. He even wanted to have children with her—"

"You're kidding?"

"No. But it never happened."

"Why not?"

"They died."

"Both of them?"

"Yes."

"How? I mean why? What—"

"Now isn't the time to drudge up this old story," he said.

I rolled my eyes.

"I will tell you, Hope. I promise, just not today."

I nodded and closed the photo album. I slipped my warm hand into his, the icy freeze of his skin enlivening me. "I guess sometimes the past is better left in the past."

"Perhaps," he said, "but not yours."

"What do you mean?"

"You've been in the dark for long enough. To know where you came from is to understand yourself." He handed me more of my grandmother's possessions. "All of this belongs to you now. It's your legacy."

My eyes lit up as I stared at the heap of stuff.

"I promised I'd give you your answers, didn't I?"

"Thank you," I said. I moved to reach for the stack when suddenly I lost my hold. Loose white pages fluttered though the air like snowflakes as they descended to the bloodstained hardwood. "No!" I panicked. Christian grabbed my hand and froze the moment. Journals hung in mid-air like birds in a painting while fallen photographs hovered above pools of blood mere instants away from being saturated.

"Salvage what you can," he said anxiously.

I nodded, grasping him tightly with one hand while striving to collect what mementos I could with the other. I grabbed a few journals and tucked them into the fold of my arm while I hurried to gather more. I reached out and snatched a handful of old photographs that were hanging together in a cluster like stars in the night sky, and that's when I noticed something.

I knelt to the floor in an effort to extract a small photograph that was about to soak through. It was the inscription on the back that caught my eye. The words *Moira and Henry 1937* were handwritten across it. "It can't be," I mumbled, plucking the picture from the air and anxiously turning it over. And then I froze. It was a wedding picture—my grandmother's wedding picture to be precise. She was young and beautiful and dressed in a lovely white lacy gown standing next to her groom—standing next to Henry.

"He wanted to tell you," Christian explained, "he just didn't know how." He batted his eyelashes at me, and time abruptly resumed mobility. Photographs fell to the floor, journals slammed against the hardwood, and loose white pages started absorbing blood.

"I don't understand." My eyes were fixed on the old wedding picture.

"He's your grandfather."

Henry could shift into anything—a raven, a butterfly, a shark even—but a grandfather … why did that seem so implausible?

"It shouldn't," Christian whispered. "See these books?" He held up a few of the bloodstained journals. "They'll teach you about Moira, but not nearly the same way that your grandfather can."

I swallowed nervously, grasping the old photograph between my thumb and index finger. I brought the brittle paper close to my heart and smiled. "This *can't* be real," I said.

"Why not?"

"Because it's crazy!"

"Crazier than the fact that I'm an immortal and you're a half-breed?"

I smiled.

"It is real, Hope. Henry is your family."

"Does he know? I mean that I'm his—"

"Granddaughter? Yes. He's always known." Christian grasped my hand. "That day in the woods, in the rain, it was the first time he'd been near you since you were a child. He was nervous and excited, and I think he—"

"Wanted to touch me," I interrupted with realization.

"He just wanted to know what you looked like."

I smiled.

"He couldn't see you in his human form, but when he left—he shifted. He took the risk of you noticing him transform just so he could get a glimpse of the beautiful woman you'd become. "Henry's so old fashioned—he's way too shy to bring it up himself." Christian grinned playfully. "But I'm not. Come with me." He tugged on my hand and led me toward the front door.

The air was filled with a blissful burst of jasmine and ginger the moment we stepped outside. I let the delightful fragrances calm my nerves as we rounded the corner of the house toward the backyard. Henry was sitting near the pool, shirtless, wearing a pair of blue swim shorts. His fair hair was spiked out in wild disarray while his eyes were hidden behind dark sunglasses. He looked like any average young guy just sitting there—except that he wasn't. He was a shape-shifter, a vampire, and my grandfather.

"I don't think I can do this," I said.

"Why not?"

"I don't know." I bit my lip. "I'm afraid."

"Afraid?" He laughed. "You really have to stop letting fear run your life."

"What do I say to him? I mean he's so young—he's younger than me!"

"He only looks younger than you. He's got a lifetime of memories to share. Some of which you were a part of."

"I was?"

"Of course." Christian squeezed my hand and pulled me against him. "Close your eyes," he whispered.

I inhaled the sweet tin-cinnamon scent of his body and closed my eyes.

"Search your memories," he implored. "Think back to the last time you were here, in Perish—when we met."

I smiled, letting the blissful recollections dance upon my thoughts.

"Now remember Henry … remember him at the house." Christian's voice was hypnotic. "Remember him here in the garden, here with your grandmother … *here with you*."

And suddenly I did remember. I opened my eyes and smiled.

"You have nothing to be afraid of," he said. "Just go to him."

I nodded and stepped lightly across the pool deck.

"Hope," Henry greeted, inhaling my scent as I neared.

"Hi," I replied nervously.

He was sitting in the red, butterfly patio chair with filigree wings, listening to some crooner on the antique radio. He leaned forward, toward me, and I happened to see the word *Moira* tattooed in an elegant script on the inside of his left, upper arm. I hadn't noticed it before; it was understated and refined—much like Henry himself. A sharp whiff of copper suddenly distracted me. It was his scent; it was strong and redolent and reminded me of pennies. *Pennies*, I contemplated, and suddenly I realized why the sheets in the master bedroom smelled so aromatic with the curious blend of lavender and pennies: it was their scents intertwined, my grandparents, *Moira and Henry*. Tears welled in my eyes.

Henry moved closer. "There, there," he whispered, listening to the subdued sounds of my sniveling. "Why are you crying?"

"Because … you, me … we're …"

Henry laughed, his mild manner even gentler than Christian's. "Don't cry, Hope," he said, extending his pale hand toward me.

I placed my hand over his and encouraged him to touch the contours of my face, allowing him the opportunity to finally feel what I looked like. Henry smiled, and I smiled too. A light breeze soared past, carrying with it the delightful scent of salt and honeysuckle. The tufts of Spanish moss swung from the banyan tree with the soft current while the melodic sounds of songbirds harmonized to Henry's old-time music on the radio. It was a blissful moment and one that I had never imagined possible. There under the blaze of the balmy southern sun against the silhouettes of the scrawny pines, I met my grandfather again for the first time.

33-The Last Kiss

La Fuente was closed for the night. A strange mélange of blood and disinfectant filled the air.

Christian lit some candles and drew the long curtains closed. He slowly sauntered toward me. "A hidden stash." He smiled mischievously, holding up a pristine glass bottle, his sweet face aglow with candlelight.

"You're such a bad-boy," I joked.

"I'm not really a boy," he purred, knowing how much his youthful appearance both unnerved and excited me.

"Maybe I should have called you Peter Pan instead of Tin Man."

"So why Tin Man then?" He popped a tiny heart-shaped candy into his mouth and smiled.

"Gee, I wonder." I inhaled the metallic cinnamon emanating from his skin. *"Oh sweet Tin man,"* I sighed in my thoughts. I moaned a little. He was enchanting; his youthfulness gleaming in the radiance of the candlelit room. Christian really was the man of my dreams, more beautiful than all of the stars in the sky, and tonight I would make him mine.

He broke out into laughter. He was listening in on my thoughts again.

"Don't be embarrassed," he whispered.

"Yeah sure," I said, mortified. "I'm like an open book to you."

"Ah, now I've made you blush," he teased.

I turned away, embarrassment driving my haste.

"You're so pretty when you blush," he said, sitting down on the black velvet couch beside me.

My body quivered nervously with his nearness, tingling awkwardly like I was a visitor in my own skin. I felt more like a girl than a woman.

"Oh c'mon," he whispered, stroking my knee with his cold hand.

I trembled a little with his touch and slowly turned toward him. "It's not fair," I complained. "I never get to hear what you think of me."

He smiled, his eyes glimmering.

"You're not going to tell me how you do it—are you? How some of your thoughts are loud and clear while others, the juicy ones, they stay private."

He laughed.

"Fine," I said. "But you will tell me one day."

"If I must," he replied jokingly with a sigh of reluctance.

I swatted him in the chest.

"You know," he said, changing the subject, "I was thinking that maybe I needed a nickname for you."

"Me?"

"It's only fair."

I waited to hear the name he'd conjured.

"Alice," he finally said. He uncorked the bottle with his teeth and spit the cork across the room.

"Alice," I replied. "How—"

"What? Trite? Cliché? Corny?"

The ambrosial aroma of the drink filled my nostrils, and I could feel my mouth beginning to water. "Christian," I sighed under my breath. I could smell his blood in the concoction. I could distinguish its sweet succulence the moment the cork left the neck. I swallowed hard and smiled. "It's perfect."

"The nickname or the drink?" he teased.

I laughed, and he laughed with me, his face soft and enchanting.

"Ever since you fell into my world, this hellish Wonderland, I've never stopped thinking about you." He handed me the opened bottle. "Now drink me, Alice."

I took the bottle from him, held it next to my mouth for a moment, and closed my eyes, inhaling the sweet smell.

"And if you hadn't fallen down the rabbit hole—"

"Then you wouldn't have been there to save me," I said, opening my eyes.

Christian smiled.

"Alice and the Tin Man," I said. I wrapped my lips around the mouth of the bottle and then downed a sip, the taste living up to my every expectation.

"Enjoy it," he said, a sorrow swelling in his eyes. "It's one of the last."

I swallowed sinfully, a blaze of guilt running down my throat as I drank.

"We'll start over," he said. "It'll take time—"

"Time," I interrupted. "Time is something you have a lot of when forever is potentially infinite." I handed the bottle back to him.

"I suppose you're right," he said. He downed a swig, spilling some of the rich drink on his chin.

Each drop was like a drug encapsulating the titillating tonic my body craved. It was irresistible. *He was irresistible.* I moved closer and tenderly licked the drops of blood with the tip of my tongue.

He moaned and pressed his hands to my back, pulling me closer. I followed his lead, allowing myself to rest upon him. I moved my lips to his mouth, and with the taste of blood on our tongues, we came together into a kiss. His touch roused me with a feeling of fervor I could barely contain. I wanted him, every part of him. I wanted to know what it was like to have him.

"Slow down," he urged, recoiling a little.

"Why?" I said softly. "It was just a kiss."

"*That* wasn't just a kiss. I've waited a long time for this with you." His voice was tender.

"And …"

"And it's your thoughts," he confessed. "I can't seem to handle listening to them while we're …"

"Then stop eavesdropping, old man," I teased. "Just let what happens happen." I ran my hands down his chest until they met with the bottom of his shirt. I began inching it off of his beautiful body.

"What if I can't stop?" he said, pulling the shirt over his head and tossing it to the floor.

I stared at his naked chest. "What if it's *me* that can't stop?" I moved closer to him and stroked his arms. I inhaled the sweet scent of his skin again and smiled. His smell left me breathless. I stared into his eyes. An animalistic night shine flooded his irises like liquid mercury, and suddenly his familiar gentleness faded—replaced by a harder, more unrefined Christian, one who was feral and hungry for both my body and my blood.

I gasped.

He grabbed my hips with his hands and pulled me against him. I bit my lip, elated with the suddenly seductive vivacity of the situation. I slid my hands down his chest until my fingers met with the tattoo of the phoenix that adorned his ribcage. I traced the ornate black lines and sighed. "Tattoo me," I said.

"My god, woman," he hissed in reply. "You want to talk about a tattoo—*right now*?"

"I do."

Christian recoiled.

"Tattoo me," I pressed.

"No," he said, running his fingers through his hair.

I smiled coyly like a little girl and even stooped to bat my eyelashes for effect.

"No," he replied rigidly, grabbing the bottle from the floor and downing another swig of blood. "It's permanent. It hurts. And you'll regret it."

"Christian ..." I grinned playfully, reaching out for him. I started tickling the tattooed feathers of the phoenix that framed the contours of his hip, and soon I could feel him easing under my touch.

He groaned with frustration. "What's so important that you'd want it permanently etched onto your body forever? And might I remind you that forever could be a very long time."

"I don't know ... I guess I just thought it would be romantic."

He shook his head. "You're so human."

"So make me unhuman then."

"No."

"Tattoo me."

"No."

"Change me."

"No."

I jerked my hands from his skin and pouted.

His eyes softened. "Why do you want a tattoo all of a sudden?"

I shrugged.

He took my arm with his hand and gently turned it around. The ghastly trail of his bite marks that scarred the inside of my wrist glistened in the soft light of the room.

"Is it to cover these?" he asked.

"No," I said, pulling my arm away.

"Then why?"

"Oh come on, Christian. People have been getting tattoos since the dawn of time, and you've been giving them for nearly that long! It's *just* a tattoo," I implored, moving my fingers back to his body, letting them crawl up his chest like a spider. "C'mon … can't I just want something without having to overanalyze it—please?"

He rolled his eyes and heaved a sigh. "I'm going to regret this," he lamented, grabbing my hands and pulling me from the couch toward one of the worktables.

He led me through the shop when suddenly the heady smell of disinfectant began unnerving me with its pungency. I looked around the room. Wires and machines and needles glistened like tools of torture in the candlelight. A chill ran down my spine. This was really going to happen, I realized. I was about to get my first tattoo.

"Yes you are," he replied.

He sat me down upon a hard, white, vinyl table and insisted I relax. A moment later, he pressed his foot on a pedal, and his tattoo machine suddenly came to life buzzing like a cicada on a hot day.

"So," Christian said softly. "What is it that you want me to tattoo on you?"

"I don't know." I shrugged.

"You want *me* to decide?" His eyes widened.

"Yeah. What's wrong with that?"

"Nothing other than the fact that you'll be wearing it for the rest of your life." He proceeded to fill a couple of little plastic cups with black ink.

"I *trust* you."

He shook his head.

"I know how you feel about me, Christian," I said confidently. "And I know you'd never do anything to hurt me." I pulled my shirt off over my head and tossed it across the room. I covered myself with my arms and turned to face him. I could feel his stare. I brushed my hair over my shoulder and caressed the nape of my neck with my fingers. "Here," I said decisively. "I want you to do it here."

Christian exhaled and ran his pale hand along his face. "Are you sure you're ready?"

"I'd be lying if I said I wasn't afraid."

"Fear again," he teased. "Think you'll ever be free of that hold it has on you?"

"Not in this lifetime. So c'mon, Christian. Just do it—tattoo me."

There was a strange faraway look in his eyes.

"What now?"

"This is your first."

"So?"

"*So*, no matter how many tattoos you end up with, you'll never forget this one." He put down his machine and stood up in front of me. He started fiddling with the top of his pants. "Look," he said, lowering his jeans just below his left hip.

There, below his hip, was a large, smudgy patch of black ink embedded into his skin.

"See this?" he said, revealing the inky patch on his upper thigh. "In its glory, it was a pre-Columbian sun-god."

I let my eyes linger on each glorious detail of his aged tattoo. It was about the size of a tangerine and barely discernible.

"I was seventeen when a tribal elder gave this to me. I was still human at the time."

I reached out and stroked the faded lines with the tips of my fingers.

"This was my *first* tattoo. And it was one of the *last* experiences I remember having as a human. I'll never forget it."

I looked into his eyes and smiled. "And this," I whispered, "with you here today—*I* will never forget it."

A reluctant smile forced its way across his pretty face. He nodded at me. A moment later, he grabbed the half-empty bottle of blood from the floor and sauntered toward me. He brought the bottle to my lips. "Drink it," he said softly in my ear. "You'll need it."

It was advice that I wasn't about to ignore. I downed a gulp just as the buzzing of his tattoo machine filled the air. I closed my eyes and pursed my lips, anticipating the pain. And then it happened. Like a razor's edge, I felt tiny needles cutting into my flesh, slicing and infusing me with ink as he drew across my neck. His movements were practiced, quick, and precise, and after a while, I grew accustomed to the sting. Blood and ink suffused the air with a marvelous mélange, and I inhaled its tart tang with pride. There would be no turning back; this tattoo would sit upon my skin forever.

Finally the weight of his hand eased, and the buzzing stopped. He was finished. My neck throbbed with a burning soreness as the stale air in the room graced my fresh abrasion. A moment later, I felt his hands on me, stroking my back. He pressed himself against me, and I moaned. Then I felt his cold lips on my skin, against my neck. The sharp edges of his teeth grazed my raw flesh, scratching me as he tongued the excess blood that dripped from my new tattoo. Suddenly, and without warning, he dug his fangs into me, piercing my skin with the force of his bite. I cried aloud, the stabbing throb of his penetration nearly breaking me with the intensity of its force. I shut my eyes hard, a burst of tin cinnamon unexpectedly invigorating my senses. It was his blood. My body came alive with a renewed vigor, and the pain I felt weakened with the craving that swelled beneath my skin to have a taste of him.

"Drink me," Christian whispered inside my thoughts.

And suddenly I really was his Alice—desperate to find a means to indulge in the Wonderland that was his blood. I opened my eyes with a ravenous fierceness to find that he was offering his pale hand to me. Fingernail-sized gouges oozed in the center of his palm. I reached for his hand and pulled him to my mouth, swallowing his sweet savor as though it were oxygen to my lungs. The taste of his blood in my mouth, rushing through my veins, roused me with an indescribable rapture. I was both weak and strong simultaneously in his arms.

"Stop," he suddenly groaned, tearing himself from my flesh. "I need to stop."

"No," I begged. "I don't want you to stop. Taste me," I urged. "Have me," I begged.

His breathing was heavy as he pondered my plea.

"Do it," I implored, the flavor of him fresh on my tongue.

He grabbed my arms with his hands and sunk his teeth into my neck again, biting through my flesh as though it were Snow White's poisoned apple. The pain was extraordinary. Blood dripped down my collarbone, overwhelming the tangle of cable chain from my necklace in a scarlet smearing. *"Christian,"* I sighed through my thoughts, lost in the painful pleasure of him upon me. He was more animal than man as he reveled in my flesh, sucking from me with a speed that quickly rendered me weak. Consciousness was fading, and soon I was little more than a drained corpse left to linger on death's doorstep. *"Christian,"* I sighed again with a soundless whisper when suddenly I felt his latch lessen.

"My god, you're turning cold." His voice was panicked.

I watched with weary eyes as he severed his wrist with his teeth, allowing a stream of blood to seep into my mouth. I swallowed, and within instants, his curative blood had already begun restoring my strength.

"I'm so sorry," he whispered, wrapping his icy arms around me. "I haven't bitten into flesh in so long." He sighed. "And to taste you …" He moaned.

"Don't," I uttered groggily. "I don't want your apology—I didn't want you to stop."

"But I could have killed you."

"Or you could have changed me," I countered. "I was close—I know you could feel it, and I had your blood in my veins already. It would have been a seamless transition."

He recoiled a little. "A seamless transition? That doesn't sound like a perfect moment. Your life only ends once, Hope. Don't settle for subtlety. You deserve sunsets. At the very least, you deserve to end your life with a sunset in the background." He smiled. "You'll get your moment. You just have to be patient."

"I'm not good with patience."

"Well you've got no other choice really. You're going back soon."

"What?"

"Your father's wedding. You promised him you'd be there."

"Ugh," I sighed.

"It won't be that bad."

"Come with me then."

"I can't."

"Why not?"

"It's complicated."

"Forget complicated," I replied. "Forget any of it. I don't want to go back to that life."

He exhaled deeply, his eyes turned hard. "We both know it would be easier if you forgot about *this* life instead."

"Don't say that," I snapped. "I lost you once—"

"You could still have a shot at a normal life, Hope, if you didn't remember me."

"Don't," I begged.

"You and I both know that there are some things better left forgotten—and I can do that for you."

"But I don't want that. I don't want to forget you again."

"But we're from two different worlds, and my world will inevitably destroy both of us."

My eyes swelled with tears. Numbness coursed through my veins.

"A simple veil—"

"No!" I barked, a stream of tears flooding my face.

"But it's the only way."

I shook my head, speechless.

"You said it yourself—I'd never do anything to hurt you." he swallowed uneasily. "Well this is me trying not to hurt you."

"I can't believe you're saying this!" I wiped the tears from my face. "On the dock, you told me that story about the siren and the sailor, and then you asked me something. Remember? What if death wasn't the end—that's what you said, wasn't it?"

He nodded.

"You asked me if I could live in a moment of happiness forever with my true love. Well that's what I want more than anything—happiness forever. I know you've had a long life with many regrets, but it's time you let go of the past, Christian. I want a future with you. I want *forever* with you."

His eyes ignited with their familiar silvery iridescence as he reached out and embraced me.

"You veiled me once," I whispered. "Don't make me lose you again."

"Shh," he cooed, his voice like a frosty zephyr against my skin. "It'll be better this way. I promise."

He pressed his soft, cold lips to mine in a kiss, and our mouths moved together to the mysterious cadence of our mismatched hearts. It was beautiful and perfect, and I could feel forever just within reach when suddenly the forlorn familiarity of a strange sensation began befalling.

"No," I urged soundlessly, *"you promised."*

But like a gentle wind, Christian began drawing streams of air from deep within me, breathing in wispy fragments of my soul, extracting my memories against my will. Tears of sorrow swelled in my eyes as I surrendered to the veil.

34-Nuptials

I was a Montague at a Capulet party; I positively didn't belong. The smell of vanilla-scented phlox and heliotropes left me with a headache. Bouquets of cream-colored orchids and ivory hibiscus adorned nearly everything in the vicinity. Even the birds of paradise stood in formation as though they were planning an attack while sweet-smelling plumeria ornamented collars like standard-issue uniforms.

"Ohana," muttered the lady with the russet-colored skin in the white sarong. She strung another lei around my neck.

"Mahalo," I replied, a phony smile plastered on my face. I stroked the soft petals with my fingers and sighed as she walked away. *Leis*, I contemplated. They were like pretty little nooses just daring me to make a wrong move.

My eyes lingered on the shoreline in the distance. The movement of the turquoise water as it skimmed over the black sand beach fascinated me; it was like watching night envelope day at dusk. I loved it out here. It was practically like paradise—practically. Just then the sharp cackle of superficial giggling forced my attention back to the reception area. I turned from the ocean toward the immense white tent up the beach. It was decorated with thousands of tiny, white twinkling lights; it was both beautiful and ostentatious—which was consistent with the tradition of all of my father's weddings. I trudged through the sand back to the reception. The sickly sweet scent of happiness pervaded the evening air. It was nauseating and made my walk a difficult one.

The tent décor was more pallid than a room full of chalk. Harmonious hues of alabaster comprised the milky centerpieces while even the guests managed to adhere to the strict snowy theme for suits and gowns. The ambiance was far from heavenly; it was hygienic. And something much more significant other than color was missing from the event as a whole: it was love. Love seemed the last thing on anyone's mind. The bride was preoccupied by the twinkle of diamonds and riches in her gold-digging doe eyes to even bother pretending that she truly cared for my father. And he, a pompous jerk to begin with, had a serial habit of assuming a new blond trophy wife every few years. The entire affair revolted me, and yet here I was paying my respects.

I finished off my glass of wine and cringed, smelling the waste of money in the air. I straightened my white, silk dress and sighed. The only thing I did appreciate at the wedding was the wine. It was a beautifully mature and complex bouquet—it was a lot like me actually. I took another sip and scanned the crowd. I didn't recognize any of the faces; most of them were either too wrinkly to remember or too surgically enhanced to recognize. Just then I felt a pair of sweaty hands on my bare shoulders. I twisted around with the fury of a tornado.

"Where have you been?" the tall, muscular, blond man with Ken-doll good looks inquired.

"Me?" I asked, recoiling from his grasp.

"Yeah you," he laughed in response, straightening his tight, white suit. "I just met this great woman over there. She's a doctor, like me," he said pompously. "Well she said that she can have that *thing* off your neck in no time."

"Excuse me?"

"We all make mistakes," he said, running his beastly hands along my shoulder blades. "But a tattoo?" he scorned, stroking the black butterfly tattooed on the back of my neck. "A tattoo is just so—"

"Don't touch me. Do I even know you?"

"Why do you keep saying that?" he fumed. "I'm your fiancée! *My name is Bradley*," he emphasized dramatically. "Maybe you'd remember if you hadn't lost the enormously expensive three-carat diamond engagement ring that I proposed to you with!"

What was he talking about? Engagement ring? Who was this barbarian? I stared into his arrogant blue eyes and tried to remember him—really tried, but there was nothing. "Look, buddy," I said, the excessively feminine and floral scent of his cologne sickening me with its stink, "I don't know you. Okay?"

"I'm glad you think this is funny. But," he said, calming down, "I'm willing to look past your little romp in Margaritaville because I care about your father—I mean you … I care about you."

I laughed. This guy was ridiculous. He didn't seem like the kind of person I'd associate with—let alone get engaged to! Just then, my father and his blushing bride, Cindy, suddenly approached.

Bradley plastered a phony smile on his chiseled face. "Doctor Havergale and the new Mrs. Havergale. Congratulations," he gushed, extending his hand to my father. "You make such a beautiful couple."

The bride threw her yoga-toned, spray-tanned arms around me and squeezed me like a tube of toothpaste. I thought I was going to regurgitate the Mahi Mahi from earlier.

"I'm so glad you came!" Her voice was high and singsong like a little girl. "And don't feel like you have to call me Mom or anything," she blurted, more bubbly than the champagne in her hand, "because that would be stupid—and plus, you're like *way* older than—"

"That's enough, Cindy," my father said. "Why don't you get Bradley another drink?"

"Richard," she giggled, "don't we have people to do that sort of thing?"

"Cindy. I want a moment with my daughter. Alone."

"Oh," Cindy replied naively. Her thick, false eyelashes fluttered like the legs of a centipede as she shifted her gaze over to me. "Sometimes your father is so complicated." She smiled. "But I'll figure him out eventually."

"Don't take too long," I said. "You've probably only got about two years or so."

Bradley whacked me in the arm with his elbow.

"C'mon, Cindy," Bradley said. "Let's give them a father-daughter moment." He ran his huge hands around her tiny waist and escorted her toward the bar.

"Sorry, Richard," I said. "Sometimes it's hard for me to restrain myself around your wives."

"That would be an understatement."

I rolled my eyes.

"Thank you for coming, Hope."

I shrugged. "Have I missed *any* of your weddings?"

"Touché." He smirked, his hardened face easing up a little.

"And lucky for you," I teased, "love is blind."

"Watch it. I'm still your father."

I smiled.

"And what about you? I haven't seen you since your return from …" He cleared his throat. "You seem different."

"I *am* different. I'm happy."

"That's all I ever wanted for you." His tone was practically kind.

"Really?" It was the first sincere thing my father had said to me in a long time—maybe ever.

Cindy and her pack of young, beautiful bridesmaids suddenly returned. The flock of Barbie girls swarmed my father like a piece of meat, pawing his overpriced designer suit with their long, fake fingernails.

"Sorry, sweetie, but we need him back!" slurred one of the blondes.

"He's all yours," I replied, a fake smile fixing itself back into position on my face.

"Another wine, *maikai wahine*?" a bronzed shirtless guy in a white sarong asked distracting me.

I eyeballed his tray of brimming wine glasses.

He winked.

"What about a bottle instead?" I teased.

"Follow me," he whispered with a smirk.

"Mahalo," I replied. I cleared my throat and then my thoughts. I followed him toward the bar when suddenly, through the corner of my eye, I spotted Bradley again. I could hear him hollering my name across the crowd. I pretended not to notice and quickened my step.

The guy in the white sarong uncorked a bottle of expensive champagne. "Here," he whispered, handing it to me, "take it."

"You're a lifesaver—really." I took the bottle from him and kicked off my uncomfortable, designer heels to a ukulele rendition of "Somewhere over the Rainbow" before slipping out of the reception tent.

A gusty breeze blanketed my skin in goose bumps the moment I stepped upon the black sand beach. I stared out at the ocean, inhaling the smell of salt in the air and smiled. Just then, I sensed someone standing behind me. "Bradley," I groaned under my breath. "Look," I snapped, my eyes still fixed on the ocean. "I don't remember you. I don't know you, and I honestly don't want anything to do with you!"

"Funny," a sweet, familiar voice replied. "I thought you wanted *forever* with me."

"Christian!" I gasped, turning around. The pair of shoes in my hand fell to the ground while the full bottle of champagne slipped from my grasp, spilling onto the black sand.

"Hello, Hope." Christian smiled, his splendor sending a jolt of electricity through me.

He was even more attractive than the moment we parted. His face was aglow in the pink light of the setting sun, and he was dressed in a white suit that clung perfectly to every defined contour of his exquisite body. "Am I dreaming again?" I moaned with delight.

Christian laughed.

"What are you doing here?" I gushed.

"I couldn't bear to be without you." He tenderly tucked a wisp of my blond hair behind my ear. "Not again—not ever."

I inhaled the sweet smell of his skin and sighed.

"We will never be torn asunder," he whispered without speaking. *"I promise you."*

I gazed into his green eyes while he stroked the butterfly tattoo on the back of my neck. "I missed you."

"I missed you too."

I pressed my head against his chest and listened to the nearly silent beating of his ancient heart. An instant later, we brought our lips together in a most rapturous reunion. The feeling of his mouth on mine left me breathless. Only he knew how to reawaken my soul. Every hair on my body stood on end as his hands touched my skin, and in our blissful moment together under the pink Hawaiian sky, I knew then that his kiss really was the most significant of all physical acts; the mere exchange of breath between us was our way sharing our souls.

I wanted to stay forever in his arms but heard my name being called.

"Damn it," I muttered, my eyes shifting to the beach. Bradley stormed along the sand like an ogre toward us. "This guy," I said, enraged. "I don't even know who he is, but he won't leave me alone."

"I'll take care of it," Christian assured me.

"Who the hell is *this*?" Bradley fumed, eyeballing Christian as he approached.

"Who the hell are *you*?" I spit back.

Christian stroked the small of my back and planted his palm on my hip. He stared into Bradley's smug blue eyes and smiled. "Hello," he chirped pleasantly in his fading English accent.

Bradley sneered, his eyes flitting over to me. "Is *this* what you've been doing in Florida?"

"That's quite enough," Christian snapped.

"I should have listened to your father all along," Bradley ranted. "He tried to warn me."

"Enough," Christian urged, moving closer, the colossal size of Bradley's frame nearly dwarfing him as he neared.

"You wanna fight me or something?" Bradley's voice wavered as he spoke.

"Fight *you*?" Christian taunted with a smirk. "Now how could *I* ever fight someone as big as you?"

"Stay away from me," Bradley insisted edgily.

"You have no idea how lucky you are that Hope *doesn't* remember you." Christian's tone was smooth.

"Oh, please," Bradley snapped.

"You didn't deserve her."

"She didn't deserve me!" he retorted.

Christian put his hand on Bradley's arm. "She's capable of unimaginable things," he whispered.

"That's ridicu—" and abruptly Bradley went quiet. His eyes looked as though they were glazing over. He didn't speak. He didn't move. Then several snowy swirls of breath suddenly emerged from Bradley's lips. They lingered for a moment before slipping away with the wind.

I watched until finally Bradley started to stir, blinking his eyes a few times as though he was waking up from a dream.

"What happened?" he asked, his voice groggy and low. "What am I doing here … at the beach … with you people?" He looked at Christian and me. "Do I know you?"

"No," Christian replied coolly.

Bradley heaved a sigh. "It must be the champagne." He smiled awkwardly. "I'm sorry I bothered you." He turned away and stomped along the beach back to the reception tent.

I laughed as he left. "That was you veiling him—wasn't it?" I grabbed Christian by the arm and pulled him close.

"Maybe," he teased, playfully moving against me.

"I rather enjoyed watching you do it. Come to think of it, I distinctly recall you doing something rather similar to me on our last night together at La Fuente."

He wrapped his strong arms around me squeezed.

I laughed.

"You didn't need to remember that guy," he whispered.

I pulled away a little. "You mean I really was engaged to that beast?"

Christian nodded. "And since it seemed as though he couldn't keep his hands off of you …"

"You veiled his memories of me."

He nodded.

"Must be nice, having such incredible power."

Christian chuckled. "Well, with great power comes great responsibility."

The gusty wind tickled my skin, its tenacious might forcing my attention back up the beach. "Oh no," I groaned.

"What is it now?"

"Richard," I grumbled, "my father."

"Your father," Christian said nervously. "I shouldn't have come."

"Why?"

"This was a bad idea. I really shouldn't be here." He began turning away when suddenly the sound of Richard's voice halted him.

"I don't believe it," my father growled as he neared. "Christian Livingston, you really haven't changed a bit in what—over twenty years?"

"Wish I could say the same about you," Christian retorted.

"You two know each other?" I said.

"Of course we know each other. Don't we, Richard?" Christian said.

"Who could forget those summers in Perish?" His eyes turned hard. "Especially your last."

"I thought I told you to stay away from Hope."

"I thought I told you I couldn't."

"Wasn't it enough that you people ruined her mother's life?"

"You people," Christian snarled. His eyes ignited like molten lava. "Time has made you weak, old man."

"This isn't my fight anymore," Richard declared.

"I'm not here to fight," Christian asserted, calming down. "I don't have any quarrel with you. You kept her safe, and I respect that tremendously."

"Don't patronize me," Richard snarled.

"I'm not. I love her. I *always* have. But then I think you already knew that."

Cindy suddenly appeared, trudging through the sand in her extravagant white gown. "So this is where you've been hiding!" she teased giddily.

"Go back to your party," Richard snapped.

"Not without my groom!" Her eyes flitted over to Christian. "And who is this?" she slurred suggestively.

"He's nobody," my father spit back.

"Some nobody," she muttered under her breath, eyeballing Christian's body.

"They're *both* nobody to me," Richard said with a hardened resolution. He grabbed his young bride and pulled her back up the beach away from us.

I felt a sinking feeling in the pit of my stomach as I watched him leave, but I didn't cry—Richard wasn't worth it. I glanced at the wedding tent one last time, watching as he rejoined the party, and when he disappeared among the crowd, so did his place in my heart.

"My old life is vanishing before my eyes," I said.

Christian put his arm around me. I inhaled the sweet smell of my Tin Man, and suddenly the sinking feeling in my stomach was gone.

"I shouldn't have come," Christian insisted.

"*I* shouldn't have come either," I added with a smile.

He laughed. "Don't regret your decision. You did the right thing."

He squeezed my hand tightly. "Richard will come around. He will. He's just too narrow-minded to recognize—"

"What the hell happened between the two of you?" I interrupted.

"It's a long story, from a long time ago." He kissed my forehead. "You were just a child. It's complicated."

"Why does he still remember you? I mean, clearly he knows what you are."

"Veiling Richard would have been an act of kindness. He needed to remember what he did."

"What did he do?"

"That's for him to tell you one day when he's ready."

I swallowed hard and shook my head. "There's such bad blood between the two of you."

"Blood," he whispered. "Somehow, it's always about blood."

I reached out and stroked the side of his face with my hand.

"Oh, you do know how to weaken me," he moaned.

I grinned. "Being here, it's made me realize something."

"What's that?"

I ran my hands up his chest. "It's made me realize how much I don't belong here anymore."

"Well then, where *do* you belong?"

I smiled. "In a moment of happiness forever."

35-Moonrise

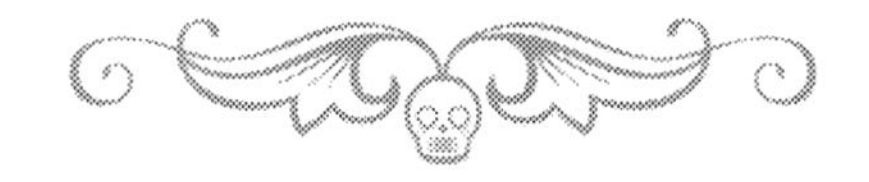

The sun was near setting time. The sky was alive with the purest palette of pinks and oranges I had ever seen. I watched as the fleeting vignettes changed with every passing moment. The granules of dark lava scoured the soles of my feet as we walked along the beach together. It wasn't Perish, but it was paradise because I was with Christian. I had long since forgotten about Bradley and Richard, the opulent wedding and the horrible way the entire affair made me feel. It wasn't about any of that anymore. It was about Christian, and it was about me, and tonight it was about the undying love we were finally pledging to each other.

"Will it always be like this?" I asked.

"Yes," he paused, "and no." He squeezed my warm hand tighter.

A cool breeze graced the edges of my skin.

"Time changes you," he explained, "maybe not physically, but intrinsically."

"I want *this* forever," I said, gesturing to the vastness of the sky above and the endless expanse of the horizon ahead of us. "Sunset forever, with you."

He stopped walking. "Then *forever* it shall be."

A strange medley of dread and desire suddenly swelled inside of me. Was this it? Had the hand of fate written this moment to be my last? I started to shiver, the cool water gracing my toes and ankles as the tide rolled in. I swallowed hard and closed my eyes. *"Tin Man,"* I purred in my thoughts. *"Tonight I give you my heart."*

"And tonight I'll have it," he replied with a whisper. "Are you sure?"

"Yes."

Living a lie wasn't an option, and I had no intention of existing as some freakish half-breed any longer. Christian was my destiny—predetermined and inevitable. I belonged with him. I wanted this more than anything. I wanted to be with him. I wanted to be like him.

A warm wind caressed my skin, carrying the smell of ocean and orchids with it. Beyond the roaring pound of my arrhythmic pulse, I could hear the sound of waves crashing against the shore and party music in a distant background. I looked to the sky. It was aglow with the lingering magnificence of the setting sun. My heart pounded like a rhythm-less drum. Its inelegant thump throbbed through the thin skin on my throat. With trembling fingers, I tore the leis from my neck, brushed the windswept hair off of my shoulders, and curved my head to the side, exposing my jugular in the clearest, most accessible manner.

"Come to me," he whispered, running his hands around my waist and pulling me into him.

I arched my back in the cold familiarity of his arms, feeling him inhale the scent of my body.

"Is this your moment, Hope Havergale?" he whispered, pressing his soft lips to my skin and gently kissing me under the angle of my jaw. "Is this the way you imagined your death?"

"Yes," I moaned in reply, craving the unbearable burn of his bite and the sting of his sharp incisors spearing their way into my flesh. "Yes," I repeated. "Love hurts."

And then he stopped. He let go of me, and I nearly fell to ground.

"Love isn't supposed to hurt," he said.

"That's not what—"

"Save it," he said, disheartened. "I can't." He ran his fingers through his hair and took a deep breath. "I can't do it. I can't hurt you."

My heart sank in my chest, deflating with defeat. "So you'd rather leave me eternally unrequited," I chastised.

He shifted his gaze away from me and toward the splendor of nightfall. He was silent—both his voice and his thoughts.

I shook my head and reached for his cold hand. "Don't you see that by denying me, you *are* hurting me?"

"Hope—"

"And sometimes love *does* hurt," I interrupted. "It hurt like hell when I left Perish." I tightened my hold on his hand. "A love like ours … a love worth fighting for is worth the pain."

"But it's your life we're talking about," he pleaded. "I've spent the last twenty years protecting you—protecting your life. How can you just suddenly expect me to take it away from you?"

"I'm not asking you to take my life. I'm inviting you to give me one anew."

He groaned with frustration.

My eyes flitted to the horizon. The sunset was breathtaking. I dug my feet into the sand when suddenly a sharp lava rock scraped my ankle. I picked up the shard and smiled.

"Hope," he scolded anxiously.

I took the jagged edge of the rock and dragged it along the inside of my right palm. My childhood scar reopened with ease. Fresh blood seeped from the cut.

"What are you doing?" he exclaimed, his eyes alive with the scent of my blood in the air.

"You know exactly what I'm doing." I grabbed his left hand and pulled the sharp ridge of the rock along his palm. His thick blood oozed from the cut.

"Don't …," he uttered with a futile plea.

I pressed my hand to his. Our fingers intertwined; our blood fused together in a seamless union.

"You've been to hell and back to be with me," I said. "You were made for me. And tonight, I will be made for you."

He exhaled deeply, his lips quivering as he struggled to resist the invitation to indulge in my flesh.

"I want this," I implored, squeezing him tighter. "I want you forever." I pulled my bloodied hand away from his and brought it close to his mouth. I opened my palm to his lips.

"Hope," he sighed softly, inhaling the fresh scent of me, and suddenly his sweet face turned severe, a silvery shine searing in his eyes. He wanted me, and this time he'd have me. His volatile stare slivered my soul with a raving intensity I'd never seen before. He ran his hand down my back and pulled me close, streaking my white, silk dress with his bloodstained palm. I elongated my neck and surrendered to him—to the moment. I closed my eyes and filled my senses with the world as I knew it. And then with an atrocious twinge, I felt the sharpness of his teeth penetrating my delicate flesh. I gasped with the force of him within me. I was suspended on a fleeting billow of bliss, dangling vulnerably in his icy arms unreservedly his for the taking. And this time, he didn't disappoint. The pain by no means abated, and soon I grew numb. Coldness enveloped me like a cloak. My breathing became shallow and quick as my heart slowed to a nearly indiscernible thump. Death was like an uninvited guest roaming the corridors of my lifeless frame, contemplating permanent possession.

When finally he stopped, only a fragment of life remained within my dying veins. Cold and weak, I hung limply in his arms. I was numbed to the pain, numbed to everything. A strange silence prevailed. I struggled to open my eyes to see the world again for the last time.

The glorious golden sun was an instant away from being consumed by the water. It was day's end in its finishing stage. Time was standing still, and we were suspended in a moment—a moment of happiness together. And there in the demise of my life, we detained the sun from setting to bid a final farewell to my humanity.

Before long, I could feel the wind upon my skin and hear the roar of waves crashing against the shore. The world was running at normal speed again. The sound of flesh being torn followed by the sweet savor of tin-cinnamon in the air immediately jolted me back to consciousness.

Christian pressed his wrist to me, his curative blood smearing against my listless lips. I opened my mouth to taste him, and soon his blood coursed through my veins like a river, breathing new life into my failing body. The numbness vanished, and the coldness subsided with him inside of me. Suddenly I simmered with verve, awakening with a renewed vitality. I could sense everything around me with a profound sensitivity, breathing in the bitter suffusion of darkness as it washed over the sky and listening to the sharp hum of the stars as they stirred above.

I withdrew from his wrist and opened my eyes for the first time once more. His beautiful face filled my sight. He was astounding, less of a boy and more of a man to me now.

"Forever," he whispered blissfully.

"Forever," I replied with a smile, watching the adoring way he stared into the golden iridescence of my new honey-colored eyes. I felt whole for the first time. I was stronger, braver, and more confident than I had ever thought possible. My skin could barely contain the excitement that was coursing through my veins. I hungered to taste this new life. I was ready and willing to explore the world. I'd lost my sense of fear for good and gained a sense of freedom I'd never expected.

Everything had changed, but somehow nothing was different. I was still just a woman in love. My life as I had known it had ended, but the one I had always dreamed of was just beginning.

"Let's go home," I whispered.

Christian beamed. We walked along the black sand beach together, hand in hand into the night, planning our happily forever after.